LILY
ROSE

a novel

DEBORAH ROBINSON

Skyhorse Publishing

To my beloved parents, Worley and Ruby Long Sturgill,
who gave me the greatest gift of a lifetime—a home

To my husband, Edward J. Robinson,
the other angel in my life who has made all the difference

Skyhorse Publishing books may be purchased in bulk at special discounts for sales promotion, corporate gifts, fund-raising, or educational purposes. Special editions can also be created to specifications. For details, contact the Special Sales Department, Skyhorse Publishing, 307 West 36th Street, 11th Floor, New York, NY 10018 or info@skyhorsepublishing.com.

Skyhorse® and Skyhorse Publishing® are registered trademarks of Skyhorse Publishing, Inc.®, a Delaware corporation.

Visit our website at www.skyhorsepublishing.com.

10 9 8 7 6 5 4 3 2 1

Library of Congress Cataloging-in-Publication Data is available on file.

Cover design by Daniel Brount

Print ISBN: 978-1-5107-6405-7
Ebook ISBN: 978-1-5107-6406-4

Printed in the United States of America

Precious memories, how they linger, how they ever flood my soul
—Traditional gospel song by J. B. F. Wright

Prologue

WHEN SHE STEPPED OUT OF the car and looked up, the large country house in front of her wasn't what she expected. The white, clapboard dwelling had sloping gray roofs, traditional black shutters on the windows, and a sunporch with wooden rocking chairs. Surrounded by oak and maple trees, and lush hydrangeas turning a soft pink in the autumnal air, the place almost looked like a family's stately, time-honored mansion deep in the woods of Connecticut. But it wasn't, she reminded herself. It was a mental hospital, and she was here to check herself in.

With trembling hands, she carried her suitcase through the front doors and walked to the intake counter, where the receptionist asked her to fill out some paperwork.

Name…Lily Rose Long

Occupation…

She paused here. She had held the job of fashion director and spokesperson for one of New York City's oldest and most prestigious department stores for almost ten years, had her own line of boutiques by the age of 33, but she wasn't sure of where she stood now.

Occupation…business owner

Marital status…

Lily paused even longer here. A few weeks ago, she would have answered confidently, but now even this was up in the air.

Marital status…single

The only thing she could write down with any certainty was her name. But maybe she should start to question that, too. After all, she had been adopted as a baby and had never really known her biological parents. What Lily knew for sure was that within the past week her life had been turned upside down, and she wasn't sure of who she was anymore.

As Lily passed her completed paperwork and ID card to the receptionist, she wondered if anyone would believe she was the same person in the photo. Certainly she looked nothing like the vibrant, smiling young woman on the card. Lily couldn't remember the last time she had washed her stringy blond hair, or even taken a shower. She was wearing an old gray sweatshirt and baggy jeans, a far cry from her usual all-black fashion armor of silk top, cigarette pants, and stiletto heels.

Her heart began to race as she lay down on a gurney by the nurse's station to be observed. Turning her head, she saw the nurse begin to remove items from her suitcase that her friends had packed—perfume, a nail file, poppy-red nail polish, and dental floss—and put them in plastic bags.

"What are you doing with my things?" Lily asked timidly.

"Honey, you'll get them back later when you're feeling better," the nurse said, placing the plastic bags in a metal container with Lily's name on it. "We can't allow you to have anything in your room that you might harm yourself with."

Lily moved her gaze to the clock on the wall. The hands seemed to creep by. Yes, she had thought of ending her life, although she hadn't told anyone except for her beloved pets—Sable, a Siberian Husky, and Hollywood, a fluffy Himalayan cat. However, it was clear that other people had felt she was capable of this act; otherwise she wouldn't be here with a stranger rummaging through her belongings.

Having finished with her task, the nurse informed her, "I'm going to give you a little something to help you sleep before we take you to your room. You need to rest now."

Lily obediently swallowed the pill and watched as the hands of the clock faded away.

When she awoke, it was the next morning and she was in what she guessed was her room. Again, it wasn't what she expected from a hospital, but a simple, airy space with a twin bed, chest of drawers, a desk, a lamp, and an armchair. Her suitcase was sitting in the middle of the floor. Lily got out of bed and began putting the rest of her things away. Since she had been in no shape to pack, her friends had packed for her—comfortable clothes like T-shirts and sweatpants, sweaters and jeans. Then she felt a little book at the bottom of the suitcase and pulled it out. Someone must have seen it lying on Lily's bedside table in her apartment and figured it was important. It was a journal that Lily had kept for years, and although it was only half-filled and she rarely wrote in it anymore, she liked to have it nearby. It was as though the thought of writing in it provided enough comfort.

Now she opened the journal to the last page, where a slip of paper lay wedged into the crack of the spine like a bookmark. She unfolded it and read what was written there in clear, graceful penmanship, as if it held the answer to the question she had been asking all her life: the name "Anna James Jefferson."

PART I: ANNA JAMES JEFFERSON

Blood is not thicker than water

Chapter 1

36 years earlier

Anna James Jefferson—known as "Jeff" to her family and friends—lay in a mass of blond curls and a tumble of covers as the October morning light streamed through her bedroom window. From her perspective all she could see was a patch of yellow-striped wallpaper, the edge of a flowered curtain, and an old doll on a bookshelf. Although she was seventeen, her room hadn't changed much from when she was a little girl, except for the number of cheerleading trophies and pennants that threatened to take over the entire space.

"Jeff, get up, now!" her mother, Jenny, hollered up the stairs. "You know you're going to be late for the bus, and I don't have time to drive you to school before work."

"Just five more minutes!" Jeff called back. It was Friday, and there was nothing going on at school except for the pep rally. Then tonight was the big football game, but the next night—that night was what Jeff really looked forward to. She rolled over and hugged her pillow, insides quivering with anticipation.

"I can't be late at the boutique, so please hurry!" The sound of Jenny's heels clicked down the hall, and before Jeff could react, her mother flung open the door like a cop executing a search warrant.

Jeff scrambled out from under the covers and ran for the shower, mumbling, "Going, going, going," as she passed Jenny.

In the bathroom, Jeff wiped steam from the mirror and widened her large blue eyes, which were never so piercing as when she stared back at the boys looking at her. Boys were always looking—trying to see what lay beneath the soft curves of her sweater, or traveling up her long, lean legs to where they disappeared beneath the short hem of her cheerleader's skirt. But no one had succeeded in getting further than that yet, as Jeff considered herself much too good for any of the boys at her high school.

Back in her room, she carefully dressed in the clothes she had laid out the night before: her favorite navy blue plaid skirt, knee socks, and cardigan sweater over a blue blouse that matched her eyes. The way she looked was very important to Jeff, although what she knew of fashion mostly came from the boutique where her mother worked, and her own after-school job at McAlpin's department store. She and her mother didn't have money for fancy clothes, especially since her father had unceremoniously up and left one night two years before, and never returned. As her mother liked to say, James Thomas Jefferson certainly hadn't lived up to his lofty name.

For much of her sophomore year, Jeff could hear her mother crying herself to sleep every night. Jeff cried, too, but mostly she was angry; she hated her father for leaving them alone, for running off without any explanation other than that he wanted to start over. She had always wondered about that—did you get "do overs" when you had a wife and child? She and her mother were making ends meet, but Jeff didn't tell anyone at school that her dad had left. How could she casually mention to her friends that her dad just didn't care about her or her mother anymore? As hard as she tried, Jeff couldn't overcome her shame or embarrassment. When Jenny received divorce papers that summer, Jeff knew her father was gone for good, and she let go of her secret.

"Bye, Mom!" As the bus honked from the street, Jeff grabbed her gym bag and cheerleading uniform and went running past Jenny and out the door like a fawn finding its first legs.

Morning classes went as usual, with Jeff being reprimanded for talking too much during French class. She was a straight-A student but never got better than a B in conduct. Right before lunch, there was the pep rally for the big football game that night where the Paris Panthers would be playing some small school from the mountains. As cheerleading captain, Jeff handled the most difficult stunts. In three neat somersaults, she landed at the top of the wobbling human pyramid. As she looked down at the cheering crowd, she thought about how much she was over all this stupid, small-town stuff. Jeff had a yearning for something else, something beyond Paris, Kentucky. She knew there was a Paris, France, out there, and she was ready to find it.

"P-A-R-I-S Paris Panthers!"

Smack! The next thing Jeff knew, the back of her head hit the shiny hardwood floor. The lights from the gymnasium ceiling multiplied and swirled above her. Faces appeared, staring down at her. She felt herself being lifted onto a stretcher and then whisked out the doors of the school, sirens wailing in the background.

Hours later Jeff woke in a hospital room with a nurse standing by her side.

"What happened?" she asked. "Where's my mother?"

"She's already been here once, and she'll be back soon," the nurse told her. "You took a nasty fall, but you're a very lucky young lady. You have some bruises, but you should be fine."

Jeff breathed a sigh of relief. She might miss tonight's game, but she would be okay for the big event the following night—the night of the party. As part of a poverty awareness tour, some rich kids from Greenwich, Connecticut, were visiting parts of Appalachia, ending up in Paris and the horse farms nearby. Jeff's class had nominated her to represent them at a mixer that was taking place at one of the farms. Jeff could just imagine the handsome young men she might meet.

In preparation, Jeff had begged Jenny to let her borrow something from the boutique where she worked, and, glad to see her daughter so excited, Jenny had obtained a French blue cashmere dress with a black satin bow at the neck. It was by far the finest thing Jeff had ever worn, and she trembled as she zipped up the back and stepped into black patent-leather pumps.

"Here," Jenny said. As a finishing touch, she added a single strand of pearls around Jeff's neck.

"Thanks, Mom," Jeff said, eyes shining. A sheer pink lipstick brought out the fullness of her lips, and her long blond hair fell to her waist, held back by a satin hairband. She didn't look like a teenager but a grown woman.

Borrowing Jenny's blue-and-white Pontiac station wagon, Jeff drove out of town to the designated horse farm, Memory Lane Farm, for the night's festivities. Although only minutes away from Paris, it was like stepping into another world. Miles of straight white fences, occasionally broken by an imposing house or barn, stretched on either side of the road. The fields were dark beneath the faint moonlight, the bluegrass lying dormant in the cold until spring. After taking several turns, Jeff drove down a long driveway to a white-columned mansion.

Two men dressed in tuxedos and carrying trays of crystal glasses greeted Jeff at the massive oak front door. After she refused refreshment, she was directed down the hall toward a group of well-dressed people gathered in a chandelier-lit room. She spotted Amanda Brown, her schoolmate who had been selected from the junior class, and went to join her. Amanda was dressed in a simple gray A-line dress with a white collar and black bow. Jeff thought she looked okay but was glad that her own dress was so much more stylish and expensive-looking than her friend's, even if it wasn't hers.

"Have you seen any of the delicious poverty hunter boys?" Jeff asked her.

"I think they're back in the library. I saw a bunch of blue blazers over there," Amanda replied.

"Paris Panthers on the prowl," Jeff whispered to Amanda and, giggling, they entered a cherry-paneled room lit by antique lamps.

Arranged around an enormous blazing fireplace were soft, deep, tobacco-colored leather sofas and matching chairs, the likes of which Jeff had never seen before. Ten or so young men dressed in navy blazers and khakis were talking together, looking not much like high school boys, she thought, but purposeful young men. After introducing themselves as student ambassadors from Paris High School, Jeff and Amanda joined their circle. Soon, Jeff discovered that they weren't discussing solutions for poverty, but rather the bluegrass farms and the famous racehorses they had seen. Although Jeff enjoyed looking at the boys, each more handsome than the next, she quickly tired of the conversation.

Then she heard one boy say, "Hey, Eric, buddy, what took you so long? Did you get lost in a barn?"

All the boys laughed as they opened their ranks and in walked the most beautiful boy Jeff had ever seen. He was over six feet tall, with a rangy, muscular body that was even more attractive standing still than in motion. Thick, pale gold hair fell across his forehead, above deep-set blue eyes that flashed the exact color of the ocean when the sun was shining through it. He had a sharp, square jaw and a smile that showed even, white teeth. Looking at him, Jeff could practically feel her heart beating out of her chest. It reminded her of getting a shot at the doctor's office, except this was a good thing.

Then she realized he was smiling at her, with his hand extended.

"I'm Eric Langvin," he said, in a voice that made Jeff's stomach flutter.

"I'm Jeff," she replied.

Eric arched one sun-bleached eyebrow. "Jeff?"

"I mean, Anna Jefferson. But everyone calls me Jeff," she felt bold enough to add.

"I was going to say, you're the prettiest Jeff I've ever seen."

As a blushing Jeff took his hand, she was overcome with the strangest sensation, one she had never felt before in all her seventeen years. Her breathing grew shallow and something between her legs began throbbing. This was some handshake.

"Let's go sit down," Eric suggested. "Do you want a drink?"

Jeff laced her hands in and out silently. "No, thank you. But I'd love to sit."

Eric led her to a comfortable sofa by the fire, and they talked about the poverty tour—apparently he was amazed at how small the entrance to one of the coal mines he had visited in eastern Kentucky was. Jeff pointed out that Paris was nothing like the poorer areas of Kentucky; it was only fifteen minutes away from Lexington and right next to the big, rich horse farms. . . . Then she fell silent. She supposed that compared to the girls Eric knew back in Greenwich, she might as well be poverty stricken, too.

Fortunately, Eric changed the subject to hobbies, and Jeff eagerly talked about her cheerleading prowess and how she was captain of the team, while he talked about how much he loved photography, basketball, and sailing on Long Island Sound. Jeff couldn't help but notice that Eric seemed to be sweating quite a bit, even at one point removing his jacket to reveal broad shoulders, although maybe it was their closeness to the fire. As for herself, Jeff could feel a spreading dampness in her underpants and hoped it wouldn't ruin her borrowed dress.

When the tension became too much to bear, she jumped up and muttered that she had to go.

Looking disappointed, Eric asked, "Can I see you again? We're going to be here the whole week."

Jeff breathlessly agreed and suggested they meet Wednesday night at seven o'clock at the Paris Grille, which despite its evocative name was little more than a hamburger joint. She wasn't sure if Eric had just asked her on a date or what, but she figured she should keep it casual.

* * *

Wednesday could not come fast enough. That night, Jeff got ready to see Eric again. She slipped into her new blue jeans, the ones that showed off her perfectly rounded bottom, and nervously buttoned her white collared shirt. Then she snipped the price tag off the new baby pink mohair sweater she'd bought with her discount at McAlpin's. This was the perfect look for tonight: in case this wasn't a date, she wasn't too dressed up; in case it was, her outfit set off her figure to its best advantage.

When Jeff arrived at the Paris Grille—again driving the lumbering station wagon, telling Jenny that she was going to meet the girls for a bite—her heart sank. Toward the back she saw several booths occupied by some of the boys from the mixer along with a few local girls (even Amanda Brown!). Then Eric turned to her, with that alluring smile he'd first greeted her with, and Jeff could only think that here she was, with him. That was all that mattered. As she slid into the seat that he'd been saving for her, he draped his arm protectively across the back of the booth. Once again the room became just about the two of them.

"I'm glad you came," she said after a while.

"How could I miss seeing the most beautiful girl in Paris again?" he replied with a lazy grin.

"Have you ever been to the real Paris in France?" Jeff asked shyly.

"Yeah, we used to go every year the week before Christmas. My mother loved going to the George V Hotel to see the decorations, and she loved shopping for presents on the Left Bank. She and my dad used to go to lots of parties while my brother and sister. . ." A troubling shadow fell over Eric's face. "We would just stay in the hotel and eat," he finished, but something had changed in his voice.

"It's great you have siblings, I always wanted brothers and sisters," Jeff said, hoping to draw him out. "What are their names?"

"I have an older brother, Christopher. He's finishing up at Harvard."

"And your sister?"

Eric took a heavy breath. "Her name was Mary. She would have been fifteen this year."

"Oh." Jeff stared down at her hands. "I'm sorry."

"It's okay," Eric said quickly. "I don't mind talking about it." He briefly relayed the details to Jeff in the monotone voice of someone who had to explain a family tragedy too often—three years ago Mary had been in a skiing accident; she'd hit her head and never regained consciousness. His mother, who had grown up in Norway and taught her children to ski as soon as they could walk, had never forgiven herself.

"She's become a totally different person," Eric said. "Before the accident we used to talk a lot. But now she's impossible to reach. She just sits around all day, drinking and taking pills to calm her nerves, she says. It's like she's a stranger."

"And your dad?" Jeff asked.

Eric shook his head. "He's always been busy with work, but now it's like he doesn't want to be around anymore. And with my brother away at school, it's just me and Mom at home. If she's really there at all." He gave Jeff a small, sad smile. "But that's enough about me. How about your family?"

"Well, my dad's not around, either. Literally." For some reason Jeff felt like she needed to lay herself bare just as Eric had. She told him about the nights when her mother had cried, the days when she had walked the halls at school, hiding the truth that her father had abandoned them. "I don't know where he is anymore," she finished. "And I don't know if I care to see him ever again."

All around them boys and girls were eating hamburgers, drinking milkshakes, talking and laughing. Suddenly Eric reached out and took Jeff's hand in his own. It wasn't like the night they'd met, when their simple handshake had thrown Jeff's hormones into turmoil. The same heat was there, but this time there was something else—a shared connection that, for a completely different reason, made Jeff's entire body tingle. Maybe someone else could really understand her.

Someone selected a familiar slow song on the old-fashioned jukebox, and now the kids were pairing off. They danced, leaning into each other after days of travel, endless lectures about poverty, and polite, stuffy adult parties. Tonight all bets were off. It didn't matter who was rich or poor, from Greenwich, Connecticut, or Paris, Kentucky. Time had stopped here.

His hand never letting go of hers, Eric pulled Jeff onto the dance floor. He took her in his arms and held her as though they had been dancing together forever. Soon their bodies drew so close it seemed like they were hugging rather than dancing. Slowly Eric's lips closed on Jeff's, soft and deep, and they swayed in an almost hypnotic haze: two beautiful, young people wrapped up in one another. Jeff had never known happiness like this, and she didn't want it to end.

* * *

Eric's last day in Paris was Sunday. Since that Wednesday night at the Paris Grille, Jeff and Eric had spent almost every evening together. She had told her mother that she was busy with cheerleading practice or studying with her friends. To her friends, she said she had to help her mother out at the boutique after hours. What was happening between her and Eric felt enough like a dream, and Jeff was afraid that if anyone else knew about it, it would fade away altogether.

She had no idea what Eric was telling his friends—they were probably ribbing him about his "Kentucky filly." She had heard nasty stories about these kinds of flings. But what she and Eric had was special; she just knew it.

Eric invited Jeff to the poverty tour's last event, a fireside supper on Sunday night at Red Rose Farm, one of the oldest bloodstock farms in the region. Not only would the other boys be there, but so would some of the top horse breeders from the area, no doubt hoping to get some business from the boys' wealthy fathers. Jeff was flattered to be invited—this was going to be no high school mixer.

Since Eric had told her event was informal, Jeff was relieved she didn't have to ask her mother to borrow another dress from the boutique. But that afternoon, when they were coming home from church, Jeff asked Jenny if they could stop by McAlpin's for just a second.

"I forgot my math textbook," she explained.

"I'll just wait in the car," Jenny said. "Don't be too long."

Jeff rushed into the store. She knew every inch of the lingerie department because over the past two years she had worked in every department. Heading straight to the lacy white bras and panties, she hoped that none of the sales clerks she knew were there that day. She had never worn anything but a plain cotton bra and unflattering cotton panties, but not tonight. She paid in cash, hurried out of the store, and ran back to the old station wagon.

"Did you find it?" asked Jenny.

"Yes!" Jeff waved her school bag with the bra and panties tucked inside. Thankfully her mother started toward home without asking any more questions.

That night, her new underwear hidden beneath a white angora sweater and crisp blue jeans, Jeff walked up the long drive lined with oak trees that led to the main house at Red Rose Farm. It was a Federal-style mansion of painted white brick with wood-shuttered windows, flanked by beds of red roses in their last bloom. In the sitting room, the boys and men were sharing some Kentucky bourbon and Rebel Yell whiskey. The only other female Jeff could see was an older woman elegantly dressed in black, sitting in a wheelchair, a handsome man standing protectively behind her. They must be the owners of the farm, she figured. Sternly watching from the side was a man dressed in neat work clothes—a servant, she presumed, acting as sergeant-at-arms this night to make sure the rich boys didn't get out of hand.

"Hi." Eric materialized by her side. "You look great."

"So do you," Jeff said. Like the other boys, he had opted for casual jeans, a cashmere sweater, and brown loafers.

"You smell great, too," he whispered into her ear, and then in front of everyone, he kissed her. The other boys were having such a grand time, though, they didn't notice.

The stern-looking man announced supper was ready and everyone filed into the dining room. On the old wooden table sat bowls of autumn's reddest apples and bouquets of blood-red roses, and more roses were wreathed around the plates. Along the walls hung photographs of famous racehorses, including the most recent Kentucky Derby winner. After a meal of luscious beef stew and Kentucky corn bread, finished off with butterscotch pie topped with fresh whipped cream, the guests headed into the sitting room for more drinks by the fire.

Eric held Jeff back and took her hand. "Come with me," he said.
"Where are we going?" she asked.

"Let's explore."

After they went upstairs, though, Eric didn't seem that interested
in exploring. He checked the first door to make sure the room behind
it was unoccupied and led Jeff into it. The room was spacious, with
walls covered in what looked like ivory satin and adorned with oil
paintings of majestic Thoroughbreds. The floor-to-ceiling windows,
framed by burgundy velvet drapes, had a view of the curving front
driveway. In the center of the room stood a dark oak, four-poster
bed that had been turned down, revealing pure ivory sheets embroidered with tiny red roses and monogrammed with the farm's crest.
An enormous Oriental rug covered the floor, and the air smelled
faintly of orange peels and roses. Jeff supposed that this was a guest
room, although it was the nicest bedroom she had ever seen, better
than the ones she had seen in the magazines she thumbed through as
she waited for her mother to finish work at the boutique.

Eric closed the door and pulled Jeff onto the bed. They leisurely
kissed, lingering on each other's lips and tongues. Eric let her long,
soft hair slip through his fingers as he pressed his body hard against
hers. Something inside of Jeff began to throb, a sweet, exquisite
pain that made her breath quicken. Eric started to unbutton her
jeans. He looked up at her, as if trying to confirm that this was what
she wanted.

"Jeff?" he asked.

All she could do was nod as the ache in her belly continued to
throb. Eric helped her take off her clothes until all she wore were
her new lacy bra and panties. Thank the Lord she wasn't wearing
her cotton briefs.

Eric stood back for a moment to gaze at her and a questioning
look crossed his face. In a panic, Jeff wondered what about her body
displeased him.

"What happened here?" With a light finger he touched the faint, yellowing bruise on her thigh from when she had fallen during the pep rally a little over a week ago. It seemed like a lifetime had passed since then, before she had met Eric.

"It's nothing," she stammered, then sucked in her breath as Eric knelt down and kissed the bruise with a tenderness she had never felt from any other boy.

"Anna James Jefferson, you are the most beautiful girl I have ever seen," he said in a husky voice.

He continued to kiss his way up her body until, reaching her bra, he pushed her breasts out of the lacy cups and sucked her nipples until they were stiff. Then his hands traveled down to caress her bottom before he slipped off her panties. Jeff half turned away but couldn't help peeking as Eric removed his own clothes. His body was as hard and chiseled as she had imagined. She liked touching his chest, but when he guided her hand lower, she hesitated.

"I don't know what to do," she confessed, not wanting to tell him this was her first time.

"Don't worry," he said, spreading her legs apart. "Just lie back."

He gently slid into her, moving back and forth with a slow but steady rhythm. Jeff couldn't quite muffle her cry of pain, but fortunately either Eric didn't hear or thought it was a sign of passion. And after a while, as she grew used to the deep, stroking motion, she started to enjoy the act. It made her feel alive.

Their bodies glistening with sweat, Eric and Jeff became lost in each other. A strange feeling was building inside of Jeff and starting to overtake everything else. Her entire body clenched, and then an uncontrollable sensation came over her like warm, undulating waves, again and again. With a final thrust, Eric collapsed next to her. After a moment he reached for her and they lay in each other's arms, their melded bodies cooling down together.

"Do you really have to leave tomorrow?" Jeff asked.

Eric kissed her forehead. "I wish I didn't have to, but yes."

"I wish you could stay," Jeff said. "At least long enough for the grass to turn blue in the spring."

Eric didn't respond. In a while, Jeff rose to use the adjacent bathroom to clean up. When she came out, she found a nervous Eric dressed and sitting on the bed. "We should go back downstairs before anyone notices we're missing," he said.

Reluctantly, Jeff agreed.

In the sitting room, the boys were saying good night to the older Kentucky gentlemen, who by now had switched to sipping single-malt scotch and smoking Cuban cigars. One of the men said, "You're a fine bunch of young men, even if you are Yankees. Tell your daddies John Henry Clayton the Third said so!" The boys laughed politely.

Eric and Jeff quickly exchanged addresses and promised to call weekly, then Jeff headed out the door. Walking to her car in the moonlight, looking at the white fences and the gentle turning of the leaves to red and gold, she knew that she too had turned. She was no longer a little girl. She was a young woman, and she was in love for the first time.

All she could think, as she drove away from Red Rose Farm, was that she had to see Eric Langvin again. She could hardly wait.

Chapter 2

Two weekends before Christmas, McAlpin's department store was bustling. In the fine china department where Jeff worked, sparkling crystal vases and gilt ornaments were flying off the shelves. Of course, it was just the time for her to get the stomach flu. She had thrown up that morning at home, and thought it was the chili dog and fries she'd eaten at the Paris Grille the night before, but whatever the cause, she knew it wasn't going to be a good day.

At lunch, since she didn't feel hungry, she decided to call Eric. In the two months since he'd left, they'd talked at least once a week. Jeff would tell him about cheerleading practice and school parties, while Eric spoke about some fancy place called Brunswick Prep. Imagining him meeting up after school with pretty girls in expensive clothes, Jeff couldn't help feeling jealous. Toward the end she would try to steer the conversation toward how they might see each other again, but Eric would become vague and say he had to get off the phone. It took all of Jeff's self control to resist telling Eric that she loved him. He must feel the same, right? She hadn't lost her virginity to him for nothing.

Sometimes at night, she would run her hands over the worn sheets of her narrow twin bed, pretending they were the luxurious ivory bedding she had lain on with Eric. Closing her eyes, she'd move her hands to her own body. He'd stroked her *here*; he'd kissed her *there*. Her nipples were especially sensitive but she touched them anyway, remembering how he'd put his mouth on them. When she couldn't stand it anymore, she slid a hand between her legs, trying to recapture the sudden surge of pleasure she'd felt with Eric. Each time she did, she missed him more than ever. She just had to hear his voice.

Jeff went to the department store's phone booth, put coins into the slot, and waited for the phone to ring.

"Langvin residence," a woman answered in a refined British accent.

"This is Anna Jefferson calling for Eric. May I speak with him please?" Jeff used her most dignified voice.

"Young Eric is not at home at the present, but I will certainly give him the message that you rang. Does he have your number?"

"Yes, ma'am," Jeff said, wanting to end the conversation as quickly as possible.

"Good day then, miss."

As Jeff hung up, her heart felt heavy. Why did she think Eric would be home on a Saturday? He was probably out with his friends—or, she shivered—some girl, driving around, grabbing a bite to eat, going to the movies. She yearned to know what he was doing at that moment without her, but knew she couldn't call him again for a while. She would just have to wait and see how long it took for him to call her back.

The rest of the day was a blur of wrapping gifts and trying to hold back her nausea. When she stepped through the front door that evening, the smell of the lasagna her mother had made for supper almost made her head straight for the bathroom.

Jenny took one look at Jeff's pale face and asked, "What's wrong with you? Don't you feel well?"

Jeff flopped down on the worn living room couch and confessed, "I feel terrible."

Jenny tucked her into bed with soup and crackers, and after nibbling a few, Jeff did feel a little better. But she was so exhausted that before she could take a sip of soup, she fell asleep, without thoughts of Eric or anything else.

The next morning, Jeff begged off from going to church, telling Jenny that she needed to rest. Once alone, she lay back in bed and tried to remember when she'd last had her period. Definitely before the whirlwind week in which she'd met Eric, because she was relieved that it wasn't going to be a problem. But since then?

Jeff hadn't thought much about her period since it had started when she was twelve, as it showed up faithfully every month. At the time, Jenny had given her a box of Kotex and a book called *Becoming a Woman*. "This book will tell you all the things you need to know, now that you're a young lady," she'd said. That was the extent of Jeff's mother teaching her how a woman's body functioned.

Jeff had thrown the book in the corner and forgotten about it. When she'd told her friends, they'd laughed together over the words *Becoming a Woman*. Later, Jeff thought that becoming a woman meant falling in love and having sex, preferably in that order. Now that she'd slept with Eric, she definitely felt she was a woman. But was there more to that? As little as she knew about periods, Jeff did know that missing one could mean something monumental . . . something that could upend her life.

She needed to see a doctor. Jenny had mentioned taking her to see their family physician that Jeff had known since she was knee high to a grasshopper, but she certainly wasn't going to see that old geezer, or for that matter, take the chance of being seen by anyone in Paris. She'd have to make a trip to Lexington, and as soon as possible. Looking through the phone book, she found a women's clinic and planned to call them first thing the next morning to make an appointment.

Monday morning, Jeff woke up feeling queasy again, her stomach churning as she dressed for school. She dabbed some blush on her pale cheeks and faked her best smile as she walked into the kitchen, sitting down at the table just as Jenny placed a sunny-side egg, two slices of bacon, and some buttered toast in front of her.

"Mom, I don't think my stomach is ready for that yet," Jeff said. "Could I just have a plain piece of toast?"

"Certainly, Jeff." Jenny looked at her, the worry lines between her eyes deepening. "Are you sure you don't want to see the doctor?"

"I don't think it's that serious," Jeff told her. "Actually, I think I might be on the mend."

After eating her toast, she regained some strength and ran to catch the bus, eager to get out from under her mother's watchful eye. At school, Jeff used the public phone to call the women's clinic and was relieved to learn she could make an appointment for the following afternoon. She'd tell her friends she had terrible cramps from her period, and ask her mother to borrow the car so that she could work extra hours at McAlpin's after school. Until then, she'd just have to try to keep herself from barfing at home or in class.

Only then did it occur to Jeff that Eric hadn't called her back that weekend, and that she had barely thought about him since the unsuccessful phone call. If she needed to tell him something . . . well, she'd deal with that later.

* * *

The next afternoon, after walking out of the clinic, Jeff sat in her car. Her heart was pounding, little beads of perspiration moistened her hairline, and her hands were icy cold. Could it really be true? She lifted her shirt and ran her hands over her belly, flat as it had always been. But something was growing in there, and she didn't know how to stop it from taking over her very being.

In a fog, Jeff drove home and walked through the door to find her mother, who had caught a ride home with a colleague, sitting in the living room.

"Everything all right, Jeff?" Jenny asked. "They're not overworking you at McAlpin's, are they?"

Jeff just shook her head, mumbled something about not being hungry, and went straight up to her room. In front of the full-length mirror she lifted up her shirt again, higher this time, trying to see any changes in her body. Her breasts were full and heavy, and her nipples ached with something more than longing. A wave of nausea rippled across her belly, the familiar feeling that had tormented her for the past few days. Gripped by a sudden rage, Jeff drove her fist into her own stomach. Breathless and stunned, she collapsed onto her bed and curled into herself, choking back sobs.

She cried until she could cry no more, and then she lay with glassy eyes staring up at the ceiling. Only one person could help her now. Eric. Eric needed to know. And when he did, he would make everything better. Jeff sat up and pushed back her hair, damp from her tears, eyes starting to glimmer with hope instead of despair. Maybe he would even want to marry her. Jeff could finish high school in Greenwich with the rest of the rich kids, and then she and Eric could start their life together. She wouldn't be Anna James Jefferson anymore. She would be Anna James Langvin.

This thought sustained Jeff enough for her to get up, wash her face, and go downstairs to face her mother. If Jenny noticed anything was different about her, she didn't show it. Instead, through dinner, she chattered away about her recent promotion to sales manager at the boutique and the pay raise that came with it. Jeff picked at her food and thought how awful it would be to be her mother's age and stuck in a thankless job, standing on her feet all day helping well-to-do women try on fancy clothes that she'd never be able to afford. Although Jeff had decided a long time ago that she was going be the one wearing the clothes, she hadn't yet been able to figure out how. Now she knew. It would be through Eric, and this baby was going to be her ticket to a better life.

Of course, if Eric ever returned her call. Jeff knew she couldn't wait that long. That night, she concocted the perfect plan. In the week between Christmas and New Year's, she'd travel to Greenwich to tell him the wonderful news in person. To her mother she'd say that the poverty awareness tour had invited the representatives from the schools they'd seen to pay them a return visit in Connecticut, all expenses paid. Didn't Jenny want Jeff to have the opportunity to see more of the world, and for free? Jeff would type up a fake permission form at school for her mother to sign, and Jenny would be too preoccupied with her new job and the holiday shopping rush at the boutique to question it.

To get to Connecticut, Jeff would need money. Luckily, back when her mother and father had gotten divorced, Jenny had set up a savings account in both her and Jeff's names in case of emergencies. Jeff even had her own checkbook, although she'd never used it before. Hopefully Jenny wouldn't find out how much money was withdrawn until much later, when Jeff was comfortably living with Eric. For a moment Jeff felt a pang of regret for abandoning her mother, but she knew Jenny would understand. What mother wouldn't want the best for her daughter's future, even if it meant being separated from her for the rest of her life?

Finally, Jeff reasoned that she would need a lavish wardrobe to look like the well-dressed girls she saw in *Couture* magazine, not like some hillbilly from Kentucky, when she would meet Eric's parents. She needed to prove to them that she looked the part of their future daughter-in-law. Thankfully, she knew just how to do this.

She would select her new wardrobe the following Saturday, the last day she worked at McAlpin's before the new year. It wouldn't be stealing, she told herself, but simply taking what she was owed after working there for so long.

Jeff had it all figured out, her set of lies, one on top of the other. While she had always told little white lies to her mother or her friends, it had never quite been on this level. But with this baby growing inside, she felt a deep, dark side of her oozing to the surface.

* * *

That Saturday, Jeff started to put her plan in motion. Although she no longer worked in the clothing department at McAlpin's, she knew it inside and out. The fashion coordinators and their assistants were always pulling clothes for fashion shows and pushing around rolling racks. The fashion assistants were constantly changing, and there was a new girl every couple of months, but you could always spot them because they were attractive and had their noses in the air. Jeff had changed her clothes immediately following school, slipping into a dress and kitten heels. Then, with a smirk on her face so not a single salesclerk would dare ask any questions, she grabbed a rolling rack and headed straight for the designer area, where all the clothes she lusted after were displayed. Everywhere she looked were satin blouses and silk scarves, cashmere sweaters and woolen trousers. Jeff loaded her rack with them, then added a few party dresses for options in case Eric wanted to take her out on New Year's Eve. She could just picture how handsome he'd look in a tuxedo.

A woman Jeff didn't recognize touched her arm, startling her out of her reverie. "Miss, I wasn't informed we were doing another fashion show right before Christmas."

"I'm so sorry no one told you," Jeff replied without missing a beat. "We're just doing a last-minute thing for gentlemen to buy Christmas gifts for their wives."

Although she still looked disapproving, the woman gave Jeff a single nod to proceed, and Jeff hastily rolled the rack out of her sight. Then, just like she had watched the fashion assistants do many times before, she rolled the rack out of the store and into the parking lot, where she laid the clothes on the back seat of the Pontiac. After returning the rack, she went back to the fine china department and finished up her shift. If all went well, this would be the last time she stepped foot in McAlpin's.

Her next stop was the bank. Jeff didn't know if she would need her mother to be with her to take out money, but the elderly teller behind the window hardly gave her a glance as Jeff handed her the withdrawal slip. With $500 in her purse, Jeff felt a little like a thief—although this was her own money, she reminded herself. She wasn't sure if the amount was enough to cover the bus and train tickets, as well as other expenses, but she figured that once she got to Greenwich, Eric and his family would take care of her.

Jeff headed home with just one more step to complete. The previous day during study hall, she'd typed up a permission form about being invited to Greenwich by Eric's school as the follow-up to their poverty awareness tour. Now, as she handed the form to her mother at the kitchen table, she explained how Amanda Brown, who had originally been selected to represent their school, had dropped out at the last minute.

"She had a family emergency . . . her grandmother passed away," Jeff made up on the spot.

"I hope she's doing all right," Jenny said.

"Oh, she's fine." Jeff wished she had left out that last part about the grandmother. "So, can you sign the form?" She pushed the paper and pen toward her mother.

Jenny read it with more care than Jeff had expected. "Are you sure they're paying for everything?" she asked. "It's a big trip." She had never let Jeff go farther from home than Lexington, or stay away longer than a weekend sleepover at a friend's house.

"Don't worry, Mom," Jeff reassured her. "I'll be perfectly safe the entire time. Just think of the places I'll see and the people I'll meet. I might never get this chance again."

Slowly signing the form, Jenny said, "I've always wanted to give you more, Jeff, you know that. But ever since your father left us, it's been hard to make ends meet. I just wish things were different."

"I understand, Mom," Jeff said, giving her a hug. "Thank you for letting me go."

Later that evening, upstairs in her room, Jeff could breathe a sigh of relief. In her closet, hidden behind her regular clothes, was her new, fancy wardrobe from McAlpin's. Tucked in her dresser drawer, beneath her underwear, was a stack of ten- and twenty-dollar bills. All she had to get through now was Christmas, which ever since her father had left had been a quiet, even somber affair, usually church followed by a lunch prepared by her mother and an exchange of presents. Jeff had gotten a porcelain vase at a discount from McAlpin's for Jenny. At the time, she'd wondered if she should buy something for Eric's parents as well, but ultimately decided against it. Nothing in Paris was good enough for them, plus wasn't the baby the real present? She could just imagine how excited they would be to find out about their grandchild.

By the following Monday she would be in Greenwich, knocking on Eric Langvin's door. Jeff loved the name of where he lived. She opened up her school notebook, where she must have written "Anna James Langvin" more than thirty times in class this past week, and had carefully copied Eric's phone number and address from the crumpled piece of paper he'd given her. She went to sleep that night with the name dancing through her dreams. Belle Haven . . . it sounded like a magical place.

Chapter 3

THAT SATURDAY AFTERNOON, SNOW WAS coming down fast as Eric Langvin hurried to his car after basketball practice. Coach Eastman liked to keep his team in fighting form over the holidays, but today he'd ended practice early, as a nor'easter was predicted for New York City, Long Island, and Connecticut. The weather forecasters were projecting winds up to 90 miles an hour in some areas, and Eric wanted to get home fast. He scraped the frozen windshield, then started up the engine of his Porsche, a gift from his parents for his seventeenth birthday. Even though Greenwich Avenue was almost deserted, he drove carefully. The last thing he needed was to total this new red beauty. If that happened, his father would ground him until he went to college. Things were so strained between his parents these days that going away couldn't come soon enough.

After pulling up to the gate at Belle Haven, Eric waited for the guard to wave him through, and then turned on to Harbor Drive. Belle Haven was one the oldest and most historic patrician enclaves located on the southernmost tip of Greenwich, on the Long Island Sound. The Grand Dames steeped in history, built in the late 1800s, sat perched right above the ocean. He passed the Belle Haven Club, which was like a second home to him. He'd spent every summer of his life there, sailing, swimming, and playing tennis. His family would eat dinner twice a week on the porch. His time spent at the club had shaped a lot of his life, and he wished all the summers of his life could be just like the ones he'd had before.

Eric was almost home. The glistening snow on the pristine street only served to accentuate the splendor of Viking Manor, the dwelling in which he'd grown up, although he'd never given the wealth or opulence of the place much thought. This was his normal. When he arrived at the large black gates, the guard immediately opened them.

"Welcome home, Master Langvin," the guard said formally.

"Thank you," Eric responded, heading up the long hill to the massive estate.

He entered the cloakroom from the garage that had been updated when the old Georgian mansion had been renovated in the late fifties, and removed his snow-covered boots, navy pea coat, and knitted ski cap. Wrinkling his nose, he caught the sumptuous aroma of dinner cooking in the oven. He thought it smelled like pot roast, one of his favorites. Intermingled with the mouthwatering odors that perfumed the air, he caught a whiff of chocolate. Most likely Chef Claudio had just whipped up hot chocolate with fresh whipped cream, a regular staple on cold winter days at the Langvin house.

These familiar smells reminded Eric of happier times when he was younger, before his sister Mary had died and his older brother Christopher was still at home. Things had been so different then; his family had been so happy. He remembered afternoons when they would hang around the large, sunny kitchen, laughing and talking after arriving home from their various sports practices. His lovely mother would come into the kitchen, just standing on the sidelines while she watched her boisterousness family, a delighted smile on her face.

Then came that fateful day three years ago when Mary had been only twelve. She had been the most promising young skier that Greenwich had ever witnessed, with everyone speculating that Olympic medals were in her future. On a day in January, the coach of the girls' ski team at Greenwich Academy invited Mary to join them for some practice runs at Mount Southington. Mary had seemed nervous that morning, but Eric knew it was just because the other girls were older and a little more seasoned. He knew how skilled his sister was; she was a natural, and he was sure that she was destined for something great. Although his Norwegian mother had taught all of them to ski—she had always declared, "We are Vikings. We were born to ski"—and Mary had quickly proved to be more talented than anyone else in the family.

But after that day, the Langvins never skied again. His parents were called to Greenwich Hospital, where they were told that Mary had died in a skiing accident. A girl on the team had collided with her from behind, causing her to go off course and crash into a tree. She had died on impact.

That was also the day Eric's family changed forever. His father had always worked a lot, but now he stayed at the office later and later. But it was his mother who seemed the most different now. Whereas she had once been warm, loving, and outgoing, she was now a recluse. Now when he came home from school, the only thing she did was hold a crystal glass filled with vodka and slices of lime in her per-fectly manicured hands. Although she still dressed to perfection, the light from her eyes had vanished. With Christopher away at medical school, Eric was always lonely in that house. Thank God there were members of the staff who were as close to him as family.

As Eric placed his book bag on the kitchen counter, Chef Claudio smiled broadly. "Eric, my boy, big storm is coming. I made you pot roast just as you like, but I have spaghetti left over from last night you can have, too, if you want."

Eric gave Claudio a bear hug, burying his head into the man's massive shoulders. He loved the way this strong, Italian man was not afraid to show how warm and kind he was. Claudio had been with the family for as long as Eric could remember. His parents had regularly eaten at a very famous restaurant in New York City where Claudio was head chef, and one day they just decided to hire him. At first Claudio was uncertain about giving up the ambitions that had brought him to America years ago from Rome, but his wife Sophie wanted a quieter life, so he finally agreed to the position. He and Sophie moved into their own cottage on the property, and he had been with the Langvins ever since. Claudio was also trying to help Eric with his Italian lessons, so sometimes they conversed only in Italian for a few hours a day. Although Eric wasn't doing too well yet, he enjoyed hearing Claudio tell stories about his childhood in Rome and put Italy at the top of his list of places to visit someday.

Eric was drinking his hot chocolate and starting on his second fresh-baked peanut butter cookie when one of the housekeepers entered the kitchen, saying that his mother wanted to see him in the Lalique Room, the place where she seemed to spend all of her time now. It was adjacent to the living room, with large French windows that looked down upon the sea. Frosted Lalique crystal, including a chene table with figurines inside it and glass shelves decorated with vases, covered every inch of the enchanted space. The vases themselves were filled with white lilies that spilled over with bloom. Two curved, tufted, velvet peacock blue love seats faced each other in the middle of the room, looking almost gray in the winter light. As Eric approached his mother sitting on one of them now, he imagined what a beautiful photograph this scene would make. He enjoyed taking pictures of people and often practiced his photography on his family.

He kissed his mother softly on the cheek. "Hi, Mom. Why don't you go in the living room and warm up by the fire? It seems a bit cold out here with the storm and all."

When his mother looked up at him, Eric was shocked at how pale and wan her face appeared, her blue eyes enormous. Had he just not been paying attention, or did he just not want to see it?

"Oh Eric, I love it right here. I can see all of my beautiful figurines and watch the snow come down. It reminds of when I was a little girl in Norway. We used to play in the snow and ski every day." Her hands begin to tremble, sloshing the liquid in her martini glass. "If only I hadn't insisted that my children learn to ski, too. Mary might still be alive."

As Eric pulled his mother into his arms, he felt his usual despair at hearing these words. She said a version of them to him almost every day. In fact, he suspected that she looked forward to when he came home from school just so that she could call him into the sitting room and blame herself for Mary's death. At first, he'd tried to soothe her, telling her that Mary's skiing accident was just that—an accident—and it had nothing to do with her. But she wouldn't listen, and soon he gave up trying. He didn't know how else to help his mother. Over the past three years she'd gone to many doctors, who'd prescribed her an assortment of pills. It saddened Eric to see her depend so much on self-medication—the pills and the alcohol—but he was only seventeen and figured those in positions of authority knew better than him.

Drawing away from her, he said, "It's okay, Mom. I'm still here."

His mother smiled distantly at him and Eric muttered some excuse about having to go to his room to do his homework. Before leaving the Lalique Room, he turned back to look at her. She was still staring vacantly at the space where he'd been standing, and he knew to a certain extent it didn't matter whether he was there or not. She was lost in the past, in her childhood, forever keeping tragedy at bay the only way she could.

Upstairs in his room, Eric flopped on the bed and entertained the idea of studying, but he still felt unsettled. The holidays this year were going to be difficult, especially since Christopher never came home from school anymore. He recalled the family Christmases they'd all spent in Paris before Mary died. There had been so much laughter then, the feeling that they would always be together as a family.

He had never talked about these memories with anyone else, even his friends. But he had revealed them to that girl Jeff, whom he'd met in Kentucky. He didn't know why, but something about her had made him open up to her, not to mention the fact that she was more beautiful than any girl he'd ever met. That night they'd spent together certainly had been something. Eric's experience with sex was limited to fooling around at parties and a short, awkward in-and-out with a Greenwich girlfriend, but even he knew what they'd had together was good, even special. Some nights he still dreamed about Jeff's luscious body, imagining her warm, supple breasts in his hands, and then he would come in an explosion just like the fireworks on the Fourth of July. He'd wake up soaked and have to change his boxers. But the real Jeff—her face, her voice— was beginning to fade.

At first, after he'd returned home to Connecticut, they'd talked quite a few times on the phone. Eric had liked listening to Jeff's jokes about cheerleading practice and what was going on among her group of friends at the Paris Grille. But in their later conversations, he couldn't help feeling that she was looking for something more from him. It had been so easy when they'd left each other to pretend that might be possible. But hadn't he done enough by giving her his phone number and address so that she could write him? What else could he do? Eric was beginning to realize that he knew very little about girls. So when a couple of weeks earlier a housekeeper told him that "Anna Jefferson" had called, he didn't call back.

And since he hadn't heard from Jeff since then, he figured that she had gotten the message and wasn't going to bother him anymore.

Lying in bed, Eric wished life was less complicated, like when he was younger. When his sister was alive, his father and brother were around, and his mother wasn't a stranger. He couldn't make that happen, but at least he could simplify things by cutting things off with a girl whom he was likely to never see again. It was for the best, he thought, if he forgot about Jeff, and she forgot about him.

Chapter 4

THE FIRST GLIMPSE JEFF HAD of Belle Haven was from the taxi she had stepped into after getting off the train in Greenwich. Prior to that she'd spent the past day and night on the train from Lexington to New York City, so agitated and nervous she could barely sleep. Instead, her mind kept replaying questions to the tune of the train's wheels rumbling along the tracks. Would Eric's family welcome her? Would they welcome the baby? Well, she thought, it was too late now. The baby was here, and growing fast. Although her morning sickness had mercifully calmed down in time for the trip, Jeff was aware every second of the little being that had taken possession of her body.

During her brief stop in Grand Central while waiting for her next train, Jeff had slipped into one of the sleazy bathroom stalls to change into a cashmere sweater, soft blue woolen trousers, and a fluffy white down coat from McAlpin's. She thought she looked just like one of the snobbish, sophisticated girls that Eric might know. Then, as if she was indeed one of those girls traveling home to Greenwich, she strolled through the station's hallowed marble halls in her shiny new loafers. In the main hall, standing beneath the constellation-covered ceiling while passengers swarmed around her, she felt like she'd finally arrived somewhere worthwhile.

Boarding the train to Greenwich, her heart began to pump hard with excitement at the thought of seeing Eric again. By this time she had convinced herself that once he heard about the baby, he would want to get married right away. Lots of girls Jeff knew in Kentucky had gotten accidentally pregnant, and their boyfriends had all married them. It wasn't that farfetched, was it? Well, Eric wasn't exactly her boyfriend, but they were in love, and this was exactly what Jeff wanted for herself: a rich, educated boyfriend, not some poor nobody without a future. Most definitely of all, she didn't want to be like her mother, alone and trapped in a dead-end job.

In the taxi, Jeff leaned forward to see everything she could of the world opening up before her. She had never seen houses this large or magnificent, each looking like it had come straight out of a storybook. A recent wintery storm had left the trees glittering with snow, but she could imagine what they must look like in the summer, lush and green, providing an extra curtain of verdant privacy.

When the taxi turned onto Harbor Drive, the Atlantic Ocean in all its glory stared back at her. She asked the taxi driver to stop for a minute so that she could drink in the view of the rough gray waves. Never having seen the sea except in pictures and postcards, she couldn't help but feel overwhelmed. She wondered what it would be like to live right beside it . . . and maybe now she would get the chance. Maybe this little monster growing inside her was a good thing after all; maybe it could land her right in the middle of the wealthy lifestyle she had always desired, and believed she deserved. In a cold and commanding voice she never knew she possessed, she said to the patiently waiting taxi driver, "Go!"

Jeff's optimism dimmed slightly when the taxi pulled up to a pair of iron gates leading up to the Langvin estate. Just beyond it she could see an enormous mansion rising above the trees—a shining beacon on the hill, yet forbidden to those who weren't welcome.

Doubts from the train ride resurfaced, but she shook them off with a toss of her abundant blond curls.

With all the confidence she could muster, she said to the guard in the gatehouse, "I'm here to see Eric Langvin."

The guard just winked at her. "Sure, miss, welcome to Viking Manor."

What did that wink mean? Did Eric have girls visit him often? Jeff squashed that thought and congratulated herself that she had managed to fool the guard, just like she had fooled everyone else so far.

After paying the taxi driver, Jeff got out with her suitcase in hand and stood before the Langvins' front door. It opened within a few seconds of her ringing the bell, as if someone had been expecting her. Rather than a maid, she was surprised to find herself face-to-face with Eric. It was as if Jeff was seeing him again for the first time—his fair hair, his square jaw—and falling straight into his sea-blue eyes without noticing the puzzled expression in them.

"Surprise!" she exclaimed, throwing her arms around him.

Eric returned her hug but his reply was less enthusiastic. "Jeff, what are you doing here? You're supposed to be in Kentucky."

"Since I hadn't heard from you for so long, I thought I would visit you so we could spend New Year's together." When he didn't say anything, she put on her most alluring pout. "Eric, aren't you glad to see me?"

"Uh, sure." Even though he was only wearing jeans and a sweat-shirt, he stepped outside and closed the door behind him.

This was not the welcome Jeff had been expecting. "Don't you want to ask me to come in?"

"It's not really a good time," Eric replied. "My parents are busy, so why don't we go for a ride and grab some hot chocolate down at the club?"

Without waiting for an answer, he took Jeff's suitcase and headed around the house toward the garage. Jeff followed him with uncertain steps, but when she saw his red Porsche, her excitement began to return. Sitting next to him in his car as they zoomed down the snowy, empty streets was like something out of the movies. What would her Kentucky girlfriends think of her now?

Eric turned off Harbor Drive and pulled up to an expansive, dignified-looking building with an American flag flying from the rooftop. This, Jeff supposed, was the Belle Haven Club, which he had mentioned to her during one of their telephone conversations. As they walked up to the entrance, Jeff snuggled into her coat with anticipation. The fact that Eric was taking her to one of his favorite places must mean something.

The interior of the club was homey, filled with overstuffed club chairs and sofas, but nearly devoid of people as Eric led Jeff to a table overlooking an expansive marina.

"Where is everyone?" Jeff asked.

"It's kind of deserted now because everyone's in Palm Beach for the winter," Eric explained. "But when it gets warm, more boats are docked out there than people to sail them."

"Do you like sailing here?" Jeff hoped that talking about sailing would put him a better mood.

"Yes, but I also like hanging out at the dock. You can get some great pictures at sunset when the light is just right. The golden hour, it's called."

Jeff recalled how enthusiastically Eric had spoken about his photography the first night they'd met. "What else do you like to take pictures of?"

"People . . . my family, mostly. There's something about being able to capture a person's essence when they're posing, or especially when they're not posing and just acting natural, doing what they normally do. It's tough, but when it happens, it's like magic."

"Well, I'd love for you to take a picture of me," she said coyly.

He only nodded as a waiter came and placed before them two steaming mugs of hot chocolate, scones, and a bowl of clotted cream. Jeff realized just then how hungry she was, having eaten nothing since boarding the train in Grand Central. Also, now that her morning sickness was no longer bothering her, she had the appetite of a mule. But she couldn't stuff herself in front of Eric. Instead, she sat back, wrapped her hands around her mug, and gazed adoringly into his eyes the way only a teenage girl can. Eric seemed to relax and smiled back at her, making Jeff feel encouraged. The feelings from their time alone together—all the lust and wonderment—came rushing back.

"Eric, please don't be mad," she entreated. "I'm so happy to see you and I just wanted to spend some time with you. I was thinking I could stay at your place and meet your parents?"

"I'm glad to see you, too," Eric responded with what sounded like genuine warmth. "But you can't stay at my house. My parents would never allow it. Maybe I could put you up at a nearby inn? I could come see you every day. How long are you planning to be here, anyway?"

As Jeff took a cautious sip of her chocolate, she began to understand what Eric meant. He didn't want her to meet his parents. He didn't want her inside his house. Instead, he wanted to keep her hidden someplace he could visit her and undoubtedly have sex with her without anybody else knowing. But Jeff hadn't schemed her way to Greenwich to be someone's dirty little secret.

"I'm afraid I can't do that," she said, folding her hands over her belly. "There's another reason I came here to see you, and I might as well tell you now."

"What is it, Jeff?" Eric asked, sounding irritated for the first time.

In a soft voice, she said, "I'm ten weeks pregnant."

Eric stared at her as if he didn't quite realize what she was getting at. Then he shook his head. "How do you know it's mine?"

A hot redness surged across Jeff's face. This certainly wasn't the way she had imagined this conversation going. "Because you're the first person I ever had sex with," she snapped. "And the last," she added for good measure.

Now Eric looked even more confused. "I didn't think you could get pregnant your first time."

"I didn't, either." Jeff tried to choke back the angry tears rising in her throat. "But between the two of us, you should have known better."

Eric looked taken aback, even abashed. "I'm sorry," he said. "I didn't mean to suggest that you were . . . I mean, you're right. I should have known better. But that doesn't change what's happened. What are you going to do now?"

"Me?" Jeff wished they were sitting next to each other instead of with the white-linen gulf of the table between them. She knew if she could just hold his hand, just touch him, she could make him understand. "Eric, I know this is scary. I'm scared, too. But I fell in love with you the minute I met you, and I knew we were meant to be together. And although I would not have planned this ever, this will bring us closer together. We just have to make some plans."

"What kind of plans? Do you think we're going to get married?"

"Well, I . . ." Jeff stopped when she saw the resolute look on Eric's face. For a moment, neither of them spoke.

"You're right, you should meet my parents," he finally said.

A glimmer of hope shot through Jeff's mind. He wanted her to meet his parents! And once she did, she was sure that they would see that she and the baby fit perfectly into their family. After all, not long ago they had lost a daughter, and now they might be gaining one.

Neither Eric nor Jeff spoke to each other during the chilly ride back to Viking Manor. Once there, Eric led Jeff through the back door and into the kitchen, where arranged on the long counter were two different kinds of pizzas, a green salad, and a hot loaf of buttered bread. It was food for a quiet family dinner, but Jeff's mouth began to water since she hadn't dared to eat a bite at the club.

"Wait here," Eric said, and Jeff stood obediently where he had left her, wondering if she might sneak a piece of bread.

When he returned, Jeff followed him into a circular sitting room that made her think of a crystal ice palace. Holding court was an elegantly tall, thin, pale blond woman who appeared as fragile as one of the glass figurines that filled the glass-fronted cabinets throughout the room. From what Eric had told Jeff about his mother since the death of his sister, she could indeed tell that something had forever frozen within Lillian Langvin. Despite being wrapped up in a cream cashmere robe, she looked as cold as the vodka on the rocks that she held in one long, delicate hand. Jeff's attention was immediately drawn to her other hand, which was adorned by a very large, square-cut diamond ring. She hoped to be wearing one at least half that size on her hand by New Year's Eve.

"Mom," Eric said, "I'd like you to meet Jeff . . . I mean, Anna Jefferson."

Lillian inclined her head in a cool nod, looking at Jeff with eyes the same unsettling aqua as Eric's.

"Nice to meet you, ma'am," Jeff stammered.

"Where's Dad?" Eric asked his mother. "I want him to meet Anna, too."

"Your father is in the family room watching the game."

"Then I think we'd all better go join him there."

Jeff was glad to leave the sitting room, being afraid she might accidentally break one of the priceless glass objects if she so much as breathed. She followed Eric and his mother down the hallway to a much cheerier space where Lars Langvin was settled in a big, brown leather cigar chair, the television playing low in the background. As he turned around and stood in the fashion of a gentleman, Jeff could see that Eric got his height and build from his father, but his coloring was all from his mother.

"Eric, my boy," Lars said, "you didn't tell me you had a date tonight." His dark eyes flickered over to Jeff in appraisal. "Come sit down and introduce me to this lovely young lady."

Eric looked as if he was about to correct his father, thought better of it, and gestured for Jeff to sit down beside him on the couch opposite his parents. "Dad, this is Anna Jefferson," he began and then faltered, unsure of how to continue.

"So Anna, do you go to Greenwich Academy?" Lars broke the silence.

Jeff supposed this must be Brunswick Prep's sister school. "No, sir," she said. "I'm from Paris—"

"Paris, Kentucky," Eric interjected. "Anna and I met when I went down for that poverty awareness tour in October. She happened to be passing through town just now and thought she would pay me a visit."

Jeff had to clench her teeth to keep from screaming. Here she sat with a baby in her belly, making her so hungry that all she could think about was the pizza sitting on the kitchen counter, and Eric wasn't even going to tell his parents the truth about why she had come to see him. Obviously she was just going to have to tell them herself.

"Mr. Langvin, Mrs. Langvin, I'm so happy to finally meet you." Jeff spoke as if she and Eric had been dating for months. "What Eric is trying to say is that we fell in love in Kentucky, and I came to spend New Year's with him."

Lars turned to Eric with a smile that appeared to be an attempt at joviality. "So I see this isn't just a date but a new girlfriend."

"I—" Eric opened and closed his mouth.

"We have some very special news to tell you," Jeff continued, looking expectantly at Eric, who was still speechless.

"Eric," Lillian said, "what in the world is this all about?"

Jeff couldn't wait any longer. "Just tell them!" she hissed at Eric. "We have a lot to plan, and being pregnant, I really need to eat!"

She felt as if she had tossed a bomb into the middle of the room, yet Eric's parents maintained an impressive level of calm. Lars sat stone faced, while Lillian's expression was unchanging, the slight shaking of her martini glass, the ice cubes tinkling, the only betrayal of her inner thoughts. Meanwhile, Eric sat with his face lowered, his ears turning bright red.

"Could you please freshen my drink?" Lillian asked her husband in a quiet voice.

Without a word, Lars took her glass and left the room, and no one else spoke until he returned. Lillian continued to look into the distance, while Eric stared at the floor, and Jeff twisted her hands in her lap, a little less sure of herself after throwing down her ace. After Lars handed Lillian her drink, Jeff noticed that she removed two tiny white pills from the pocket of her robe and slipped then under her tongue.

"Well, kids," Lars said in that same, falsely jovial voice, "that's certainly some big news."

That released something in Eric, who cried, "Dad, neither of us meant for this to happen! It was all a mistake. I'm so sorry."

A mistake? Jeff glared at Eric, forgetting that she hadn't planned this pregnancy any more than he had, having persuaded herself that the baby was their love child.

"I know you didn't, son," Lars soothed. "And I know that Anna here didn't, either, but now we have to make plans for what comes next. Now, Anna," he turned to Jeff, "why don't you go to the kitchen and get some dinner? You said you were hungry, and you need to keep up your strength. Eric can accompany you."

Eric gave his father a pleading look as if he didn't want to be left alone with her, which annoyed Jeff. Ever since she'd arrived in

Greenwich, she'd had to do everything, from telling Eric she loved him to revealing the news of the baby to his parents. He'd done nothing but apologize to his parents when he should be apologizing to *her* for getting her pregnant. Still, Jeff thought, he could make up for all of that with a sizeable ring.

"Anna," Lars said, "do you have a place to stay tonight? I thought not. I'll have a suite prepared for you and your suitcase delivered to it. We can talk tomorrow morning when we've all had a chance to get some sleep."

"Yes," Lillian agreed, as if this were the time of day she looked forward to the most. "I'm going to bed right now."

Jeff followed Eric back into the kitchen, where they sat on stools at the counter. Ravenously hungry, she dug into the pizza without any thought of how it might look to him. She was done with pretending now that the secret was out. Eric, she noticed, hardly ate anything but stared out the window, deep in thought.

After a while, he asked sheepishly, "Are you feeling better?"

Jeff nodded. "I feel a lot better now that your parents know about us. I was so worried about what they would say when they found out about the baby."

"You don't need to worry," Eric replied, as if more to himself than to her. "My father will know what to do."

Jeff hoped that after dinner he might take her on a tour of the house, but Eric seemed in no hurry to leave the kitchen. If the tables were turned, she'd want to be alone in his bedroom with him as soon as possible. She wondered if he might find her body less attractive now that she pregnant, although she didn't know why; her breasts were larger than ever, and her stomach wasn't showing in the least bit. Maybe she just needed to remind him that she was the same person he couldn't keep his hands off of in Kentucky.

"Should we go upstairs?" she suggested. "I've had such a long trip and I'm so tired."

Eric blinked as if awakening from a dream and stood up. "Of course. Most of the staff is off tonight, so I'll show you to your room."

Playfully, Jeff held out her hand for him to help her down from her stool. When he took it, she pretended to stumble and fell hard against him. His arms automatically went around her, and she looked up at him with pleading eyes. Their lips met, and in an instant they were transported back to the dance floor at the Paris Grille, the bedroom at Red Rose Farm. He pressed her against the counter as his appetite for her returned with an intensity that surprised them both. Taking his hands from around her waist, she guided them underneath her sweater to her breasts, then moved her own hands to the front of his jeans. He groaned and lifted her onto the counter, kissing her lips, her neck, and lifting her sweater, between her breasts, moving down her body.

He had just reached her stomach when the sound of forceful footsteps approaching made them both freeze, breathing hard.

"My dad," Eric whispered.

Jeff landed back on the floor with a thud and adjusted her clothes as Eric quickly moved to put the counter between them. Seconds later, Lars walked into the room, looking from one telltale flushed face to the other. Nervously, Jeff ran her tongue over her swollen lips.

"I was just about to take Jeff to her room," Eric explained, although no question had been asked.

"I'll take her," Lars said. "Go to your room, Eric."

Meekly, Eric turned and left without glancing at Jeff.

"Come, Miss Jefferson." With a stern face, Lars escorted Jeff upstairs to the door of her suite. "Your suitcase is inside," he informed her. "Someone will come get you in the morning. Have a good night."

As Jeff watched Eric's father retreat down the hall, she wondered what would have happened if he hadn't shown up in the kitchen. She knew she hadn't imagined the fervor with which Eric had kissed and touched her. But she didn't know if he would dare try anything with her again under his parents' roof; hopefully they could go somewhere private for New Year's Eve. The most important thing, she reminded herself, was that Eric still desired her. He still loved her.

Although she was exhausted, Jeff felt a wave of triumph suffuse her body. This morning on the train she had been a poor girl with an unwanted baby in her belly. Now she was staying in the finest home she had ever laid eyes on, and someday it could all be hers. With a full stomach and full heart, she turned the doorknob and stepped over the threshold into her new life.

Chapter 5

OPENING HER EYES THE NEXT morning, Jeff felt as though she were waking up in her scrapbook back home in Kentucky. From the time she was a little girl, she had cut out pictures of bedrooms from magazines like *Veranda* and *Town & Country* that her mother had brought home from work. Now she was in one of those extraordinary rooms.

As she snuggled in her canopy bed, which was draped with an embroidered indigo cover, she looked around the room with its soothing dove-white walls. Every single detail was exquisite to her eyes. The white mantle above the fireplace was adorned with Chinese blue vases and chairs. A window seat served as an ideal reading nook, framed by an entire wall covered with books. From the Palladian window she could see the serene, snowy landscape outside. The room even had a skirted dressing table topped with antique perfume bottles and a large silver mirror that she could imagine looking into while putting on her makeup for New Year's Eve.

Her thoughts were interrupted by a soft knock at the door.

"Come in," she called, drawing the blanket up over her chest, half expecting it to be Eric himself.

Instead, the door opened to reveal a fresh-faced young woman dressed in a black- and-white maid's uniform and holding a silver tray. She looked to be only a few years older than Jeff.

"May I come in, Miss Anna?" she asked sweetly. "I'm Linda, one of the housekeepers. I've brought you some breakfast. Please be downstairs in the living room at nine o'clock and leave out any clothing you would like cleaned or pressed. I will take care of it when I clean your room."

"Thank you," Jeff replied, in wonderment at the service. Now this was the way to live.

Her breakfast tray was filled with eggs, bacon, and buttered toast; obviously someone had taken into consideration she was eating for two, and Jeff ate every morsel. Then she took a shower in her very own bathroom that also had a soaking tub. She couldn't help comparing it to home where she and her mother shared a bathroom with a pink plastic shower curtain and a rickety old medicine cabinet that hung crookedly on the wall. How could she go back to that after experiencing such heavenly bliss?

After leaving out her travel clothes and the clothes she'd worn the previous day for Linda to get cleaned, Jeff went downstairs to the living room, which was adjacent to the Lalique room where she had met Lillian Langvin the day before.

Although she knew she wasn't late, everyone else was already assembled in the palatial living room. Below a ceiling etched with delicate molding, the furnishings were all in various shades of white, from linen and cream to a snowy white. Eric sat on a deep cream sofa with his parents on either side. He wore a navy blazer and gray slacks, and a penitent expression on his face. Lars was similarly attired, but it was Lillian that Jeff's eyes were immediately drawn to.

Lillian Langvin wore an ivory fitted dress that danced just below her knees, fine hosiery that made her slender legs shimmer, and cream crocodile pumps that were fitted perfectly to her feet.

Through the thick waves of her platinum hair winked opal earrings encrusted with diamonds, and around her swanlike neck rested a single-strand diamond necklace. Jeff had never seen one person wear so many diamonds before.

"Now that we're all here, we can proceed," Lars said. "Please sit down, Anna."

Jeff felt somehow dwarfed, minimalized, as she sank into one of the sofas opposite the Langvins. Shouldn't Eric be sitting next to her rather than in between his parents? She tried to catch his eye, but he refused to look at her, focusing instead on the coffee table separating them.

Lars continued to address her. "May I introduce you to Phillip Harris?"

A dark-haired, clerical-looking man stepped forth from the shadows. In his gray vested suit and a sleek, monochromatic tie, Jeff thought he looked like he was going to a funeral. Could he be a minister? No, she was jumping ahead of herself. She and Eric hadn't discussed marriage yet, and she was not going to be talked out of having a big wedding.

"Anna, where do you want to go to college next year?" Lars asked.

This unexpected question took Jeff by surprise. She had not given much thought about what would happen after she graduated from Paris High School. Perhaps she'd take some classes at the local community college while continuing to work at McAlpin's; that is, until something better came along. In all honesty, she had hoped that her life would take a substantial turn before then, although she had never envisioned anything as substantial as getting pregnant.

"I don't know," she admitted.

"That's too bad. Because Eric is going to Harvard next fall, just like his brother and I did before him. And he's going to go to business school after that."

"Dad, I haven't decided yet," Eric muttered, showing a spark of defiance for the first time.

"What's there to decide?" Lars scoffed. "What's good enough for the other men in the Langvin family is good enough for you. Don't think some hobby like taking photos is going to amount to anything."

"Some people make a good living from photography," Eric pointed out. "And they're able to hold onto their souls while doing it—"

"Enough!" Lars roared. "Eric, you've done quite enough here. I would advise you to keep quiet." Composing himself, he turned his attention to Jeff again. "Eric's mother and I have discussed this, and we're sure that your parents must feel the same way. Since you and Eric are so young, and you both have such bright futures ahead of you, you mustn't let a baby get in the way."

This was the first time since arriving in Greenwich that Jeff felt her plan start to tilt to the side, like a ship hitting a reef. "I'm having this baby," she said in a shaky voice.

"We're not asking you to do anything that would put you or the baby in danger," Lillian spoke up.

Lars looked to Phillip Harris, who now stepped into the spotlight. "Miss Jefferson, the Langvins are prepared to pay you $100,000 in increments of $25,000 a year if you will simply agree to put the baby up for adoption. You must also sign a confidentiality agreement that the father's name will not appear on the birth certificate and that you will never reveal his identity to anyone."

Now Jeff was starting to get the picture, and it was not a pretty one. The Langvins wanted her to go away because she and the baby weren't good enough for Eric. The Langvins didn't want anyone to know about them.

She looked beseechingly at Eric. "But we're in love." She paused. "Aren't we?"

Eric's gaze seemed to have moved from the coffee table to the floor. "I'm sorry, Jeff, but I agree that this is for the best."

In that moment Jeff knew that he would not help her. He was too cowed by his father, too afraid of his family to go against them. She was completely, utterly on her own.

"*You're* sorry?" she cried. "I'm the one with the little monster in my stomach, not you! Now I have to go through this all by myself. You can't just buy me off with a little bit of money and get me to go away."

Lars shook his head. "I don't think the amount is insignificant. In addition, you have your mother and father to support you through this time."

"My father left two years ago and my mother doesn't know I'm pregnant. She doesn't know I've come up here. Nobody knows about me and Eric, I didn't even tell my friends. So much for my support! Not everyone lives like your family, Mr. Langvin." With that final shot, Jeff sprang to her feet and ran upstairs to her suite, barely able to keep back the tears.

In her room, Jeff lay in a crumpled heap on her bed, her hopes dashed. Now she would never become the wife of a multimillionaire, or live like the beautiful young women whose lives unfolded in the pages of her scrapbook. She cried for her mother and for the hours Jenny spent standing on her feet working at the boutique. She cried for her father, who had felt so trapped that he had no choice except to leave his family. She couldn't stop the tears for her small-town friends, whose visions for their futures were nothing more than attending a no-name college, finding a husband, and having a baby, just like the one in her stomach. What dismal and mundane lives they would lead, never realizing what they were missing.

But most of all, she grieved for herself, for the happy, innocent girl she had once been. Now that she had a taste of what this kind of lifestyle could be like, she knew she could never go back. Only she had no idea how she was going to get there now.

* * *

For the next three days, Jeff stayed in her suite. She hadn't realized how physically exhausted she was from the trip and the pregnancy, and emotionally exhausted from the grim realities of her situation, which seemed to expand with each passing day. All she wanted to do was sleep. Safe in the veil of her dreams, she turned further into herself.

During this time, she was vaguely aware of knocks at her door, someone quietly entering to leave freshly laundered clothes and trays, and departing just as quietly. She left the food untouched, ignoring the baby's desperate cry for nourishment that she felt deep inside her. When she was awake, she noticed that snow was falling fast outside the window, cloaking the room in perpetual dusk. Sometimes she opened her eyes to find a fire burning in the fireplace, but it didn't bring her warmth. Instead, she felt cold like the snow piling up on the streets outside, numb like the ice glistening on the lawns. She was like a princess trapped in the tower of a grand castle, except she was the one who had engineered her own imprisonment.

On the third morning, she woke up to find Linda, the young housekeeper, standing next to her bed.

"Miss Anna, I brought you food," she said. "You must eat something, especially in your condition."

Jeff looked at her with bleary eyes. "What do you know about my condition?"

"I know that it's made the Langvins very upset." Linda leaned in closer. "I'm not supposed to talk to you, but I overheard Mr. Langvin say that if you don't come out of your room soon, he's going to call the police. They won't let you stay here much longer."

With a sigh, Jeff lay back on her pillow. "They can't just throw me out."

"They can, and they will. Take my word for it. These people don't care about anyone but themselves, they're only concerned about how their family looks. I've just been here six months, but I've worked for other people just like them. And I have seen situations like this."

"So what would you suggest I do?" Jeff asked.

"Take their offer and triple it," Linda replied without hesitation. "Take what you can from them and go."

Gazing into the young woman's earnest face, Jeff saw that she spoke the truth. But before she could thank Linda for the advice, the young housekeeper said, "I have to get to work now. If I get caught talking to you, I'm out of a job," whereupon she turned and rushed from the room.

Linda was right. Jeff knew she didn't have time to lie in bed and wait for the axe to fall. As she tried to get out of bed, she realized how shaky she had become without eating any food for the past few days. She didn't feel particularly hungry, but she knew she had to eat, although certainly not for the little monster inside her, who had caused all this trouble. No, she would eat for her own strength, to prepare for the battle ahead. Jeff started slowly with the scrambled eggs, then as her hunger grew, demolished the bacon and oatmeal. A large glass of milk sat next to her tray, which she knew had been put there because of her pregnancy. Jeff immediately took it and poured it down the toilet. *Nothing for the baby! Nothing!* Grimly, she watched the white liquid disappear down the drain.

She began pacing the room like an animal in a cage, desperate to devise a way she could outsmart Lars Langvin and Phillip Harris, whom she now assumed to be the family lawyer. They were the ones with the money, the experience, and the authority. The only thing she had in her favor was the baby in her belly. But just maybe that was enough.

Jeff sat down at the Queen Anne desk in her room and opened her school notebook that she had brought with her. The page on which she had written "Anna James Langvin" over and over in class stared back at her. With a swift tug she yanked the page out and threw it away. Then she started to furiously write down her demands.

Studying her list a few hours later, she heard a soft knock at the door and knew it was Linda. The housekeeper smiled when she saw the empty tray.

"Linda," Jeff said, "please tell the Langvins that I will meet with them in the living room at six o'clock this evening to tell them my decision regarding their offer."

Linda simply nodded, picked up the tray, and left the room.

For the rest of the afternoon, Jeff walked around the room, practicing what she had to say. The only time she'd ever had to make a case was in debate class at school, but never with such high stakes. This time, whether she won or lost would determine the shape of her future.

* * *

At six o'clock that evening, Jeff sat in the middle of a sofa in the Langvins' living room, having arrived a few minutes early. She wore a black cashmere sweater, black trousers, and black flats. Her long blond hair was pulled back with a black bow. Although she didn't wear any makeup, that only made her eyes even more blue and penetrating.

Lars Langvin and Phillip Harris entered together, seating themselves on chairs opposite her. That was when Jeff understood no one else was coming. While she hadn't expected Lillian, due to the woman's brittle constitution, she was a little disappointed that Eric wasn't there, even if he wasn't of much use to her anymore.

"Where's Eric?" she couldn't help asking.

"He's staying with a family friend," Lars informed her. "He won't be back until the day before school starts up again."

So she was truly alone.

The three of them bypassed pleasantries, as they all knew this gathering was not going to be particularly pleasant.

"So, Anna, have you given some thought to our proposal?" Lars looked straight into her eyes, as she imagined he might when trying to close a big business deal.

Never once looking away, Jeff replied, "Yes, I have, and it is unacceptable." She paused and then said with more assurance than she felt, "I have a proposal for you, and this is all I will accept."

"The Langvins have made you a fine offer—" Phillip Harris started to say.

Lars held up a hand. "No, Phil. Let's hear what she has to say."

Jeff stood, holding the yellow piece of lined paper from her notebook that contained her list of demands in return for putting the baby up for adoption and her secrecy. She had no intention of keeping the baby after it was born; they didn't have to worry about that. But she was going to get what he owed to her. During the three days and nights that she had lain in despair in her bedroom, she had thought about all the things that she had yearned for over the course of her young life: money, status, a big house, and to be a socialite. *She so wanted to be a socialite!* She didn't know exactly what a socialite was, except that such a person was wealthy, glamorous, and desired by everyone. Someone like Lillian Langvin. If she couldn't marry Eric, Jeff would find someone from a family with an even more renowned pedigree. She would go to a college where she would join the most prestigious sorority, date the richest fraternity boys, and then marry the one from the best family.

"First," she said, "Mr. Langvin will use his connections to get me into a good college in the south."

Laughing a little, Lars shook his head. "I'm afraid I can't do that."

Jeff glared at him through narrowed eyes. "Surely you know people who can help you do that."

Phillip Harris looked like he was about to protest, but Lars waved him down once again. "Please continue."

"You will give me $100,000 up front and $50,000 each year for the next four years. In return, I will do as you ask and not put Eric's name on the birth certificate, or ever reveal that he is the father of the baby."

Finished with her announcement, Jeff handed Lars the piece of yellow notebook paper. She had written her demands in perfect, block-styled handwriting and signed them with a bold, oversize signature—*Anna James Jefferson*. Lars glanced at it, then handed the paper to Phillip Harris, who quickly scanned it.

"Miss Jefferson," the lawyer said, "you are seeking a very large sum of money for your silence, don't you think?"

"I thought my silence was the most important thing in the world to the Langvin family," Jeff responded, her hands folded calmly in her lap.

"We feel that $100,000 is more than adequate for you to begin a new life after the baby is born and you get back to school."

"I don't have any idea how my health is going to be during this pregnancy. There could be complications, and the baby's life could be in danger. There isn't any amount of money that you could compensate me with if something happened to either of us."

"Of course." Lars tried to placate her. "However, none of that would be our fault."

"Fault?" Jeff raised an eyebrow. "Who put me in this position? You know, I have quite a good story to tell. One about how a rich boy on a poverty awareness tour took advantage of a poor girl from Kentucky. I'm sure your local paper would be interested in that."

Lars sprang to his feet. "Why, you little—" He would have said more, perhaps done more, had his lawyer not restrained him.

Jeff moved not an inch from her position on the sofa. She knew she had Lars Langvin by the throat. Linda had said that these people were most concerned about how they appeared to others, and while Jeff didn't know how she could make good on her threat, she knew it was potent enough if it got Lars Langvin to drop his mask. She had come to understand that while money was important to a family like the Langvins, what was more important was how their family looked. They had already lost a child; they couldn't afford to lose another to scandal and disgrace.

"Miss Jefferson," Phillip Harris said, "can you please excuse us for a moment?"

He drew Lars away from Jeff and into the Lalique room, where their murmuring voices were lost behind the crystal figurines. On the sofa, Jeff continued to sit calmly. While she would not have believed three days ago that she, a seventeen-year-old girl from Kentucky, could have outwitted the patriarch of an affluent Connecticut family and his lawyer, now her confidence was unshakeable. The baby in her belly had given her that power.

In a few minutes the two men returned with solemn expressions. Phillip Harris was the one who spoke. "We will honor your requests with the following conditions, providing you follow them."

Jeff's expression did not change, although inside she felt victorious. Her crazy teenage love for Eric was over. She couldn't think about how he had let her down and not supported her. All that mattered was that she had won the battle. "What are your conditions?"

"Upon the baby's birth, you will give it up for adoption to social services. You will provide a clean birth certificate with the state seal omitting the name Eric Edward Langvin as the father. You will disclose to no one that he is the father of this baby. Ever. You will not discuss your visit to Greenwich and the Langvin residence with anyone, now or ever." He paused briefly and then continued, "Tomorrow, you will fly first class back to Lexington and a car service will take you home. From then on you will not contact any-one in the Langvin family ever again. All questions—and I trust there will be none—will be directed to me."

"And the money?"

"You will receive $100,000 up front, which will be wired to a Lexington bank that we deem is most appropriate. The other $200,000 will be placed in a New York bank trust, which will provide you $50,000 each year for the next four years. This agreement is to be discussed with no other party. Is this understood?"

"Yes," Jeff answered simply. "What about college?"

Visibly wincing, Lars cleared his throat. "The admissions dean at Emory University owes me a favor. I assume that school is acceptable to you?"

"It is."

Holding Jeff's school notebook paper by the edge, as if he could barely stand to touch it, Phillip Harris said, "I will go prepare the document and we will sign in the morning."

He stepped out of the room, leaving Jeff and Lars Langvin facing each other. Slowly, Jeff got to her feet and, with her back absolutely straight, looked at Lars with unwavering eyes. She held out her hand.

"I appreciate doing business with you, Mr. Langvin."

Lars took her hand and gave her a begrudging bow. "Good luck, Ms. Jefferson."

* * *

As the black town car drove away from Viking Manor, Jeff turned once to look back at the house that she had once hoped would have welcomed her. For weeks she had dreamed of being in Eric's arms, a declaration of love from him, a fancy ring, a family that would embrace her into their exclusive fold. Maybe she'd gotten something better though: her freedom.

She imagined herself on a warm and sunny campus in Atlanta where she would meet new people and become an entirely new person. All she had to do was make it to her due date. The baby was the last obstacle in her path, and after it was given up for adoption, she would truly be free to be whoever she wanted to be.

The last glimpse of Viking Manor disappeared behind the trees, and Jeff turned to face the front. She was leaving the old Jeff behind her—the young girl who believed in fairy tales and romance, love at first sight, all of that childish nonsense. The new Jeff was savvier than that. She now understood that what she really wanted could only be gotten with cold, hard cash, and that someday she'd look back at this little interlude up north as the beginning of her education.

Chapter 6

AFTER JEFF RETURNED TO PARIS, what had happened to her in Belle Haven almost seemed like a dream. Except in a bank in Lexington was $100,000 that had been wired to her within a few days of her return. Now, rather than simply dreaming about Eric Langvin during her spare time as she had before the holidays, Jeff imagined the real things she would buy with her newfound fortune. Designer clothes, for one, and jewelry. Maybe a car that was a million times better than her mother's old Pontiac. But all that would have to wait until after she had the baby, and after she had left home for college. She counted on Lars Langvin to hold up that part of the deal as well.

As the months went by, Jeff had more pressing matters to think about; namely, how to hide her pregnancy from her mother and her friends at school. Fortunately, basketball season had ended without the team going to the state championships, so she had an excuse for not participating in cheerleading practice anymore. Her uniform no longer fit anyway. Otherwise, she dressed in baggy clothes, transitioning from oversize winter sweaters to blousy tops and loose dresses when the weather grew warmer. She was lucky that her height, and the fact that she carried the baby low, made her protruding stomach easier to disguise. Her friends were either oblivious or too involved with prom to take much notice.

Jenny proved to be more difficult to fool.

"You seem to be putting on weight, Jeff," she observed one day. "Is everything all right?"

"Mom!" Jeff feigned hurt and dismay. "I guess I've been drinking too many milkshakes at the Paris Grille lately."

Jenny stepped back to look at her with a critical eye. "It just seems so unusual for you. Maybe you should go see a doctor."

"That's not necessary, Mom, I just need to go on a diet. I promise I'll go on a diet right this minute!" Covering her face with her hands, Jeff pretended to tear up.

"I guess I could stand to lose a few pounds, too," Jenny admitted. "I'm sorry, Jeff.

She moved to give her daughter a hug, but Jeff ducked away, not wanting her mother to discover that what was making her shirt billow out was not too much junk food, but the hard, round ball of her stomach.

Jeff was already seeing a doctor—a female gynecologist in Lexington who had been recommended by the women's clinic. To cover up her appointments, she told her mother that she was going to work at McAlpin's after school, but she had actually quit her job at the beginning of the year, never having returned the fancy clothes she'd stolen. On those afternoons, when she left school, she would walk around the corner to the town car she'd hired for herself, which took her to Lexington.

Sitting in the waiting room at the doctor's made Jeff feel young and inadequate. Many of the other women came with their partners, and if they didn't, Jeff would check their left hands to see if they were married. All of them were. She felt so self-conscious about it that she took the gold wedding ring from the jewelry box where her mother had put it after her father left, and wore it to her appointments. Even if no one else cared, it made her feel less alone.

At her twenty-week appointment, her doctor asked if she wanted to find out whether the baby was a boy or a girl.

"No thanks," Jeff replied, then thinking that she sounded too callous, added, "I want it to be a surprise."

To tell the truth, she didn't care what sex the baby was. It was going to be given up for adoption right after it was born, so why bother? Jeff refused to think of the creature she was carrying in her belly in that way. She didn't think of names, she didn't think of tiny fingers and toes—she didn't think about anything beyond making it to July 4th, her due date. The Fourth of July was sure going to be explosive this year.

After her appointments, Jeff would have her town car drop her off in the shopping district and she would stroll around the stores, getting a preview of what she could buy. Once, she was walking down a street when the window display in a children's clothing store caught her eye. She couldn't help stopping to stare at the exquisite, embroidered pink dress on a white-limbed, headless child mannequin. In that moment she allowed herself to imagine what it would look like on a real child, with flaxen hair and aquamarine eyes. Then, with a shake of her head, she tried to push the vision from her mind.

To distract herself, she stopped in front of the entrance to a five-star hotel and stepped inside. The sound of a tinkling fountain met her ears, as well as the hushed murmur of guests' voices echoing off the marble floor.

"May I help you, miss?" a concierge asked.

"I was just looking for the bar," Jeff said. She might as well have a drink, since she had an hour to kill before the town car picked her up.

The interior of the bar reflected the Thoroughbred horse world, with its brown leather furnishings, tartan plaid chairs, and subdued lighting. Large framed prints of famous Kentucky Derby winners marched across the wine-colored walls. Sitting at the counter, Jeff tried to think of what to order. She knew she shouldn't because she was pregnant, but surely one drink couldn't hurt. It'd have to be something special. She pictured Lillian Langvin in her crystal sitting room, eyes glittering like blue glass, a martini in her hand.

"I'll have a vodka on the rocks," she told the bartender.

The first sip had its intended effect of completely clearing Jeff's head of any thoughts related to the reason she was in Lexington in the first place. It also emboldened her to look around at the other patrons. Since it was early evening by now, the bar was starting to fill with men getting off from work; some meeting their female companions, but others by themselves and giving off a faintly predatory vibe. Jeff knew that with her stomach concealed beneath a floaty dress, her pregnancy had made her face fuller and more appealing. She must look at least 22, judging by how openly some men were staring at her.

Basking in the attention, she didn't notice the man who slid into the seat next to her until he cleared his throat. He was tall, dark-haired and dark-eyed, moderately attractive in a well-cut blue suit. In his mid to late twenties, he was not her type—although, she reminded herself, Eric Langvin was no longer her type, either.

"What's a beautiful girl like you doing here?" he asked.

"Waiting for someone." As she lifted her glass, Jeff made sure that the light caught her mother's wedding ring on her hand.

Noticing it, he chuckled. "Everyone here is waiting for someone, just not the person you'd think. So tell me why you shouldn't be waiting for me."

Jeff smiled sweetly. "Because I'm seventeen, and I'm pregnant." She shifted slightly in her seat so that the curve of her belly became apparent, then laughed as the man stammered an excuse and moved away from her faster than if she'd suddenly sprouted horns.

Still, she thought, it was nice to be appreciated. For the first time since she'd been with Eric, she felt the tingle of possibility. At the end of the hour, with the aftertaste of vodka bitter on her breath, she got into the town car and watched as the lights of Lexington faded into the bluegrass.

* * *

The second of July was a hot, muggy day, with storm clouds threatening on the horizon, and Jeff was absolutely miserable. Her entire body was drenched with sweat, and as the baby was almost due, she could hardly move. She just sat on the front porch, fanning herself, not caring who might drive by and see her.

The only saving grace was that her mother was gone for the weekend with her new boyfriend, Dodge Atkins, an army veteran she had met through a coworker at the boutique. Dodge was a good old southern boy and seemed to truly love Jenny. Once, he even told Jeff that her mother was the best thing that had ever happened to him. Jeff was glad that her mother had found someone like him, although primarily she was glad that he occupied most of Jenny's time. On the occasions that he was over at their house, Jeff just smiled at him and served him sweet iced tea like a dutiful daughter.

On that Saturday morning, Jeff sat on her mother's bed, watching her pack for her trip to Lake Cumberland with Dodge.

"Jeff, what if he proposes?" Jenny asked, her eyes alight in a way that made Jeff wonder who was the teenager here.

"If he does," she told her mother gently, "you should say yes."

She waved her mother and Dodge goodbye in his pickup truck, then spent the next few hours watching television and eating an entire bag of chips with sour cream dip, until indigestion and the heat drove her outside. Now she watched idly as a few streaks of lightning arced across the sky. She'd better go in before the rain hit.

But just as another bolt of lightning flashed, she felt a stab of pain in her midsection. As she struggled to her feet, a gush of warm water trickled down her leg. She looked down to see a pool of clear, colorless liquid spreading across the floorboards.

The time had come.

Cursing the baby's early arrival—it clearly had plans of its own—Jeff staggered into the house and called her doctor, just as another contraction brought her to her knees. She knew she couldn't hold off much longer; the next phone call she made was for an ambulance.

Lying in a bed in Lexington Memorial Hospital, the thunderstorm raging outside, Jeff gritted her teeth and tried to think of anything but the red-hot waves rippling across her belly. She had never experienced pain like this before. It felt like something was trying to claw its way out of her, to rip her apart from the inside. She almost broke down crying when her doctor arrived and said she was too far along for an epidural. For the first time since she'd gotten pregnant, she wished her mother was with her.

"Push!" the doctor ordered. "The baby's head is crowning!"

Through a haze of sweat, Jeff overhead one nurse say to the other under her breath, "The ring of fire."

It really did feel like she was on fire. This must be the ninth circle of hell, she thought as she gave one last push with all the strength she possessed.

"Here she is!" the doctor said. "A beautiful baby girl."

Jeff heard a high-pitched cry, but before she could see where it was coming from, the nurse whisked the baby away. Exhausted and overwhelmed, she soon fell into a deep sleep.

Disoriented, she woke to the nurse saying, "Would you like to hold the baby to say goodbye?"

Jeff awkwardly took the small bundle wrapped in a pink blanket into her arms. Looking down, she knew one thing for certain: this baby was indeed beautiful. The features of her face, from the almost transparent wisps of her eyebrows, to her tiny nose, to her rosebud lips, were perfectly formed. Jeff knew that many babies were born with blue eyes that later changed color, but these eyes were the haunting sea-blue that belonged to Eric Langvin and his mother, and perhaps no one else on earth. A sudden thought occurred to her: would this baby ever know why she had such unusually colored eyes?

Then Jeff was aware that another woman had entered the room. She was not a nurse, but introduced herself as Miss Johnson from social services.

"Anna, are you feeling well enough to fill out the paperwork?" Miss Johnson asked.

"Yes," Jeff said. But as the nurse started to take the baby away from her, she blurted out, "Please, can she stay here a bit longer?"

The nurse looked questioningly at Miss Johnson, who nodded permission. So the baby remained in the room as Jeff, too tired to read through everything that had been handed to her, hastily signed at the bottom of each page as instructed.

"What would you like to name her?" Miss Johnson asked.

For a long time Jeff had not intended to give the baby a name. But after gazing into those blue eyes, she knew exactly what the baby should be called, to remind her of where she came from.

"Her name is Lily," Jeff told Miss Johnson. No matter where she ended up, Lily would always carry some part of her grandmother, Lillian Langvin, with her.

Miss Johnson gave her a searching look, as if trying to gauge how she really felt about giving up the baby. "Don't worry," she said. "We'll find a good home for her."

Jeff supposed that this was when a lot of girls changed their mind or doubted their decision. She wasn't one of those girls, but something made her want to keep the baby in her sight. "May I hold her again?" she asked.

"I'm sorry, but we have to go," Miss Johnson responded, gently but firmly.

"Goodbye, Lily," Jeff murmured, and lay back as the nurse took the baby away from her for the last time.

As soon as she was left alone, Jeff looked through her purse for her firecracker-red nail polish. Now that the baby was gone for good, she might as well celebrate the Fourth of July in style.

* * *

The rest of the summer passed swiftly. Jeff had gotten her body back sooner than she'd expected, allowing her to spend the warm, sluggish days of August sunbathing in the backyard. She went out with friends and even kissed a couple of boys, things that she hadn't dared to do during the school year from fear of being found out. It was quite possible, it turned out, for her to pretend that nothing out of the ordinary had happened over the Fourth of July weekend.

Jenny had returned from her Lake Cumberland trip with an engagement ring on her finger, and most of her time was spent making plans for her future with Dodge. Would he be moving in with them? Would they go back to Tennessee where he was from, to take care of his ailing mother? When Jeff announced that she'd been accepted to Emory University on a full scholarship, she could tell that her mother was both impressed and relieved. No matter what she and Dodge decided to do, she wouldn't have to worry about what would happen to Jeff.

Jenny and Dodge got married at the church the last weekend in August, and the day after that Jeff headed down to Atlanta before classes started.

"Don't you want us to come with you?" Jenny asked.

"You should enjoy your honeymoon, Mom," Jeff replied. "You deserve it."

As she hugged her mother goodbye, she felt a faint pang of guilt for not telling Jenny about the baby, who was, after all, her grandchild. Who knew if she would ever have another one? Jeff didn't know. But revealing the truth to Jenny would have exposed the web of lies she had spun for months. No, it was better this way.

Also, Jeff didn't want her mother to come with her to Atlanta, because she didn't want anyone to interfere with her plans. With her fat bank account, she bought a whole new wardrobe and got a makeover by a well-known stylist she had read about in a fashion magazine. When she arrived on the Emory campus, wearing the latest designer clothes and platinum blond waves framing her face, she had transformed from a poor Kentucky girl into a southern belle, for all appearances from a very fine family.

Within a few weeks, Jeff had woven herself into the fabric of college life. Although she thought her classes were boring, she decided she would become a psychology major, because she was interested in how other people's minds worked. She went through rush week and became a proud Sigma Chi, the sorority of her choice. Her roommate, Haley McKinney, was small-town girl from Athens, Georgia, and Jeff was able to play her like an old-time fiddle.

"My daddy owns a horse farm in Kentucky," Jeff told her when they met.

"Like a Thoroughbred horse farm?" Haley asked, her eyes wide.

"Just one of the biggest in the state. Why, we've had five Kentucky Derby winners over the years."

Haley quickly came to regard Jeff as the height of sophistication and worldliness. Together, they decorated their room in shades of pink, from expensive hot-pink bed linens and comforters to fluffy fuchsia throw rugs. All their dorm mates loved to gather in their room because it was so cheerful and fun. But while Jeff enjoyed their company, something important was missing from her social activities. The next step in her plan was to find a handsome, wealthy boyfriend, and so far, no one that she'd met was up to the grade.

The few frat parties she had gone to had left Jeff sorely disappointed. Sure, there were some nice-looking guys that came from well-to-do southern families, but no one stood out to her. They were all still boys, not much more refined than the pimply adolescents at Paris High School. She knew she was subconsciously comparing them to Eric; she supposed he had started at Harvard by now, if he hadn't found a way to stand up to his father. If she had any hope of banishing Eric from her memory, she needed to find the right man who could do it.

So one night Jeff did what would soon become a ritual for her. After asking around, she discovered that all the deep southern dining and drinking spots were in a swanky part of Atlanta called Buckhead, and the best place to go there was the Ritz-Carlton. As she had done when she'd gone into Lexington, she hired a town car to take her to the hotel. But when she stepped out of the back seat, she would have been unrecognizable to anyone she'd known back home in Paris. She wore a silk ivory dress that whispered just below her knees and nude kitten heels that accentuated her long, slender legs. Her blond hair, piled high on her head, was held with a diamond clasp. Around her neck was draped a necklace with a one-carat diamond pendant that rested just above her cleavage. Jeff didn't look like an eighteen-year-old college freshman, but a young woman on the prowl.

The Ritz was certainly a big step up from anything in Lexington, with its sparkling chandeliers, Oriental rugs, and old-world charm. Jeff sat down at a table near the bar and watched the gentlemen and their guests smoke fine Cuban cigars and drink scotch that was probably older than she was. She found this all very exciting and glamorous, although she had never smoked before. Perhaps she would start. She had seen some girls on campus smoking a long, thin, brown cigarette called "More," and thought it looked very sexy.

When the waiter came around, she ordered a martini with fresh limes that in her mind she called a "Lillian Langvin." Later, it would become her signature drink. ("I'll have a Lillian Langvin straight up!" she would say to the puzzled waiter.) Then she ordered shrimp cocktail, followed by a rare steak. She'd never had meat this bloody before, where it practically oozed at the touch of a knife. But it tasted incredible, the salty essence of life seeping out onto her plate. When she was done, she daintily wiped her mouth with a napkin.

While dining, she had ignored the many male eyes that became fixed on her. Now that her performance was over, it was her turn to do the evaluating. These men were in their twenties and early thirties, certainly a cut above the inexperienced boys at Emory. But they had no idea that Jeff was the one who had the power to pick and choose among them, and that whomever she did choose would be the luckiest man in the room that night.

Glancing around, she caught the eye of a man closer to thirty than twenty, whose cheekbones and sharp green eyes gave him a wolfish look that she found appealing. After she gave him an almost imperceptible nod, he stood and made his way to her.

"What's your name, darlin'?" he asked.

"Anna James Jefferson," she replied.

She didn't mind giving him her real name. She was done with hiding, with secrets, and she was determined that no man she met from now on would ever forget her.

PART II: LILY ROSE LONG

Lies live long after death

Chapter 7

At 4:30 a.m. on a cold, snowy morning, Carrie Ellen Long switched on a small lamp in the corner to start her day with some ironing. The clothes were neatly rolled in the basket and spritzed with water, waiting for her touch. Carrie Ellen turned the radio on to her favorite country station, just as Dolly Parton was singing "My Blue Ridge Mountain Boy." Although snow was falling in the mountains and clouds hovered low over the valley, she hummed along with Dolly. She could not have been happier. It had been just about a month since she and her husband, Alexander, had adopted the sweet baby girl that lay in the crib nearby.

Carrie Ellen and Alexander Long lived in the small town of Cumberland Falls, in the shadow of the Cumberland Mountains in southeastern Kentucky. It was a picturesque place, although rumors around town suggested a dirty little secret: the coal mines that had operated for decades without complying with safety regulations had filled the lungs of their workers with the deadly black dust that eventually killed many of them. Growing up, Carrie Ellen had hoped to become a clothing designer or an artist, but after she finished college, her mother and father had gotten sick. Since her only sister, Martha, had married a wealthy horse farmer and lived three hours away near Lexington, she took on the responsibility of caring for her parents. They had passed away only a few years earlier, leaving Carrie Ellen bereft, but she always believed that when one door closed, another one opened.

For eighteen years, since they had first gotten married, Carrie Ellen and Alexander had hoped to start a family. They'd watched their friends and neighbors have children, expressed happiness for them, all the while wondering if it would ever be their turn. As they had grown older, and adoption become the only option, there had been endless home visits, waiting, writing letters, and more waiting. But finally—like the thrill of seeing a snow-white dove spreading its wings—it happened. Just days before Christmas, a case worker called.

"Mrs. Long, this is Miss Johnson from state social services. We think we may have the perfect baby for you and Mr. Long. Can you come to Lexington on Friday to meet her?"

Carrie Ellen's breath caught; everything seemed to stop in that instant. "Yes, Miss Johnson, we'd love to meet the baby."

After she hung up the phone, Carrie Ellen's mind raced with plans. Friday was only four days away. She needed to unpack all of the newborn items she had Alexander had saved over the years, in the event they were allowed to take the baby home the same day. She didn't know if that was how the process worked, but she couldn't wait any longer to hold her child.

When Alexander came home that night from his job as a vet, Carrie Ellen could hardly contain her excitement.

"Alex, she's here . . . our baby is here!" she cried.

Dropping his workbag by the door, Alexander took her in his arms. "I can't believe it," he murmured into her hair. Then he pulled back, looking intently into her china blue eyes. "My dear, I don't want you to get your hopes up. What if the baby isn't right for us?"

"What do you mean? Of course she's the one."

Drawing her in close again, Alexander said, "God will let us know."

While he was overjoyed about the news, Alexander didn't want Carrie Ellen to get hurt. It had been such a long wait, and he worried that one more setback would break her spirit. Carrie Ellen was desperate to be a mother; she felt that her life wasn't complete without a child. But no matter what happened, Alexander had faith that God would lead them.

Carrie Ellen and Alexander were so excited that they decided to drive to Lexington on Thursday afternoon to see if they could visit the baby early.

When they got into town, Carrie Ellen called Miss Johnson from a pay phone. "I know our appointment isn't until tomorrow, but we're already here. Could we stop by and see the baby for a little while today?"

Miss Johnson, however, was firm. "Mrs. Long, I know how eager you are, but rules are rules. You'll have to wait. So go out and have a nice supper, get some sleep tonight, and tomorrow will be here before you know it."

Although Carrie Ellen expected this answer, she was still disappointed.

"What did she say?" Alexander asked as she got back into the car.

Carrie Ellen could only shake her head, not trusting herself to speak. Despite eighteen years of waiting, one more day was still excruciating to her.

Early Friday morning, before the sun had come up, Carrie Ellen and Alexander got into their shiny new gray Plymouth and made the long drive back to Lexington. They arrived at social services at 9 a.m. sharp and sat in the waiting room, holding hands. Both of them looked their absolute best. Alexander wore a fine gray suit that set off his slicked-back black hair and emerald green eyes, while Carrie Ellen was dressed in a tailored navy suit with a white-lace-collared blouse and pearls, her heart-shaped face framed by a mass of wavy brown hair. She twisted one of her mother's embroidered white hankies in her small hands. Neither she nor Alexander were able to speak; they were caught up in the most important moment of their lives, simultaneously ecstatic and terrified.

Finally Miss Johnson came into the room and walked toward them with a bright smile. "Good morning, Mr. and Mrs. Long," she said, shaking both their hands warmly. "Shall we go in and visit with the baby I think would be just perfect for you?"

Carrie Ellen led the way, holding Alexander's hand as they entered the infant room together. Her heart broke to see so many babies in cribs, their lost eyes looking into space, their arms no longer outstretched to be held. The room was eerily quiet, as if the babies had long since learned that crying didn't bring anyone to comfort them.

Then they stopped in front of a crib where a six-month-old baby girl was propped up, as if she was too weak to sit. She wore a clean but shabby dress and dirty white shoes, both of the kind that had been worn far too many times before by too many other babies. Carrie Ellen only glanced once at this poor attempt to spruce her up; her eyes went straight to the baby's delicate, angelic face and soft wisps of flaxen hair. She gasped when she saw the eyes that gazed unwaveringly back into her own.

"Look, Alex," she whispered. "Her eyes are the most beautiful shade of blue."

"They look like the ocean on a summer's day," Alexander replied, even though in his almost forty years on earth he was yet to see the shining sea in person.

The little girl looked back at these two strangers with her haunting eyes and broke the tension with a big, toothless smile. Carrie Ellen could feel tears running down her cheeks as she gently picked up the baby. As she held her ever so tightly, she knew what "just perfect for you" meant.

That had been a month ago. Since coming home, the baby had

changed significantly under Carrie Ellen and Alexander's care. Instead of lying sad and uneasy in her crib, she was alert and sat up on her own, babbling brightly to whoever would listen. Her little body had grown chubby and strong, clothed in Carrie Ellen's painstakingly hand-sewn outfits. And Carrie Ellen and Alexander couldn't have been more enchanted by their little girl. Every day they thanked God that she had come into their lives.

Carrie Ellen had ironed halfway through the basket of laundry. The snow had stopped and a sliver of sunlight peeked over the mountaintops. Having awoken, the baby began to gurgle in her crib.

Picking her up, Carrie Ellen said tenderly, "Good morning, my Lily Rose."

Lily Rose felt her mama's face in her hands and smelled her sweet, flowery scent. They held each other close, deep in love.

* * *

Lily Rose had grown up listening to the story of her adoption many times. She loved hearing about the telephone call from social services, the hand-me-down clothes she was wearing—which Carrie Ellen still kept in a dresser drawer—and meeting her parents. She liked knowing the origin of her name, that "Lily" was the name on her birth certificate while "Rose" was the name of Carrie Ellen's mother. When she was three, her parents had told her she was adopted, which she took to mean that they had paid money for her. "How much did your parents pay for you?" she liked to ask other children.

Lily never wondered about her life before that, or where she had come from, even though now, at age seven, she was old enough to know what being adopted really meant. All she knew was that Carrie Ellen and Alexander were her parents, and that she loved them more than anything in the world, along with Rebel, her German Shepherd.

Sitting in class at the end of the day, Lily thought about how Rebel would be waiting for her by the schoolhouse door as he always did. At 2:30, when she emerged, he ran to her and jumped up, pushing his warm muzzle as close to her as he possibly could without knocking her down. She threw her arms around him, kissing him and cooing, "Rebel, my good boy. Thank you for waiting for me."

Then they walked up the street two blocks to her daddy's veterinary office right off Main Street, where an assortment of dogs, cats, and even a bird waited with their owners. Lily was known as the vice president in charge of "Pet Soothing." She put Rebel behind the counter in his bed for a nap, then went around the waiting room, playing with the animals who seemed especially nervous and talking to their owners.

"Now what seems to be the problem here?" she asked a man whose cat was cowering in the back of its carrier.

"I'm sure he'll be fine," she assured a woman as she stroked the head of her dog, who had an injured leg.

Although she was only in the second grade, she had learned from her father the valuable lesson of treating both people and their animals with respect and kindness.

"Lily," Alexander said, coming out of his office. "Don't forget that your mama wants you home soon."

"Yes, Daddy," Lily replied obediently.

She was only allowed to spend an hour at her father's office on the weekdays and a half day on Saturdays because Carrie Ellen was afraid she would become too attached to the animals. Occasionally an owner would leave a dog or cat behind, and it would inevitably make its way into the Long family. Now they had six dogs. Since Lily was an only child, her parents let her have as many pets as she wanted, but there had to be some limits.

Lily and Rebel continued on their way home, and soon they arrived at the Long family homestead at the top of the hill on Weeping Willow Lane, so called because of the two giant weeping willow trees in the front of the yard. A stone path lined with orange African tiger lilies led up to the house, a 1920s white colonial with a mahogany front door and shutters. The wraparound porch, which had been added in the 1950s, looked inviting with pots of blue hydrangeas, white rocking chairs, and a front porch swing that many generations of the family had at one time or another quietly swung in on a lazy Sunday afternoon. Behind the house, a back lawn led deep into the hills filled with pine trees that Lily's great-grandfather had planted years ago. To the east was the majestic Black Mountain that looked toward Virginia, and beyond that the rugged Blue Ridge Mountains, surrounding the Longs with the most scenic views imaginable.

Entering the front door, Lily hollered, "Mama, we're home!"

"Well, I can see that, Lily. I was just fixing you an afternoon snack." After giving her a hug, Carrie Ellen placed a plate of chocolate chip pecan cookies and a glass of sweet iced tea on the oak kitchen table. "How was school today?"

"Josie Collins stepped on the back of my shoe when we were in line going to the playground." Lily stuck out her white tennis shoe, which indeed had a black mark on the heel. "The teacher had to stop the line so I could put my shoe back on, and Josie laughed at me."

"Did you say anything to Josie?"

Lily furrowed her brow. "No."

"Why not?"

"I didn't want her to get mad. Josie is popular and has lots of friends. I want to be her friend, too," Lily admitted in a small voice.

Carrie Ellen put her arm around Lily's shoulder. "Don't fret so much about it, I'm sure Josie was just joking. Now, let's go pick some flowers for dinner."

Lily followed her mother to the garden, but her stomach continued to churn over what had happened at school that day. Why hadn't
she said anything to Josie? Why hadn't she told the teacher? Instead,
she'd let Josie laugh at her, as her face grew hot and flustered. As
was her habit when she was worried, she chewed the insides of her
cheeks. Sometimes she bit down so hard that her mouth bled and
sores formed. Carrie Ellen repeatedly asked her why she did this to
herself, but Lily could only shake her head and run away. She didn't
know why she was compelled to hurt herself, and her mother didn't
know how to make it stop, so they just didn't talk about it.

After gathering a bouquet of old-fashioned pink tea roses, light
green hydrangeas, and multicolored delphiniums from the garden,
Lily and Carrie Ellen arranged them in a Tiffany vase that Aunt
Martha had given Carrie Ellen for Christmas. Lily always looked
forward to visiting Aunt Martha and Uncle Grant at their horse
farm near Lexington. With its white fences and large barn, it was
just about the prettiest place she had ever seen. She couldn't wait
until she was old enough to spend summers there—Uncle Grant
had promised he would teach her to ride—when she could walk
out in the morning and see that the grass really was blue.

While Lily knew her mother looked forward to when Lily could
get to know her only relatives better, she also dreaded it because she
would miss her daughter dearly. Carrie Ellen and Lily were as close
as a mother and daughter could be. There was nothing more Lily
liked than to be by her mother's side, helping her make clothes, cook
meals, or tend to the garden. Everything Carrie Ellen touched was
a declaration of love for her family, for her house. As she arranged
the flowers, she positioned the blooms loose and lovely, brimming
with life. Lily thought they couldn't have looked better than if they
had been painted in a picture.

"How do you know what colors go together?" she asked.

Carrie Ellen gestured out the open window to the panorama of the mountains in the distance. "Look at nature, and God will tell you," she said.

Although she squinted until her eyes crossed, Lily wasn't sure if she was getting God's message.

"Now," Carrie Ellen said, "help me set the table before your daddy gets home from work. Unless he has an emergency, you know he likes to eat right on time."

Lily got the dishes from the old pie safe and started setting the table. "When Daddy gets home, can I ask him about taking piano lessons?"

"Haven't I always told you to never ask your daddy, or any man for that matter, anything until after he eats? Then, see what kind of mood he's in. After Daddy's done eating, and if he seems to be in a good mood, then you can ask."

Lily nodded without really understanding, but she squirrelled this piece of advice away for the day when she imagined that she would have a husband of her own.

When Alexander walked through the door, he was greeted with the pleasant sight of family life. Carrie Ellen, wearing a blue floral housedress underneath a hand-embroidered apron, dusted off her hands and pushed her brown curls from her glowing face. Kissing him on the cheek, she asked, "Alex, honey, did you take good care of all those dogs and cats today?"

Lily came skipping up behind her and hugged him around the waist. "Daddy, I'm so glad you're home. I taught the dogs how to howl all at once. Want to hear?"

Alexander sat down at the kitchen table while Lily lined up the six dogs with their tails wagging. As she proceeded to sing off key, they began to bark in a variety of tones, culminating in a full-throated howl. Laughing, Alexander could only give them a standing ovation, smiling broadly but privately hoping that the performance would end soon.

After they sat down for supper, Lily Rose reached for her parents' hands to say grace, as they always did before each meal. She did the honors on this night. "Dear God, Thank you for our food, for Mommy and Daddy, Aunt Martha and Uncle Grant, and our entire family, including Rebel and all my other pets. Please keep us all safe. Amen."

"Amen," Carrie Ellen and Alexander echoed.

Carrie Ellen started to pass around the chicken and dumplings, green beans, and creamed corn. For dessert, there was a pineapple cream pie waiting in the kitchen that she had baked earlier in the afternoon.

Carefully watching every bite her father took, Lily waited until he set down his fork, patting his belly with satisfaction, before she spoke up. "Daddy, can I please take piano lessons? I'll practice and work real hard."

Placing his napkin on the table, Alexander pretended to think about it. "I'll tell you what, Lily," he said. "You can learn how to play the piano if you make me one promise."

Lily nodded vigorously, her eyes wide. "Of course, Daddy. What is it?"

"That you teach your pets"—he indicated the dogs lying around their feet under the table and winked at her—"how to properly sing."

"Yes!" Lily exclaimed. "Thank you so much, Daddy!"

Alexander's eyes met Carrie Ellen's over the table, and both of them smiled at their daughter's enthusiasm and their good fortune. They truly felt blessed now that their family was complete.

The Long family chattered happily as they finished their meal, and the sun slowly set behind the towering mountains.

Chapter 8

LILY ROSE SMILED AS SHE looked out the window of the study at Red Rose Farm, at how the bluegrass she loved so much in summer was just as magical in winter. The late afternoon sunshine cast long shadows over the pristine white landscape and made the snow glisten on the bare branches of the oak trees. In the countryside just beyond the side yard, a ranch hand was walking a majestic black stallion that was acting a bit frisky because of the cold. Tossing his thick, silky mane, he picked up his feet gingerly, sending tiny puffs of snow in the air with each step. Clearly, he was enjoying the outdoors as much as the farm dogs that chased him alongside the white fence. Lily giggled when she saw her dog Rebel keeping up with the others, racing and tumbling through the snow until his normally black-brown coat turned pure white.

Red Rose Farm was like a second home to her. Every year, her parents and Aunt Martha and Uncle Grant switched off where they spent Christmas, and each place made the holiday special in its own way. The previous year, when Aunt Martha and Uncle Grant arrived in Cumberland Falls with their car laden with presents, the Longs' house was decked out with homemade decorations. The air was permeated with the lingering scents of vanilla and chocolate, due to Carrie Ellen baking all week long. As was the old southern tradition, on a round, lace-covered sweets table lay dark chocolate fudge, a chocolate Bundt cake, hand-pulled taffy, and many other delicious baked goods for guests who dropped by. Also in the living room was the Christmas tree, cut down from the family's own proud stand of pines that Lily's great-grandfather had planted. Beside it, Lily played carols on the piano with a few missed notes here and there, accompanied by the howling of the family's menagerie.

Christmas at Red Rose Farm was a more elegant affair, although every bit as festive. The facade of the white-brick mansion twinkled with white lights, while the old wooden front door was adorned with wreathed branches of fresh Douglas fir and dogwood berries that surrounded a burnished horseshoe in the center. The polished wooden horse stalls were each decorated with the same wreaths, as well as red ribbons and holly.

Of course, Lily knew Red Rose best when the oak trees were dense with foliage and the bluegrass was lush. For the past three years, since she had turned ten, Carrie Ellen had allowed her to spend summers with Aunt Martha and Uncle Grant. Accompanied by Rebel, Lily would walk the fields with Uncle Grant, hearing about the inner workings of a Thoroughbred horse farm. She learned how to ride from the longtime farm manager, Ray, and she came to adore the short, taciturn man whose preferred facial expression was dour for nearly everyone but her.

Lily Rose also enjoyed spending time with Aunt Martha, Carrie Ellen's older sister. Aunt Martha had been in a wheelchair ever since a childhood bout of polio, but she moved with more grace than anyone Lily knew. She had Carrie Ellen's deep blue eyes and glossy dark brown hair, and she was always elegantly dressed in black, with jewels winking at her throat and wrists. Lily could just imagine how beautiful she must have been as a young woman when Uncle Grant came to court her.

The story that Aunt Martha told Lily about how she'd met Uncle Grant sounded like a fairy tale. Her parents had despaired of her ever getting married; while she'd met a number of eligible young men, none of them had been willing to see past her physical limitations. But one night at dinner, her father brought home a young man he'd met through a friend. Just out of the Air Force, Grant Jenkins was dashing in his uniform, his easy smile charming the entire table. Everyone else was already seated when he took the chair next to Aunt Martha, and for the next hour he was captivated by her. He didn't realize she was in a wheelchair until after dinner, when he stood up and offered her his arm to escort her into the sitting room. In the silence that followed, Aunt Martha stared down at the table, her ears burning with mortification at the trick her well-meaning father had played on this poor, unsuspecting young man. But when she glanced up, she saw in Uncle Grant's eyes genuine respect and admiration. In that moment she fell in love, and within the year she and Uncle Grant were married.

Lily listened to this story with her eyes wide. Aunt Martha really was Cinderella. She'd gone from being the underappreciated sister to a princess, not of a castle but one of Kentucky's largest bloodstock horse farms, which in Lily's view was even better. Although Aunt Martha couldn't have children, she lived a rich life, and in Uncle Grant she'd found a man who loved her as much as she deserved. Lily wondered what it would be like to fall in love one day, like Aunt Martha and Uncle Grant, or her own parents. She was old enough now to notice the tender way in which Carrie Ellen and Alexander spoke to each other, the unseen affection of a hand gently placed on a shoulder or a shared smile before they parted. If she could only have one tenth of what her mother and father had, Lily thought she would be lucky.

At thirteen, Lily was not without her own feelings toward boys. But that was all it was so far—feelings, whether it was noticing how

Mitch Adams pitched a baseball for the school team, or Duncan Rice walking past her every day to math class. She also was aware of how boys were starting to look at her, at the bob of her flaxen ponytail and the way she held her books to her chest. But she wasn't in a hurry to grow up. She was content to wear the clothes that Carrie Ellen made for her, which were as stylish and well made as anything in her friends' closets. And while she didn't spend as much time at Alexander's office anymore, her pets remained the joys of her young life, and she couldn't imagine being apart from Rebel.

Turning from the view of Rebel and the farm dogs playing in the yard, Lily tried to focus on the book in front of her, *The House of Mirth* by Edith Wharton. She'd discovered the gilt-edged, leather-bound tome on one of the shelves in the study, and after opening it and discovering that the main character's name was the same as her own, decided to try and read it. But the archaic language was too difficult, and all she could tell was that it was set in a long-ago New York, before she closed it in favor of dreaming about the present-day New York, which she knew not through ancient books but from glitzy magazines and movies and television shows. Everyone looked glamorous in this New York, as if they lived on another planet of high fashion and fine culture, impeccably styled. Lily didn't know what one did to get there, especially from the backwoods of Kentucky, but it must be possible.

"Lily!" Carrie Ellen called from the doorway. "Dinner's almost ready."

"I'll be right there," Lily replied, slipping the book back onto its shelf.

Sitting down to Christmas dinner in Red Rose Farm's old oak dining room was always a treat. Candlelight flickered on the images of famous racehorses parading across the walls, forever frozen in their moments of glory. The massive table was spread with turkey, cornbread stuffing, gravy, sweet potato casserole, scalloped potatoes, cranberry sauce, and honey buttermilk dinner rolls—all concocted by Aunt Martha and Uncle Grant's superb chef. For dessert, there were Carrie Ellen's specialties of chocolate cream and pineapple cream pies. Everyone ate until they were bursting, and then Uncle Grant and Alexander broke out the whiskey and their stories. Alexander described one of his more unique cases, a parrot who had swallowed the pearls off a necklace, and Uncle Grant talked about a recent sale to a wealthy businessman from Connecticut.

"Half a million dollars for a horse?" Carrie Ellen asked in disbelief.

"Flew down in his private jet for the afternoon to take a look," Uncle Grant replied. "Pretty much just checked its teeth and said he would sign the check."

Carrie Ellen wrinkled her nose. "Those people must think they can buy their way into anything."

"Now what I would like to buy," Uncle Grant said, "is a farm in Argentina. That's where those people's polo ponies are coming from these days. And they may end up being more profitable in the long run."

"Why, how have sales been?" Alexander asked with concern.

"Let's just say they aren't what they were when I inherited this farm. But, not to worry, we may still be around in time for Lily Rose to take over. Right, Little Rosie?" Uncle Grant raised his glass to her.

Lily Rose smiled, but she had only been half following the adults' conversation. Sipping her hot cocoa, with Rebel lying at her feet, she had been more involved with taking in the scene before her: Uncle Grant and her father chatting about business, her mother interjecting once in a while. Although Aunt Martha had not spoken much that evening, Lily had never seen her appear lovelier, her serene face framed by a cloud of dark hair, her fine-boned hands folded in front of her. Lily knew that without children, Aunt Martha considered her to be like her own, and Lily truly treasured her summers with her aunt and uncle. She didn't want to think about a future when they couldn't run the farm any more, or to even begin to contemplate a future where there might be no farm at all. For now she wanted to bask in the sounds of their voices, the candlelight illuminating their faces, the softness of Rebel's fur against her legs—taking comfort in being surrounded by family.

* * *

After Christmas, and the Long family had returned home, school started up again. Lily was eager to compare notes on the holidays with her best friend, Elizabeth Barnes. A tall, slender girl with strawberry blond hair, Elizabeth had moved to Cumberland Falls from Harlan when both girls were in second grade. The first time Lily met her was when they'd been playing dolls with some classmates. While the others talked about who their Barbies would marry and how many babies they'd have, Elizabeth impatiently asked, "But what will your Barbie *do*?" That was when Lily knew she'd found a kindred spirit.

Since then, the girls were nearly inseparable. Because her parents both worked—her father as a research scientist and her mother as a teacher—Elizabeth often ended up at the Longs' house after school, which turned into dinner, and then an invitation to spend the night. Carrie Ellen always treated Elizabeth like another daughter, and Lily considered her best friend better than having a sister. So, after being apart for almost two weeks, Lily and Elizabeth had a lot to catch up on. The first time Elizabeth spent the night after the new year, Carrie Ellen made cabbage rolls for dinner because she knew how much Elizabeth loved them.

After tucking them into bed, Carrie Ellen said with a wink, "I know you girls aren't going to sleep right away, but please don't stay up too late. You have school tomorrow, you know."

"We won't," the girls chorused.

But at ten o'clock, after her parents had gone to bed and the house was still, Lily and Elizabeth were still awake, sitting cross-legged and facing each other on Lily's bed.

"You know what we should do?" Elizabeth said.

Lily shook her head.

"Go out and slide on the river. It's iced over tonight."

A worried look creased Lily's brow. "Isn't that dangerous?"

"Of course. But you have to take risks if you want to experience something wonderful. Don't you think so?"

Although she still had some misgivings, Lily agreed that the iced-over Cumberland River would be a wonderful sight. It rarely froze, but this winter had been unusually cold, with fierce snowstorms up in the mountains that moved down into the valley with their strength hardly diminished.

The girls bundled up and, giggling, snuck past Carrie Ellen and Alexander's door, where Alexander was heard to be mightily snoring, and went downstairs. The moment they entered the kitchen, Rebel raised his head and padded after them, eager to join in the adventure, but Lily stopped him at the door. She couldn't risk having Rebel outside and running around with them.

"I'm sorry, boy, but you can't come with us," she whispered as Rebel whined in protest.

Bracing themselves against the frigid temperatures, Lily and Elizabeth walked down the street to its end, where the Cumberland River normally roared. Tonight, though, it was eerily silent. Moonlight shone on the sparkling ice stretching before them, eclipsing the few lights from houses along the shore. When Lily turned back to look at the sleeping town, she thought how no one would know if she and Elizabeth disappeared beneath the surface of the river. Facing forward again, she saw that Elizabeth had already walked out onto the ice.

"Come on!" she shouted to Lily.

Tentatively, Lily edged out onto the river, sliding a little in her smooth-soled school shoes. Although she had gone ice skating a few times, she never felt comfortable with the ever-present sensation of almost falling, with losing control over the very ground beneath her. When she reached Elizabeth, she just stood there, hoping to keep her balance. Elizabeth, however, was taking full advantage of the slipperiness and trying to twirl with her arms flung wide. Opening her mouth, she gave out a pure scream of joy that echoed through the wintery night.

"Elizabeth!" Lily hissed. "What if someone hears you?"

After giving an exaggerated look around, Elizabeth said, "Who's going to hear me? Everyone's in bed. Why don't you try it?"

"Me?" Lily squeaked, then cleared her throat. "Ahhhh!"

"Ahhhh!" Elizabeth imitated her in a high-pitched, whiny voice. "You can do better than that."

Doubling up her fists, Lily threw her head back to the big black sky and screamed so loudly that Elizabeth clapped her hands over her ears. But when she lowered her hands, she was smiling.

"That's more like it. How did it feel?"

"Good," Lily replied, surprised at herself. As soon as the sound had left her throat, it was as if something had been cleared away and her senses were now heightened. The moon seemed brighter, the cold sharper; she had never felt more alive.

"Okay. Now let's try something else." Crouching down and then jumping up into the air, Elizabeth declared to the sky, "I'm going to be an astronaut when I grow up!"

Lily paused for a moment as she regarded her closest friend with new curiosity. "Do you really think you're going to do that?" she asked, although she had no doubt that Elizabeth could and would do anything she set her mind to.

"Of course, I am! What do you want to do?"

Lily took a moment to consider. If anyone else had asked her, like one of their classmates at school, she would have replied with what was expected, that she wanted to find a husband and have a family. But she knew this answer wouldn't satisfy Elizabeth, and come to think of it, it wouldn't satisfy her, either. Thinking back to Christmas at Red Rose Farm, Lily remembered sitting in the study and dreaming of going away. It wasn't that she didn't love spending time at the farm, or respect where her parents were from, but she knew there was more for her out there, beyond Appalachia.

"I want to go to New York City," she confessed.

"But you've never been to New York City," Elizabeth pointed out, ever practical. "What are you going to do there?"

"I don't know," Lily said quietly, "but I'll think of it when I get there." In that instant, she was never more sure of anything in her life. It wasn't a question of if she would get to New York City, it was when. Maybe she could go to school there, then maybe she could find a job after completing school. However long it took, she would find her way to the big city.

"That'll be fun," Elizabeth quipped. "Me the astronaut in the stars and you the . . . whatever you'll be . . . in New York City."

"At least New York is closer," Lily countered.

Elizabeth laughed. "You're right. But let's promise each other that we'll make it happen."

"Okay," Lily replied, taking her friend's hands. The moment she did, Elizabeth pulled her farther out onto the ice, making her give a yelp in terror.

"How do you think you're going to handle living in New York if you can't do this?" Elizabeth asked. "Just let go and try to enjoy yourself."

Closing her eyes, Lily allowed Elizabeth to pull her around in a circle until they were spinning, feeding off each other's momentum, creating their own little orbit. When she opened her eyes again, she felt like she was about to take flight. Laughing, clutching each other, so dizzy they could hardly feel each other's freezing hands in the cold, the two girls twirled under a moonlit sky bright with possibilities.

* * *

On a Sunday in the beginning of February, Lily Rose sat in the little white church in town, holding her mother's hand. In a ritual that had been in the Long family as long as Lily could remember, she and Carrie Ellen sang hymns they both knew by heart while Alexander proudly sang in the choir. As the last notes faded away, she had already started dreaming about the lunch that sat waiting for them on the stove back home: chicken and dumplings, green beans, creamed corn, and a pineapple cream pie. During the walk home from church, Lily noticed how low the fog was and how a light, cold rain had begun to fall. She stared up at the big, pine-covered mountain that almost began in her backyard and thought how beautiful the snow would be up there by now. She hoped the rain might turn to snow and that they might get an inch or two so that she and the dogs could play outside.

After the family had finished lunch, the telephone rang. As Alexander went to get it, Lily thought about the day's sermon about helping one's neighbor. "Greater love has no one than this: to lay down one's life for one's friends," the minister had quoted. Dimly, Lily overheard her father give reassurance to the person on the other end of the line before coming back to his family.

"Farmer Evans' mare is getting ready to foal and he needs someone to come out to help," he announced. Although Alexander mostly treated dogs, cats, and other small animals at his office in town, he was trained to care for farm animals as well. When no one else was available, the local farmers often called on him for aid, and he was never known to refuse anyone.

"Doesn't Farmer Evans live over in Eolia across the mountain?" Carrie Ellen asked. "Surely you're not thinking of going over there in this weather."

Lily turned to look out the window, where the gray fog now lay across the valley like a thick blanket, and rain continued to fall in a steely mist.

"The foal is breech and needs to be turned," Alexander explained. "If there's any chance of saving both it and the mare, I need to go."

"All right," Carrie Ellen relented. "Will you need me to come with you?"

"Yes, another pair of hands would be useful." Alexander smiled gratefully at his wife.

"Can I come too?" Lily spoke up. She'd seen horses give birth at Red Rose Farm and marveled at the way the newborn foals were able to stand just moments after taking their first breaths.

"You'd better stay here," Carrie Ellen told her. "Your father and I might be late, and you have school tomorrow."

So reluctantly, Lily watched as Alexander collected his medical bag and Carrie Ellen other necessities for their trip. She and Rebel stood in the doorway and she waved her parents goodbye as they got into the van with the words long veterinary home on the side and headed down the lane. After the van turned at the end of the street and disappeared, she settled down by the fireplace for an afternoon of reading with Rebel lying comfortingly beside her.

Rather than focus on her book, however, Lily started to daydream as the afternoon wore on. This year her school was celebrating Valentine's Day with a Sadie Hawkins dance, and Lily was trying to muster up enough courage to ask Duncan Rice to be her date. By now they'd more than just noticed each other in the hallway, and had even spent some time talking to each other by the water fountain. Lily liked how Duncan always had a smile on his freckled face; the fact that his ears stuck out didn't bother her, nor that his shaggy, sandy hair desperately needed a trim. He made her laugh, and she thought that maybe it would be fun to go to her first dance with him.

"Lily and Duncan sitting in a tree . . ." Elizabeth would whisper whenever he approached Lily at school. "Just go ahead and ask him already."

But Lily was too shy to bring it up. Maybe she would do it first thing Monday morning, since the dance was just over a week away, and then she could start thinking about what she would wear. She was sure that her mother would have some ideas, and Carrie Ellen was such a good seamstress that she could finish a dress in no time at all.

With that important matter settled, Lily glanced out the window and noticed that the ice was growing thick on the sidewalk. She wondered what was taking her parents so long to get home, but knew that if it was snowing heavily on the mountain, they would have to stop to put chains on the tires. Her heart quickened as she thought of the times her father had gotten out of the car in the relentless snow while she and her mother looked down into the long, oh-so-murky ravine. She always wondered why there weren't guardrails, not understanding the politics of impoverished areas like eastern Kentucky. What she did know was that it could take an hour or more for her father to finish putting on the chains, and then it would be a long drive down the mountain to get home.

Various scenarios started to flood Lily's mind as she and Rebel kept vigil by the window. To calm herself, she put her arm around Rebel's neck and laid her cheek against the dog's soft fur. Rebel gave her face a comforting lick and settled his nose between his paws, as if to indicate he would stay by Lily's side no matter what happened. As the day started to fade, Lily searched in vain for the lights of her parents' car at the end of the street. Any moment now, she reasoned, she would see the van turn the corner. Her parents would come through the door, Alexander would set his medical bag down by the stairs, and Carrie Ellen would say they were sorry for being late. Then she'd start dinner, and at the table Alexander would tell the story of the foaling. Lily would be so proud of her father for helping his neighbor, for bringing new life into the world.

Looking at her reflection in the window and the dark street beyond it, Lily could envision all this happening. But what she finally saw hours later was a silent, flashing blue light making its way up Weeping Willow Lane and turning into her driveway. As if in a dream, two officers got out of the car, and with that Lily Rose's young life was forever divided into a before, and an after.

Chapter 9

WHEN THE LAST BELL RANG at school, Lily Rose walked into the hallway, holding her math textbook with purpose as around her swirled her classmates talking, laughing, and making plans for the weekend. This was her third year at Lexington Academy, but she hadn't made any friends to speak of, or made much of an attempt to be a part of school life. Ever since her parents had passed away, it was as if a sheet of glass separated her from the rest of the world, and through it she watched other kids being typical teenagers while she wondered what it would be like to have a normal family.

It wasn't that Lily didn't appreciate everything Aunt Martha and Uncle Grant were doing for her. She knew that Aunt Martha was devastated by the loss of Carrie Ellen and wanted the best for her. But she couldn't help feeling like it was all a nightmare, and one day she'd wake up back at her house on Weeping Willow Lane, hearing the sounds of her mother in the kitchen preparing breakfast and her father getting ready to go to the office. Returning to Cumberland Falls was an impossibility, though. The Long homestead had been sold, and the family belongings moved to Red Rose Farm along with Lily, Rebel, her other dogs, and her little cat, Grey. Lily had sobbed uncontrollably when she had to say goodbye to her friends, especially Elizabeth. Their bond of big hopes and dreams was so strong that Lily was not ready to let go of her beloved friend, and finally Uncle Grant had to gently but firmly place her in a tearful heap into the car. Elizabeth promised to see her soon, but a year later, she and her family moved to Atlanta, and it would be a long time before Lily encountered her childhood best friend again.

For the first two months Lily Rose lay in the big bedroom at Red Rose Farm with Rebel and her menagerie of pets surrounding her. Winter slowly turned to spring while she gazed out at the beautiful Thoroughbreds grazing in the grass that was beginning to turn blue. Aunt Martha was so concerned about Lily's health that she had the pediatrician come by weekly, and he suggested that a grief therapist might also be of assistance. The first day in late April when Lily went out with Rebel and sat under one of the flowering dogwood trees, Aunt Martha broke down in tears of relief. She had prayed that this would mean that there was hope for Lily Rose, and so there would be. Lily slowly commenced to ride some of the older horses with Uncle Grant around the farm, and it became an everyday ritual for her to visit the horse barns and decorate the front of their stalls. Throughout the summer, she was able to heal in the comfort of the farm, but when fall came she had to start life without her parents at a brand-new high school.

As her freshman and sophomore years passed in a haze, and she went through the motions of participating in school, come junior year Lily realized that she needed to wake up and improve her grades. That was her moment of reckoning—understanding that what her life had become was the last thing her parents would have wanted for her. If only for them, she had to do better. Back at school in Cumberland Falls, Lily had always made straight As—except for conduct, of course, because she was always caught talking too much. She didn't talk nearly as much now, but she knew it was in her best interest to start talking to someone who might help her with geometry. While Aunt Martha had suggested getting a tutor,

Lily thought that was terribly demeaning. After getting a D on her most recent test, though, she decided she might be able to swallow her pride for the sake of a decent grade.

She had heard that Finn Macarney seemed to be her man. He was a senior and had scored in the top one percent in math and science on the SATs. Word had it that he rarely bothered with tutoring because he preferred playing guitar in his band, but he occasionally did have philanthropic interests. Lily didn't know what was charitable about her challenging math skills, but she was certainly going to try to get him to help her. Knowing he had history as his last class of the day, she walked down the hallway toward him, and—using the oldest trick in the book—bumped into him, dropping everything in her arms on the floor.

"Oh, how clumsy of me!" she exclaimed as Finn gallantly began picking up her things. "I'm so glad I ran into you. I know how smart you are, and I was wondering if you could help me with my geometry homework? I just don't understand anything Mr. Donahue says, and if I can't pass this class . . ."

Lily continued to jabber, not even sure of what she was saying, but it appeared to work. Finn looked as if he didn't care if she asked him to wash her car because she was too stupid to turn on the hose—he would have done it.

"Sure, I'll help you," was all he said.

"That would be great. When are you available?"

Finn handed her the last book, maybe taking a little too much time to release it so that their fingertips almost touched. "How about right now?"

So they went to the school library, which on a sunny Friday afternoon was almost deserted, but Lily didn't mind. Although she was trying her hardest to concentrate on what Finn was telling her, she was distracted by his closeness. He was tall, with gleaming dark brown hair and warm brown eyes, and when he looked at her, earnestly explaining something about complementary angles, her mind wandered off to other places.

"So the thing to remember about complementary angles is that they always come in pairs . . . Lily?"

"Yes?" Lily blushed, embarrassed at being caught, but Finn only smiled.

"I don't blame you for not being able to concentrate. Why don't we stop here? It's getting late and you probably have plans for tonight."

"None at all," Lily blurted out. "I don't have a boyfriend." It was only from the widening grin on Finn's face that she realized he hadn't been asking her if she had a date.

"Do you need a ride home?" he asked, and she gladly accepted.

Sitting beside Finn in his old convertible Porsche that really belonged to his father, Lily didn't wonder why he knew to drive her to Red Rose Farm. Many of her classmates were aware of her story, that she was an orphan living with her aunt and uncle at what was still one of Kentucky's most notable horse farms. What Lily didn't know, as Finn later told her, after a few weeks of tutoring and he finally got up the nerve to ask her out on a real date, was that he had long since noticed her, way before she'd come up with the transparent idea of running into him in the hallway at school.

As fall turned into winter, Lily and Finn's tutoring sessions moved from the school library to Red Rose Farm, where they sat at a proper distance apart from each other at the dining room table. Lily was careful of how she and Finn acted around each other in her aunt and uncle's home, but she needn't have worried. Aunt Martha and Uncle Grant adored Finn, not only because he was helping Lily improve her math grades, but because he was helping to bring Lily back to life. They were more than happy to have him around, and, knowing his family, who were highly respected in the area, on late nights they invited him to stay over in a guest bedroom.

When that happened, Lily lay in bed, trying not to think about Finn just a few doors away down the hall. So far they held hands almost everywhere they could, and indulged in heavy petting in his car and a few other places that only Finn could come up with, but Lily couldn't help wondering what it would feel like to go further. She remembered what her mother had told her when she'd first gotten her period, that she now had a responsibility to her body and what it was capable of doing. She didn't want to accidentally get pregnant, like some girls at her school. But at the same time her body yearned for Finn, and he was relentless in his pursuit to be her first and only love. She adored watching him play the guitar, his long, meticulous fingers delicately stroking the chords. She was certain that those nimble fingers would be gentle and sure with her, but at what cost? Lily was overrun with guilt, as her parents had strong, religious beliefs that sex before marriage was a sin. She certainly didn't want to bring shame to their memory. It would help so much if Finn would only just say he loved her and wanted to marry her someday.

At least part of that happened one warm night when Finn arrived at Red Rose Farm to take Lily to the spring dance. Aunt Martha snapped a picture of the shiny young couple, Lily in a daffodil yellow taffeta dress and Finn in a white dinner jacket and black trousers. Before they left for the dance, Finn presented her with a gift-wrapped box. After Lily opened it to reveal a bottle of Chanel perfume, he said, "This is what my mother says you should bring the first girl you fall in love with." Lily's hungry heart soaked up these words, and in that moment she felt she wanted to give Finn everything.

That summer Lily and Finn did almost everything together. She watched him play baseball; even though the season had ended, he had started his own league. At night they lay under the stars at Red Rose Farm and listened to Beatles songs. Finn felt there wasn't another band on earth that could compare to them, so Lily learned many of their love songs by heart, her heart soaring with the music.

Other times, she and Finn literally flew together. Finn had access
to his father's small planes, which were kept on the family's tiny,
private airstrip. On Sunday afternoons, with a picnic lunch in tow,
they would fly a Cessna to the Eastern Kentucky Mountains and
land on Pine Mountain, which Lily remembered seeing off in the
distance from the back of her house in Cumberland Falls. As they
hiked the trails, Lily would tell Finn everything about her parents
and how much she missed them. He always listened, taking her
hand in sympathy, and it made her love him even more. Once, Finn
took her back to the family cemetery where her parents were buried. After climbing the steep hill there, they sat beside her parents'
graves in silence. Lily was overcome with sadness but found some
peace in being there. That feeling would be part of the bond she'd
have with Finn for the rest of her life.

As the lush green of August gave way to the faded gold and red
of September, the reality of forever set in. Finn was leaving to go to
Georgia Tech in Atlanta, hundreds of miles away, to study aeronautical engineering like his father and grandfather. Lily was terrified at
the prospect of him leaving her. She was also afraid whenever Aunt
Martha and Uncle Grant left the farm together, even if just for an
afternoon; her grief therapist had told her that this was a natural
reaction due to the way her parents had died. During these sessions,
Lily had often sat in stony silence and wondered just what this therapist knew about grief. Had she ever lost anyone or really grieved, or
was that just what she had learned to say in school? Did the therapist
know about the fear that welled up inside of Lily that made her heart
beat so fast, she thought she would faint? The fear that made her feel
as if she couldn't catch her breath? Yes, Lily was afraid for anyone to
leave, period. She felt like fear was her constant companion. And it
was just her fate that her first boyfriend—the first love of her life—
was leaving her, too, less than a year after being together.

Lily fully expected Finn to propose breaking up, but he had

other ideas. "We need to give this a chance," he told her. "We need to see what this could be." Finn gave Lily a gold necklace with a tiny airplane and a heart pendant to represent their love, and she saw him off to college with tears in her eyes but conviction in her heart that they were meant for each other.

* * *

When it came time early in her senior year to think about college, Lily had already made up her mind. Uncle Grant's health had not been well for some time, and he'd gradually ceded most of the decisions about the farm to his longtime manager Ray. Aunt Martha had always been in a fragile state. Lily couldn't in good conscience leave her ailing relatives, not when they'd taken her in after her parents' deaths; not when they were the only family she had left. With their approval, she applied to the University of Kentucky in Lexington. The campus was a mere 15-minute drive away, so she could live at home while attending classes. Maybe she'd miss out on some of the more social aspects of going to college, but she wasn't angling to find a man—she had Finn, and even at a distance their relationship remained firm and true.

The day she received her college acceptance letter, Lily eagerly called Finn with the good news.

"Do you really want to know what I think about it?" he asked.

"Of course I do," Lily replied cautiously, knowing by his tone of voice that she wasn't going to like what he had to say.

"You should have aspired to an Ivy League school. Why don't you think about your future?"

"Because my future is with you," Lily said. "And because I want to stay here. Besides, what does it matter? You're still so far away."

"But I have plans to be an aeronautical engineer. What do you want to do?

"Well, I thought we would get engaged soon. . . ."

"Why is it that all girls from Kentucky think about is getting married? Don't you want a career?" Finn's voice evinced a hint of disdain.

Despite herself, tears crept into Lily's eyes. She blinked them away, glad that they were on the phone so that Finn couldn't see them fall. "You don't think I have any dreams? Don't you think better of me than that?"

"You never talk about them," he pointed out.

"Well, I do."

At least, she did. In the days that followed, Lily thought about her dreams of going to New York. How long ago they seemed! When her parents had died, the part of her that had those hopes for her future had died, too. What Finn had said rekindled something in her, though. She'd show him and everyone else that she had big plans for herself, that she wasn't just going to be the girl who stayed in Appalachia, got married, and had babies. No, she was going somewhere that would allow her to rise to the very top—a place where she would finally feel like she belonged.

That fall, when she enrolled at the sprawling, picturesque campus of the University of Kentucky, Lily decided to become a business major with an emphasis on marketing. As lofty as her renewed desire to go to New York was, she was practical enough to realize that she needed a solid plan and real-world experience to get there. Remembering the beautiful clothes that her mother had made for her, she decided to get a part-time job at a designer boutique in town, because she honestly loved fashion. Aunt Martha and Uncle Grant weren't too pleased, as they feared it would interfere with her studies, but, as Uncle Grant liked to say, "It's best to let this filly frolic a bit."

Although, Lily and Finn made up quickly after their conversation on the phone, she didn't forget how he had chastised her for not having dreams of her own. He was also starting to bring up the idea that they should "go all the way." It was a reasonable request, Lily thought; after all, they'd been together for over two years. Although Finn never pressured her, she knew it was on his mind, and it had been on hers, too, more than he was aware. Her old fears of getting accidentally pregnant and her parents' religious beliefs pricked at her mind. But she was an adult now, and she made the adult decision of going to the school clinic to get birth control pills, just in case, for the next time she saw Finn.

She thought it would be over the Thanksgiving holiday, but one gorgeous afternoon in October, when the leaves on the giant old oak trees shimmered gold in the late afternoon sun and the bluegrass was still thick, there came a knock on the door at Red Rose Farm. The man in front of her wore a baggy shirt and jeans, carried a rucksack, and had a guitar slung over his shoulder. A few days' growth of beard covered his face, but his brown eyes were as twinkling as ever.

"Finn!" Lily exclaimed. "What are you doing here?"

"I thought I would surprise you. I hitchhiked all the way up from Georgia Tech."

Throwing her arms around his neck, Lily kissed him, then whispered in his ear, "Aunt Martha and Uncle Grant are home."

"Then we'll have to go somewhere else," he whispered back, and she giggled at the secrecy of it all.

After telling Aunt Martha that she was going out for a drive—even though she was eighteen, she still felt obligated to let her aunt know where she was while living under her roof—Lily and Finn got into her car. She knew exactly where they'd go: a romantic little inn they'd passed dozens of times before.

The room was perfect and cozy. There was an old-fashioned, four-poster oak bed and two wingback chairs covered in red tartan plaid in front of a blazing stone fireplace that filled the space with a golden light. While the walls were all rough-hewn wood, soft lace curtains hung from the windows. Lily couldn't help feeling nervous now that the moment had come. She was about to bare herself, body and soul, to the man she loved, and she didn't know how it would change her. But then Finn emerged from the bathroom in a cloud of steam, his dark hair gleaming, a towel wrapped around his fit, trim torso, and she knew she had made the right decision.

Afterward, as Lily lay in Finn's arms, she thought she had never felt closer to another person. Finally, she knew this was what love felt like.

*　*　*

Over the following two years, Finn's love kept Lily afloat during difficult times. During her sophomore year, her beloved dog Rebel passed away at the ripe old age of 14. He was buried at Red Rose Farm under one of Lily's favorite grassy knolls, with a special granite stone marker bought especially for him by Uncle Grant. The occasion Uncle Grant took Lily to see it would be one of the last times the two of them would ride side by side out into the far reaches of the farm. For at the beginning of her junior year, Uncle Grant suffered a fatal stroke, plunging both her and Aunt Martha deep into grief. With his passing, Red Rose Farm remained a working farm but not nearly as active as it had been in its prime. The plans that Lily had slowly but surely been building to move to New York after college suddenly felt hollow. How could she leave the place that had nurtured her in the raw, immediate aftermath of her parents' death? How could she leave Aunt Martha, who had become like a second mother to her?

One day, Aunt Martha asked Lily to sit down close by the side of her wheelchair. Reaching for both her hands, she said, "I don't want to you set aside your aspirations, my dear. Your mother would not want you to give up, not ever. She had big dreams herself of being a designer or artist, but got caught up taking care of her parents in Cumberland Falls, where she could never have followed through with them. She would want you to go find those dreams and make them real."

So in honor of Carrie Ellen, and with Aunt Martha's blessing, Lily decided she would continue to work toward the goal of New York. She had not, however, revealed to Finn the seriousness of her plans. At the end of her junior year in college, and the end of his senior year, Finn called her on the phone.

"Listen, I have some great news," he said. "I've gotten a job offer in Houston, at NASA. They want me to be part of their flight systems team."

"That's wonderful, Finn." Of course Lily was happy for him, but her joy was tempered with the question of what this would mean for her—for them.

Finn quickly filled the silence that followed. "I know you probably want to stay with your aunt at the farm now that she's alone. But would you maybe consider coming out to Houston after you graduate?"

Lily's heart was torn at the hopeful note in his voice. It was as if he already knew what her answer was, although it wasn't for the reason he thought. "I'm not going to stay at Red Rose Farm after I graduate," she said. "I'm going to New York."

"What on earth? Lily, why would you want to do that?"

"I'm thinking about my future, like you told me."

"When did I say that?" Finn sounded genuinely puzzled.

"Four years ago, you told me I should have applied to an Ivy League school. That I didn't have any goals or career plans. Well, I have them now, and I'm going to follow them."

"I didn't mean—"

"I know," Lily interjected gently. "But I have to thank you for what you said that day, Finn. Without it, I might not have thought about leaving home." *And leaving you.*

When Lily said goodbye to Finn that evening, she knew it wasn't just the end of that conversation, but the end of what had been the most solid thing in her life for the past five years. She wasn't sure it was the right decision, but she knew that she had to find out why New York City had intrigued her since she was a little girl. It was without question that she would always love Finn. He had brought some joy and optimism back after the death of her parents, showed her what it meant to be loved by a good man. She knew there would never be a true end for her and Finn, but it was over for now. After college graduation she would be off in pursuit of the dreams he had revived in her from deep within her soul.

* * *

The week that Lily prepared herself to leave for New York was a blur. Her stomach was aflutter with apprehension and fear, but she was excited, too. She had done as much as she could to get ready for the move to the big city, with some help. Aunt Martha had let her pick out some furniture and decorative items from the farm to make her new Upper East Side apartment feel warm and homey. Her aunt had also chosen the location and secured the deposit so that Lily would have an advantage that many young New Yorkers couldn't afford. The job Lily had secured as an assistant fashion coordinator at a large department store was a very stylish position, but it would not pay for a chic or fancy apartment.

Late afternoon on the day before she left for New York, Lily went out to the stables and tacked up one of her favorite horses, who was gentle and well suited to a leisurely, calm ride. They slowly made their way across the miles of the farm she now loved so much, stopping so that she could put red roses on Rebel's grave. As she looked around, she knew that no matter where she went, Kentucky would always be her home. Her heart belonged to the mountains to the east and the bluegrass under her feet. Slowly riding back to the farmhouse, Lily somehow knew that things would never be the same.

While she was putting the final touches on her packing, Aunt Martha called her downstairs, telling her that she had something important to give her. Lily expected some kind of memento, maybe a good-luck charm, but instead her aunt handed her a small, folded piece of paper that was yellowed with age. As she opened it, her hands started to tremble when she recognized the elegant penmanship of her mother, Carrie Ellen. But the words written there—"Anna James Jefferson"—meant nothing to her.

Lily turned questioning eyes to her aunt. "What does it mean?"

"This is the name of your birth mother," Aunt Martha explained. "Many years before your mother passed away, she told me she wanted to give this to you. She thought that if anything ever happened to her, maybe you would want to find your birth mother. Of course, your mother died when you were so young, I didn't think it was the right time. But now is the right time." Aunt Martha looked at Lily with concern. "Should I have waited this long?"

Leaning forward, Lily embraced her frail aunt. "Of course, Aunt Martha. It wouldn't have meant anything to me back then. It doesn't really now. But I'll have it, just in case."

Just in case of what, Lily didn't know. But after she went back upstairs to resume packing, she didn't wonder who her birth mother was. The idea was still so abstract in her mind that this Anna James Jefferson might as well have been an imaginary figure, a character in a story. Instead, Lily was overwhelmed with thoughts of Carrie Ellen, her *real* mother: her soothing touch, her loving words, the way she made Lily feel safe. Although she missed Carrie Ellen every day, the feeling now hit her as strongly as if the wind had been knocked out of her. She was resolved that there would never be anyone else she called her mother, no matter who appeared in her life.

Still, Lily slipped the piece of paper into her suitcase. Someday she might need it, or she might forget about it. Either way, it didn't change the fact that she was on the brink of starting a new chapter in her life, alone but determined to succeed.

Chapter 10

It was almost midnight, but Lily Rose couldn't sleep. The next morning she'd be on a plane to Palm Beach, where she was getting married to Richard "Peyton" Reynolds III, sole heir to R. R. Peyton's, the oldest and most prestigious department store in New York. All the fashion magazines and private social clubs in the city were not-so-politely whispering about her upcoming nuptials, as if a commoner was being married off to a crown prince. Rumor had it that there was no prenuptial agreement, and that Richard senior was secretly mad as a hornet and his long-suffering wife Lisa had turned into a shrieking maniac. Could they stop the wedding? Would the Reynolds family fortune ultimately rest in the hands of an interloper? Turn to Page Six to find out.

Snuggling into her comforter, Lily smiled at the memory of how she and Peyton had laughed at the tabloids. Peyton, of course, coming from the family he did, was used to being written about in all kinds of light. Naturally shy and retiring, at first Lily was mortified at the sight of her name plastered in black-and-white print. What would her friends, especially those back in Kentucky, think of her? But Peyton tried to be reassuring: "Once the wedding is over and we're married, everyone's interest will move on to something else. You can't let gossip control your life." Lily looked into his eyes and believed him with all her heart. It didn't matter what other people thought, even what his parents thought. She and Peyton were deeply in love—had been ever since they met two years ago—and nothing could tear them apart.

Lily's wedding attire and honeymoon clothes had been shipped to The Waves, one of the finest resorts in Palm Beach, and Peyton was already down on the island for his bachelor's parties, so all she had to do now was get a good night's sleep. Still, rest remained elusive. This was the last night she would spend in her apartment as a single woman. Lily Rose lived in a prewar Upper East Side building that was usually way out of the price range for a single girl in her mid twenties. While she had risen from being an assistant fashion coordinator at a large department store to the fashion director and spokeswoman at Peyton's, even that certainly would not pay the rent in this zip code. Not even her most trusted friends knew that Lily had inherited a sizable amount of money when her Aunt Martha had died after her first year in New York and left her the entirety of Red Rose Farm.

Lily had tried to make her apartment as close to home as possible, bringing a few antiques and other decorative pieces from Kentucky. The place had strong bones to begin with: floor-to-ceiling windows, solid oak floors, and handcrafted moldings on the graciously high ceilings. In the living room, an oriental rug covered the floor in soft blues and light pinks. Aunt Martha's white Louis XIII sofa sat in front of a marble fireplace, the mantelpiece lined with blue-and-white Foo dog ginger jars. On either side were two matching French blue slipper chairs covered with Carrie Ellen's needlepoint dog pillows. Also on proud display were the intricate quilts that Carrie Ellen's mother and her mother's friends had made at quilting bees when Lily had been adopted. Each person had embroidered squares with birds, flowers, children, and their own names to welcome Lily into their lives. These quilts may have seemed out of place in the hard glitz and glamour of Lily's life now, but they were deeply imprinted on her heart. Another keepsake served as a firm reminder of her past. On her coffee table she always had a finely cut crystal bowl filled with the dried petals of roses from bouquets that had been given to her over the years by friends and lovers alike. They were all memories of the people who had passed through her life.

To the side of the room, in front of one of the big windows overlooking Park Avenue, Lily had placed Alexander's old oak office desk from his veterinary practice. At the moment, it was covered with dress designs, color swatches for the upcoming season, and fashion articles about the store, as well as sterling-silver–framed photos of her beloved parents and aunt and uncle. Lily never sat there in the quiet evenings without first thinking about the family she had lost.

She wished fervently that they could be here to see her get married—her mother to help her get dressed, and her father to walk her down the aisle. Would they have liked Peyton? Would they have approved of all this? Lily knew they would have been proud of everything she had accomplished in only three years in New York, but would they like the direction in which her life was heading? What kind of advice would her mother have given her about marriage and being a good wife? Her mother had left her at such a young age, when Lily was barely a teenager, that they had hardly spoken of these things.

Aunt Martha, however, had been around as Lily grew into a young woman, experienced Lily's meeting and breakup with her first love, Finn Macarney. While she did not have the strict religious beliefs that Lily's parents did, she also was cautious when it came to matters of love and sex. "Whatever you do, Lily," she cautioned her niece when Lily was determined to move to New York, "don't live with a man before getting married. He's isn't going to want to marry you if he already has all the comforts of marriage without making it official." Laughing, Lily had assured her aunt that she wouldn't, never thinking what New York City had in store for her.

* * *

Lily Rose had been at work in the middle of the day when she received the phone call that Aunt Martha had passed away. Although her health had not been robust in recent years, especially after the death of her husband, Aunt Martha had never let on to Lily how poorly she was doing. The heart attack, Aunt Martha's doctor told Lily, was related to her childhood illness of polio— assuring her that there was nothing Lily could have done about it. Still, Lily blamed herself for not being there in Aunt Martha's last moments. After the funeral, she walked out into the vast fields of Red Rose Farm, heartsick, and buried her hands in the tall bluegrass. Aunt Martha's lawyer had told her that she would be inheriting the farm, which was still a very valuable property, but she would give it away in a second if it could bring her family back. Now she was truly alone.

While she would never consider selling Red Rose Farm, Lily knew she couldn't stay there, either. The farm was filled with the essence of all she had loved and lost, and now she had established a new life for herself in New York. Ray, who had lived most of his life at the farm, would keep the place running, and Lily would come down as needed, maybe for the holidays. She was glad to be able to board a plane for New York and immerse herself into work again.

For the past year, Lily had worked as one of five assistant fashion coordinators at a small department store. She reported to the fashion director, pulling together the clothes for every in-store fashion show, the new looks for each season, and what went on the mannequins. She took her role very seriously and sometimes wondered what her mother, Carrie Ellen, would think if she saw her now, brushing elbows with designers and models. However, Lily knew early on that this job wouldn't be enough for her. She wanted to make her own fashion decisions, create her own style team. Aiming high, she'd applied for and miraculously gotten a job as a fashion coordinator at R. R. Peyton's, and was set to start the week after she returned from Kentucky.

R. R. Peyton's was a paradise, nine floors of luxurious goods housed in a grand Beaux Arts building. Dating from the turn of the century, it was the city's most prominent department store and was owned by the Reynolds family, headed by Richard Reynolds. Lily had seen pictures of him, tall and stern looking, in the business sections of newspapers. His twenty-five-year-old son, known as Peyton, was more a fixture of the tabloids for his presence on the party circuit. He was known for being kicked out of bars for drinking too much, throwing money at nightclub owners after trashing private rooms, and doing lines of coke off the backs of models in bathrooms. This was only what Lily had read; she had no idea what he was really like, until two months after she'd started her new job.

She and her friend Catherine Cole were having drinks at Lloyds, a bar on the Upper East Side that many of the fashion and advertising people frequented after work. It was raining hard that evening, but everyone in the room was still looking forward to a good start to the weekend in the city. Then Lily glanced up from her chardonnay and saw Peyton Reynolds casually walk in. Everything about his appearance spoke of an easy confidence, of someone who knew he was attractive to women without even trying. He wore a long, gray raincoat over a tailored suit, his tie hanging loose around his neck. His wavy dark brown hair was just long enough to brush against his shirt collar, and his tan suggested he had just come back from an island somewhere. The moment Lily saw him, she knew the reason she hadn't wanted to date anyone since she'd moved to the city was because she had never been in the presence of a man like Peyton Reynolds.

As if her gaze was magically drawing him in, Peyton strode over to the bar and stood next to her. "The usual, please," he told the bartender as he brushed his hand absently through his sleek, slightly damp hair. Then he glanced down at Lily, as though noticing her for the first time. "Don't you work at R. R. Peyton's?"

Ignoring Catherine's knowing look, Lily said, "Yes, I'm on the designer floor."

"I knew you looked familiar." Peyton smoothly inserted himself into the space between Lily and Catherine. "So how do you like working for us?"

As Lily made small talk with Peyton, she felt a quickening sensation of desire deep in her belly just from being close to him. She had never felt this way before with a man, especially one she'd just met. Her sensual experiences had been with her former boyfriend Finn, and he had been soothing and comfortable, like a warm cashmere sweater you never wanted to give away. No, something deeply sexual and lustful was stirring in Lily, and she wasn't trying very hard to stop it.

Over Peyton's shoulder, Catherine had raised her eyebrows so high that they were ready to join her hairline. But Lily chose to ignore her friend's warning signals and let herself get lost in Peyton's deep brown eyes.

"So, Lily," Peyton said, "how would you like to join me for dinner?"

"I, uh, don't think so," Lily stammered, thinking she couldn't just leave with a man she really didn't know, and especially since he was her boss.

Peyton finished his drink and got to his feet. "Just consider it. I'll be back."

Lily could only nod as he disappeared into the crowd that had assembled at the bar.

After he left, Catherine hissed, "Lily, are you insane? He has a terrible reputation with women. Why would you even think about going out with him? We should leave *now*."

"He said he'd be back."

"Not if he finds another girl he wants to go to dinner with. He's probably left already. Do you even see him anymore?"

Stubbornly, Lily continued to scan the room until she had to admit that Catherine was likely right. She was waiting by the door, her coat on, while Catherine was in the restroom, when she felt someone spin her around. Without a word, Peyton pulled her into his arms and kissed her, long and slow, one hand around her slender waist and the other entwined in her long blond hair.

"Let's get out of here," he mumbled into her ear, and she could smell the alcohol on his breath.

Taking his hand, Lily let Peyton Reynolds lead her out of Lloyds and into another world.

First, they dined at a restaurant that was normally booked months ahead, where the chef surprised Peyton by bringing over luscious langostino tails piled high, in olive oil and lemon, and an exquisite bottle of white burgundy. This intoxicatingly delicious dinner climaxed with a dark chocolate mousse that Lily practically devoured on her own.

Then they went back to Lily's apartment and fucked each other's brains out all night long.

The next morning, after Peyton had gotten dressed and left, Lily lay in bed, thinking about how what had just happened seemed like a dream, if it weren't for the soreness of her body in all the right places and Peyton's scent still permeating her sheets. She called Catherine, knowing that she needed to apologize to her friend for leaving her at Lloyds, and feeling like she needed to tell someone in order for it to feel real.

"Spare me the details," Catherine cut in before Lily could get very far. Then she added more gently, "Watch yourself with him, Lily. You know what they say about Peyton Reynolds."

"Those are just stories people tell to sell papers."

"But usually there's some truth to them. Be careful, Lily. I don't want to see you get hurt."

Lily assured Catherine that she'd take care of herself, then spent the rest of the weekend luxuriating in the memory of Peyton, flushing a little when she recalled what they'd done to each other in certain areas of the apartment or on what furniture. She didn't expect him to try and get in touch with her—they hadn't exchanged numbers—although her heart jumped a little every time her phone rang. It wasn't until Sunday afternoon when she wondered if they'd run into each other at work the next day. The corporate offices at R. R. Peyton's were at the top of the building and she'd never seen him on the floor.

Monday morning passed without any sign of Peyton, and Lily thought she was in the clear. But then in the afternoon she received word that management wanted to see her.

Glad that she'd dressed that day in an ensemble—white cotton shirt, black pencil skirt, and black patent-leather pumps—that was both modest and showed off her figure, she took the elevator to the top floor. An assistant led her down the hall lined with portraits of the important players in the department store's history, from the English settler who started a small men's clothing store to Richard Reynolds himself. Then Lily was taken into Peyton's office overlooking Central Park.

The office was just as posh as Lily had expected, with panoramic views overlooking the Great Lawn. The windowsills, painted a high gloss black, stood out against the dove white walls. Shimmering in the sun was Peyton's glass desk with black leather spindle legs, in front of a sleek black leather chair. Behind that, on a chic leather credenza, sat a few family photos and mementos, all suggesting a single, high-profile, young man's bored attempt at filling the space. Above it hung a painting in brilliant red that bore the signature of Georgia O'Keeffe. The other side of the room contained a conference area with sumptuous black leather couches and chairs that indicated a relaxed way of doing business.

"Well, hello," Peyton said from his chair, and his tone of voice made Lily's body tremble. He looked her up and down, as if he would have liked to fuck her on his desk if his father wasn't sitting right down the hall. "I was wondering if you wanted to have dinner again with me tonight."

This time Lily answered without hesitation.

Within a week, she was calling him "Pey," and within two he had virtually moved into her apartment. While she didn't see Peyton often at work, and for a long time no one knew that they were dating, outside of it they were as domestic as could be. Except that their physical attraction to one another never waned. Lily had never felt this magnetic pull toward another person before, as if the core of her being couldn't be away from him. And, under her influence, Peyton barely made it into the tabloids anymore. He admitted to her that he'd been under some bad influences, but now that he had her, he didn't need his former vices. "You make me want to be a better person," he told her, and Lily believed it.

The first year of their relationship passed swiftly, with Lily meeting Peyton's parents, Richard and Lisa Reynolds, at their house in Palm Beach over the holidays. In person, Richard Reynolds appeared more like a former quarterback than a corporate tycoon. A statuesque six-foot-five, he had thick black hair streaked with silver and hazel eyes in a weathered yet chiseled face. Lily thought he looked like a man's man. A former model, Lisa Reynolds had been a beauty in her youth, but she had put on a few pounds and seen too many plastic surgeons. Her best feature had been her thick dark brown hair, but after it had turned gray, she had decided to go blond, which looked fine, if a bit fake. All in all she was still attractive, but Lily could tell that with her beauty fading, she clung to her husband with tight, perfectly manicured claws.

At work, Lily was rising to new heights. Although still a fashion coordinator, she produced some of the store's most dramatic and creative fashion shows. With her in charge, models slinked down the catwalk in perfect synchronization to a live band. Peyton, now president of the company under the supervision of his father, was pleased to see her career grow, telling her many times how proud he was that his girlfriend was making the store look so good. Around their anniversary, he suggested that they move into a new place together.

"I'm never at my apartment downtown," he said. "Let's find a place of our own. Maybe we could even get a pet. You're always talking about dogs and cats."

As much as Lily loved the idea of them living together and getting a dog and cat, she remembered Aunt Martha's advice. "It's not that I don't want to with you," she replied. "I just don't want to live with anyone until I'm engaged."

"I see," Peyton merely said, as if the very idea was a novel one.

Lily wondered if she had scared him off. But a few months later, on Valentine's Day, Peyton took her to one of New York's most romantic restaurants on the East River. After dessert, he excused himself and Lily sat in her chair, looking at the couples around her. She thought about which of them were married or just dating, and if the latter, which ones were living together. Maybe it didn't matter whether you lived together before you were married. Maybe Aunt Martha's advice was old fashioned and outdated. Why shouldn't she live with Peyton? But she didn't want to leave her Upper East

Side apartment, which she'd lived in since she'd moved to the city and which meant so much to her. Perhaps she should ask Peyton to formally move in. But that was assuming he still wanted to live with her anyway.

These thoughts occupied so much of her mind that she only then noticed that Peyton had returned to the table with a huge bouquet of red roses, each huge bloom round and perfect.

"Oh, Pey," Lily breathed. "These are beautiful."

"Not as much as you."

Before Lily's disbelieving eyes, Peyton got down on one knee. From his pocket he produced a small, red velvet box and opened it to reveal a family heirloom ring that sparkled up at her. Passed down from Peyton's great-grandmother, it was a perfect stone set in a miner cut, surrounded by tiny emeralds and diamonds. It nearly took Lily's breath away.

"Lily Rose Long, will you marry me?"

Lily looked down into his dark, earnest eyes and said, "Yes, Peyton. Of course, I'll marry you."

Now all the other couples were staring at them, but Lily didn't care. So what if this made it into the papers the next day? DEPART-MENT STORE HEIR TO WED EMPLOYEE. Who cared? Overjoyed, Peyton immediately called his parents to tell them the good news. From his side of the conversation, it sounded like they were pleased. He put Lily briefly on the phone with them, too. "Welcome to the family, my dear," Richard Reynolds boomed, and behind him called Lisa's fainter voice: "I'm so happy for you two."

Of course, Lily had no family on her side to inform, but later she called Catherine, who said, "At least I didn't have to say, 'I told you so.' Honestly, Lily, this isn't where I thought the two of you would end up, but it doesn't matter. You're going to be the envy of every socialite in town for taking away their most eligible bachelor."

Lily soon discovered that she had no idea what getting married to someone like Peyton Reynolds meant. When she suggested having the wedding at Red Rose Farm, he said, "Of course not. Can you imagine my parents' friends on a horse farm? We're getting married in Palm Beach." While Lily had told Peyton about inheriting the farm, he didn't seem particularly interested in her "little hobby" and had never talked about visiting it with her. So while it would have meant a great deal to Lily to get married with her family surrounding her in memory, if not in the flesh, she acquiesced to Peyton's decision, thinking he knew best.

She also agreed with Peyton that there should be no prenuptial agreement. While she was aware that unions between someone of comparatively less means, such as herself, with someone who was set to inherit an entire corporate legacy usually included a prenup, she was swept away by Peyton's declaration that they were so much in love that they were going to stay together forever. And if there was any pressure on Peyton's side from his parents about this, she was unaware of it. Perhaps in the beginning Richard and Lisa Reynolds had looked askance at the willowy blond, aqua-eyed girl that their only son had brought home to meet them, but as Lily proved herself over and over again at work, Richard certainly appeared to look favorably upon her. She felt less sure of herself with Lisa, who had been married to Richard for more than thirty years *with* a prenup, so it wouldn't be surprising if Lisa thought her fly-by-the-seat-of-her-pants son had literally given away the store. But Lisa would come around, too, Lily thought, when there were grandbabies in the picture.

In the weeks leading up to the wedding, she couldn't wait to gain a new father-in-law and mother-in-law. And she couldn't wait for her and Peyton to start a family of their own.

* * *

In the Little White Chapel by the Sea in Palm Beach, Lily Rose Long said "I do" to Richard "Peyton" Reynolds III. She was wearing a dove-white dress covered with crystals and pearls, looking like a princess. In a black tux and white waistcoat, Peyton was every inch her Prince Charming. After the ceremony, they headed back to the hotel to change before the reception, which they had decided was going to be one big lavish celebration on the beach—a time to celebrate with all their New York and international friends.

Lily had planned everything to perfection. On one secluded area of the beach, there were tents covered with flowing white gauze with chandeliers sparkling inside, each one waving gently in the seaside breeze. Inside this tented wonderland, tables covered in white gauze were adorned with lush garden arrangements of Lily's signature fuchsia-pink roses mixed with hydrangeas. Crystal pendants hung from the ceiling at different lengths, catching the candlelight and creating the enchanting atmosphere of a brightly lit palace. Each of the ladies had received a rose-pink sarong and matching pink blouse, and each gentleman a loose-fitting, white linen shirt and a pair of khakis, to change into. The guests were served pink grapefruit martinis as soon as they arrived.

Occasionally, Lily felt pangs of regret that she had no one from her family present. But she had Catherine as her maid-of-honor, and Richard Reynolds danced with her during the father of the bride dance. As soon as the song ended, Lisa Reynolds came and pulled him away, but Lily wasn't aware of it. She and Peyton didn't notice his parents much that night; they were far too much in love with each other. They danced late into the night with their friends, throwing roses and lilies out into sea all night long.

The next morning a private jet whisked them off for a blissful, two-week honeymoon in the Virgin Gorda, part of the British Virgin Islands. While Lily Rose continued to miss her own family, she reminded herself that this was her new beginning. As Peyton swam in the ocean, she rested on the white beach, daydreaming about what their children would look like: a little, flaxen-haired Lily and a tiny, brown-haired Pey frolicking in the sand together. She reasoned that she was only twenty-five, and she had years ahead of her to make this dream happen. Years later, she would remember this trip as one of the happiest times of her life.

Chapter 11

LILY ROSE STOOD AT THE window of her Upper East Side apartment, looking down into the wide boulevard of Park Avenue. Although it was almost midnight on a weekday, a few people could be seen walking back late from a bar or the gym or wherever they went to relieve stress after work. She wondered if from this distance she could spot Peyton heading toward their building, coming home from yet another late night at the office—or so he said.

It had been five years since Lily and Peyton had said "I do" on the white sands of Palm Beach, and since then, Lily's star had risen fast. Not only was she the fashion director and spokesperson at R. R. Peyton's, but Richard Reynolds was giving her her very own boutique within the department store. "The World of Lily Rose" was scheduled to open in just a few months, and Lily spent every waking moment preparing for it. Sometimes she wondered if Richard had given her the boutique because he thought it was a sound business investment, or because he was sorry for the fact that she and Peyton were still unable to conceive. She didn't know how much Peyton confided in his parents, but she was sure they knew something was wrong by now.

Lily had wanted to start trying to have a baby right away, since she'd always dreamed of having six kids. But Peyton insisted they wait, reasoning that they were young and that their careers must come first. "We have so much time ahead of us," he'd said, and so instead they'd done the next best thing and adopted a dog and a cat—a Siberian Husky named Sable and a Himalayan cat named Hollywood, both of whom provided Lily with much comfort as she waited for Peyton to come around. They started trying the previous year, when Lily turned twenty-nine. She was sure that they'd get pregnant immediately—after all, they'd had plenty of practice, and their attraction to each other was as strong as ever—but every month the pregnancy test came up negative. Lily's doctor had told her not to worry, that if they weren't pregnant after a year of trying, then they would look into it. Well, that year mark was coming up soon, and Lily wanted answers. She was beginning to suspect that maybe she wasn't the problem, but Peyton. But of course she could never bring that up to him herself.

Neither did she want to confront him about the latest rumors in the tabloids. Supposedly, while she'd been away on a buying trip for the boutique this past week, Peyton had been seen out having dinner with a gaggle of high-profile models, and had left the restaurant with one particularly delicious supermodel hanging on his arm. Reports from the scene also stated that a white powder and one-hundred-dollar bills were in abundance on the table. The only person Lily could talk about this with was Catherine, who cautiously acknowledged that she knew who the model was, and that the girl had a certain reputation with married men.

"So you think it's true?" Lily asked.

"Lily," Catherine replied, "nine times out of ten, what you read in the tabloids isn't true. But it's the tenth time that counts. Why don't you ask Peyton about it?"

"I can't," Lily confessed. "I'd rather not know. Maybe nothing happened . . . or maybe it was just this one time."

Catherine sighed. "You knew who Peyton was when you married him."

Lily thought she knew, and she thought she knew what her values were, but now she was finding herself nervously waiting for her husband to come home, not sure how she should confront him about his debauchery—his alleged debauchery, she kept telling herself.

When she heard the key in the lock, and Peyton's step in the hallway, she turned around slowly to face him. He looked exhausted; his eyes bloodshot, his shirt soaked with sweat. For a moment her heart went out to him and how hard it must be to work under his exacting father, but then she remembered the rumors about the supermodel—she was barely twenty-two!—and she hardened her grip on the edge of the chair next to her.

"How was your day?" she asked, following him into the kitchen where he barely looked at the roast chicken and salad she'd prepared and left out for him on the counter.

"Long," he simply replied, disappearing into their bedroom.

After he'd come back, having changed into a T-shirt and sweatpants that accentuated the lean lines of his body, she said in the same, bright tone, "I have some good news to tell you."

"Oh?" He sat down at the counter, giving Sable an absentminded pat.

"You know how *Couture* magazine is planning to do a cover story on the boutique? They've managed to get an amazing photographer for the shoot—"

"When is that shoot again?" Peyton interrupted.

"Next week."

"Good, because I'll be in town then."

"What do you mean?"

Peyton looked at her as if she were dense. "They're going to want me to be in the shoot, right? As the heir to R. R. Peyton's? Not to mention, your husband. If it weren't for me, the World of Lily Rose wouldn't exist."

"Actually, Pey," Lily gently corrected, "your father is the one who gave me the boutique."

At the sound of his fist slamming down on the counter, Lily jumped, and Sable gave a small yelp. "The reason you're where you are at all is because you're married to me, Lily," Peyton growled. "And don't you forget it."

Unable to answer him, Lily looked down, her face pale but her entire being burning with resentment. She had worked too hard for these past seven years, sacrificed too much of herself, to take this slight from anyone, even her husband. When Peyton reached out to her, she recoiled from his touch.

Sighing, he lowered his hand to his side and said, "I'm sorry, Lily. I've been under a lot of pressure at work."

Her head snapped up. "So much pressure that you've been able to go out to restaurants with models?"

To her surprise, he started to laugh. "You're upset about that? Lily, I was entertaining a client. Luis Montenegro. You've heard what he's like."

Indeed, Lily had heard stories about the head of one of Europe's most notable fashion houses and his appetites. "What about the supermodel you left with?" she asked, unable to suppress the quiver in her voice.

"She's hardly a supermodel. The poor girl could hardly stand up straight by the end of the night. I had to walk her to the corner to get a cab or else Luis would have gotten his paws on her."

"How chivalrous of you," Lily commented with a sniff, but the lines of her body were beginning to relax.

"Like I've told you before, Lily," Peyton said, "you can't let these tabloids dictate your life. You have to believe what's in here." Taking her hand in his own, he placed it over her heart, then drew her in for a lingering kiss. Despite herself, Lily could feel her body reacting to his, to the heat that penetrated the thin fabric separating them.

"It's too late—" she protested.

"No, it isn't," he murmured against her hair.

Still, something in Lily made her pull apart from him. Indicating the food on the counter, she said, "Let me put this away if you're not hungry."

"Okay," Peyton said, getting up from his seat to head to the bedroom. "Don't be too long, though." At the doorway, he turned around. "By the way, I'm glad to hear about the cover shoot. What did you say the photographer's name was?"

"Eric Langvin," Lily replied as she began to clear the counter. "The magazine said we were very lucky to get him, because he usually only shoots celebrities. But he agreed to do it this one time."

* * *

Sitting in the town car on the way to the *Couture* magazine photo shoot, Lily wondered what had convinced Eric Langvin to take the job. Like anyone in the fashion business, she had heard about his meteoric rise to fame twenty-five years ago, photographing portraits of famous people around the world. He was especially known for his uncanny ability to capture the essence of his subject in just a few frames. Not only had he done cover shoots for celebrities, but for those who would become celebrities. It was as if he had the Midas touch; if anyone caught in his transformative lens wasn't already well known, they would be well on their way to stardom after.

As for his personal life, not much was known about the mysterious Mr. Langvin. According to the few profiles about him, he had forsaken his wealthy family and Ivy League education for an artist's life in New York and Rome during his twenties. Then, at the height of his fame, he had settled in rural Connecticut with his Italian wife and children, and in recent years had become a virtual recluse. Now, it was rare that his photos graced the top fashion and celebrity magazines, but when they did, the public took notice.

Lily hoped he would be easy to work with. Lying in the back seat of the car next to her, head in her lap, was her red-and-white Siberian Husky, Sable. She'd decided at the last minute to take Sable with her, thinking that the husky would enjoy getting out of the city. The main reason, though, was that Lily wanted to have someone on her side. Having never been the subject of a photo shoot before, she was nervous about it and counted on Sable to help her relax.

When the car pulled up to the location in Bedford, Connecticut, her mind was immediately set at ease. Before her was an idyllic old farmhouse surrounded by white fences that reminded her of the horse farms in Kentucky. A crew member greeted her when she and Sable got out of the car, and led them into the gray stone kitchen. Lily was admiring the display of copper pots and pans on the rack overhead when Sable alerted her to someone else's presence in the room. Tail wagging, the husky ran up to a tall man with thick, wavy blond hair who bent to ruffle her fur. When he looked up, Lily saw that his eyes were a remarkable, bright blue that reflected the depths of the ocean.

"You must be Lily Rose Reynolds." His voice was deep but kind, as if a smile was hidden somewhere inside.

"Yes. Mr. Langvin?"

"Please sit down. And please call me Eric."

He gestured to the table, and Lily sat, as did Sable at her feet. She couldn't help but notice what an attractive older man Eric Langvin was, maybe close to fifty, but good-looking nonetheless. His was a rugged handsomeness, the lines on his face speaking to hours spent in the sun, enjoying the outdoors or searching for the perfect shot. And, of course, there were his magnetic eyes, the shade of which Lily had never seen before on another person. Strangers often commented on how unusual her own eyes were, but at this moment she supposed that they weren't so unique after all. She realized she had actually seen Eric a couple of times before at charity events or galas, but only at a glance. With his presence he could have been a movie star instead of the person who photographed them, but she supposed that wouldn't have interested him since he was so private.

"I'm so glad we have this opportunity to work together," he continued. "I hope you don't mind the rustic location."

"Not at all, it's beautiful," Lily assured him. "It reminds me of where I grew up."

"And where was that?"

"Kentucky, near Lexington. Have you ever been there?"

"Once, a long time ago. I remember the grand horse farms and the rolling fields, they made a great impression on me. Do you still have family there?"

"Not anymore, unfortunately."

As if Eric could tell this was a painful memory for her, he changed the topic of conversation. "In case you're wondering, I chose this place not just because of the atmosphere, but because it's a few minutes from where I live. The easy commute sold it."

Lily smiled at this, and knew that she didn't have to worry anymore about feeling uncomfortable on the shoot. She and Eric continued to talk, which was customary for a photographer to get to know his subject, but in this case she got the sense that he was truly interested in her as a person and wanted to get to know her. Easily, she told him about her dreams of moving to New York, her early years working in fashion, and meeting Peyton.

After a while, he left so that she could get dressed for the cover shoot. For that, she lay on a bed of lush, hot pink and red tea roses, wearing an off-the-shoulder pale pink chiffon dress, her flaxen hair long and tousled. In another shot, she stood against a white fence-post in a blue cashmere sweater, jeans, and a pair of boots, her hair gathered in a loose ponytail. For a third, she sat on the front steps of the farmhouse in a slinky green gown, her feet bare but her hair swept up. Aside from a few directions, Eric stayed silent and simply shot, encouraging Lily to act as natural as possible and not to be self-conscious.

Before they finished, he motioned for Sable, who'd been obediently sitting on the sidelines, to join Lily.

"Are you sure?" Lily asked, putting her arms around her dog and burying her face in her soft fur.

Eric grinned. "She's a natural, just like you. Also, I thought you might like a little souvenir from the shoot."

After she had changed back into her regular clothes, Lily went through some of the photos with Eric on his laptop. She was amazed by how he had managed to capture her every expression, the faintest hint of a smile on her face, or sorrow in her downcast eyes. It was as if his camera was a portal to her soul, and she was incapable of hiding her innermost feelings from him.

At one point, Eric placed a finger on the screen. "There's a certain sadness here. What were you thinking about?"

"I'm not sure," Lily admitted, although she knew very well what had been on her mind. She had been thinking about how pleasant the farmhouse was, and if she ever had a country home someday with Peyton and their children, she would want something just like this. *If* she and Peyton ever had children.

Abruptly, she asked Eric, "Do you have kids?"

Surprised, he answered, "I have two."

"What are they like?"

"Well, Emily is twelve and obsessed with horses. You know how that is. We're hoping she'll grow out of it. Chloe is eight and the most stubborn girl you'll ever meet, but her mother and I wouldn't have it any other way."

"They sound lovely." Taking a deep breath, Lily confided, "My husband and I would like very much to have children. That is, I would like it very much."

"And your husband?"

"He doesn't think it's as important as I do. He isn't in any rush." Lily shook her head. "I don't know why I'm telling you this."

"Because," Eric said softly, "you have to tell *someone*."

"Yes. And why not a stranger?"

He gave her a half smile. "You're right, sometimes it's easier to talk to a person you've just met than the person who needs to hear it."

"He'll have to hear it at some point." *When I get the courage*, Lily added to herself.

Continuing to scroll through the photos, Eric stopped on the last sequence of her with Sable. The dog's mouth was open, tongue hanging out. She was clearly laughing, and when Lily looked closely, there was something like joy in her own eyes, too.

"Remember this moment," Eric said softly.

"I will," Lily replied. "Thank you."

After she got into the town car with Sable, exhausted from the shoot but strangely exhilarated, she looked through the window at her photographer. He lifted his hand in farewell, and she did, too. Maybe she would never see Eric Langvin again, but he had given her a precious gift that day, restoring a side of herself that she had almost forgotten, and she would long remember him for it.

* * *

The next few months were a whirlwind of getting the World of Lily Rose ready for opening day. Lily had decided the boutique would feature one-of-kind gifts from around the world to please the most discerning customers. On a buying trip she visited South Africa and brought back tribal necklaces and colorful abstract dinnerware. She traveled to the far reaches of Iceland and found the softest, warmest, and most water-resistant fishermen's sweaters. The Parisian markets and their finely crafted furniture enthralled her, as did the Istanbul bazaars with their hand-woven goods from local weavers.

In contrast to the international flavor of the items being sold, the look of the boutique itself was a reflection of Lily's upbringing on a Kentucky Thoroughbred horse farm. The space was adorned with luscious red roses in large sterling-silver chalices. The floors were old, weathered barn wood that had been refinished to a gleaming rich brown, with crystal chandeliers sparkling down on white marble counters. Lily had personally overseen every inch of the boutique herself. She didn't trust anyone else to carry out her vision, and she knew that a lot was riding on its success.

Gold engraved invitations on cream-colored cardstock were sent out well in advance of the opening day. Lily had included one to Eric Langvin, but she didn't expect him to come, and neither did she receive a reply. She'd gotten the photo he'd taken of her and Sable printed and framed, and it sat on her father's old desk along with the other pictures of her family. Whenever she looked at it, sometimes she thought about the photographer behind it, but ultimately concluded he was one of those people that you met at a certain, pivotal point in your life, and then your paths would never cross again.

Lily Rose was sparkling that night as all of New York fashion and society turned out for her big opening. She was divinely dressed in a lavender Oscar de la Renta off-the-shoulder dress with cropped three-quarter-length sleeves and a flared, feminine hemline. Her hair was pulled loosely back in a chic chignon, and her graceful neck was adorned with a single strand of pearls. Lily's only other jewelry were the tiny diamond stud earrings that Peyton had given her on their first wedding anniversary, and of course her engagement and wedding rings.

The next day, the society pages would run pictures of her, declaring her the new face of New York fashion with her "simplistic beauty" and anointing her as "R. R. Peyton's crown jewel." Some of these photos would include Peyton, handsome despite his glower, but more often they would show Lily with Richard Reynolds, the CEO and chairman of R. R. Peyton's towering over his petite daughter-in-law as she cut the red ribbon marking the opening of the boutique, or later posed with well-known people in the fashion industry. None of them featured Lisa Reynolds, who had completely overdressed for the occasion with too many diamonds. Listening to her friends gush over how "genius" Lily's business sense was, she wondered if any of them knew that lilies were poisonous?

During a lull in the evening, Richard Reynolds drew Lily aside. Indicating the boutique and its accents, he said, "This turned out to be quite charming. Is it similar to the place it's based on?"

"Yes, Red Rose Farm is truly magical," Lily replied. "Someday I'll take you to see it, if you'd like."

"I'd like that." Richard then asked, "Is this all to your satisfaction, my dear?"

"It's wonderful," Lily said. "And I have you to thank for it. For believing in me."

"I just want you to be happy. And Peyton, of course. Lisa and I know that it hasn't been easy for you two in starting your own family."

"But how did you—"

"Peyton tells his mother everything. They've always been very close."

Lily was simultaneously mortified and relieved that Richard knew about her and Peyton's private struggles.

"Whatever you two decide to do," he continued, "we're on your side.

In a fit of spontaneous gratitude, Lily stood on tiptoe to give Richard a hug. He was in many ways like a second father to her, as Uncle Grant had been.

The opening was in every way a triumph, Lily thought as she and Peyton rode in the town car back to their apartment that night. Peyton was uncharacteristically silent, but, being tired herself, she didn't feel like talking, either. Throughout the evening she'd been too busy dealing with the press and well-wishers to keep tabs on him, but she thought he might have disappeared a couple of times. The old doubts crept up on her, but she shook them away. Since the night she'd confronted him about the supermodel, he hadn't done anything to raise her suspicions. Maybe he'd been even more attentive to her, and despite their busy schedules and her preoccupation with the boutique's opening, they'd managed to sneak in a few baby-making sessions when the time was right.

Back in the apartment, suddenly tired, Lily changed out of her dress and wiped off her makeup. Looking into the mirror, she could feel her transformation back into little old Lily Rose, like Cinderella after the ball. Wrapping herself in a crisp linen bathrobe, she went into the bedroom to look for Peyton. He was standing at the window, looking out at a breathtaking view of the Manhattan skyline.

"Is everything all right, Pey?" she asked.

He didn't turn around, but when he spoke, she knew the look he would have on his face, the corner of his mouth turned up in a smirk. "Congratulations, Lily, on becoming the toast of New York fashion."

She decided to play it straight. "I thought tonight went well."

"*Well?*" Peyton snorted. "You were a smashing success! Everyone was talking about you! Everyone was singing your praises! Even my father."

"Peyton, your father is proud of you too—"

She stopped when he lifted a finger. "Don't tell me that. I know exactly where I stand with my father."

"He didn't just give me the boutique because it was good business," Lily tried to explain. "He thought it might help me. Help us."

"Help us how?"

"To take our mind off of not having a baby yet." Taking a deep breath, Lily continued, "Peyton, we need to talk about this. What if something's wrong with me that's keeping me from getting pregnant? Or something's wrong with you?"

"There's nothing wrong. We just need to keep trying, until—"

"Until what? Until it's too late?"

Peyton turned back to the glass and stared stonily out into the glittering lights of the city.

"Peyton," Lily entreated, "please say something."

"All right," he finally said. "You should see a fertility specialist if you want to. Let's start there."

Although it wasn't the total agreement she had been hoping for, Lily knew this was a big concession on Peyton's part. They'd begin with her, and hopefully the problem was something they could get taken care of, medically.

That night, Lily lay awake next to Peyton. Although he'd fallen asleep quickly, she couldn't relax. Adrenaline was still rushing through her veins from excitement over the boutique opening and the call she'd make to her doctor the next morning. Beside her, Peyton's heart was thumping so loudly that Lily felt it was about to leap out of his chest. She had no idea what he was dreaming about. Turning over, she closed her eyes, hoping to see the baby she just knew was in their future.

Chapter 12

Anyone passing by Lily Rose on Madison Avenue that summer morning would have thought her life was nearly perfect. Her flaxen hair was shiny and smooth, her complexion flawless and fair. Her white silk Valentino blouse and slim black skirt looked like they had been tailored to fit her slender, lithe figure, which was accentuated by black Louboutin heels. As she walked down the street, her fresh lipstick catching the light and her diamonds glittering in the sun, she looked like she had everything money could buy and more. But it was all fashion armor, hiding a fragile heart. Outwardly she was Lily Rose Reynolds, the gatekeeper of New York fashion and a member of the famed Reynolds clan, whose playgrounds were Manhattan and Palm Beach. Inside she was Lily Rose Long, the little girl from Appalachia who had lost her entire family, and now it seemed like she was going to lose another that turned out to only exist in her imagination.

Lily was meeting that morning with the psychiatrist she had been going to see for the past three years, ever since she and Peyton sought medical help to have a baby. Every month while taking the fertility drugs, Lily had felt herself swinging between the extremes of joy and despair like a pendulum. Each of the procedures had been filled at first with hopes and dreams, dreams of finally being pregnant, of having a swelling belly and then holding a beautiful baby of her own in her arms. Finally she would see someone who looked like her, a tiny body with the same blood running through his or her veins. Although Lily had never loved anyone in her life more than her parents, she still wanted to see her genetics at work. Over the years, she had heard the innocent comments of people to each other: "Your face is so much like your mother's" or "You have your father's eyes." No one who knew Lily's past ever said that to her. Her face was one without an origin, without a birthright.

Then, with each procedure's failure, came the inevitable low. The only thing that kept Lily going was her boutique, The World of Lily Rose, which had expanded to five locations. In addition to New York, stores had opened in Chicago, Los Angeles, Dallas, and Atlanta. Although each one had its own dedicated team, Lily spent a great deal of time on planes flying from place to the other, as well as going on international buying trips. All of this took away from her private life and her private struggle, which no one understood, not even Peyton. Her doctor had advised that she find a psychiatrist, and Lily had agreed, although with misgivings. The idea of therapy did not bring her much comfort, as her only previous experience had been with a grief counselor when her parents had died.

After a short wait, the receptionist called Lily Rose's name. She stepped into an elegant office that was filled with orchids, leather-bound books, and a couch covered in thick, royal blue velvet. Everything about the decor was supposed to make a patient feel comfortable, and Lily could feel her anxiety subside when she entered.

"Hello, Lily."

The sight of her doctor also made Lily feel better. Well into her fifties, Dr. Raven Atwood was one of the most prestigious psychiatrists in the country, as well as a frequent feature in the fashion pages for her impeccable taste and classic style. With her dark hair swept up in a sleek chignon against her pale white skin, she was dressed in a peacock blue, summer Oscar de la Renta suit that matched her eyes and Manolo sling backs. Over the years Lily had come to trust her completely, opening up to her not only about her troubles with trying to conceive, but her grief over the loss of her parents.

"How have you been this week?" Dr. Atwood asked.

Her eyes downcast, Lily started haltingly, "We went to see the fertility specialist and . . . and he said . . ."

"Go on," Dr. Atwood urged.

It was a moment Lily would never forget. She and Peyton had been sitting side by side in Dr. MacGregory's office on the Upper East Side, waiting to get the results from tests that had been done on Peyton, for once. Lily had already been through tests that determined her reproductive organs were fine and perfectly capable of having a baby. Although it had been suggested many times to Peyton that he undergo similar examination, he had refused, insisting that nothing was wrong with him. After months, Lily wore him down and he got his sperm tested.

"Well, Peyton," Dr. MacGregory said, "it seems like you have a low sperm count."

Peyton's brows drew together in a scowl. "What do you mean?"

"Shall we say, the little fellows just don't swim or move well. You know, like all the crowds on New Year's Eve at Times Square." Dr. MacGregory laughed at his own bad joke.

Peyton looked furious. Lily, too, was shocked. Although she had suspected for a long time that there might be something wrong on Peyton's end that was preventing them from conceiving, she had never thought it might be this. And, she had to admit, she was somewhat relieved that the blame was not to be completely laid on her. But Peyton, she knew, would never admit to having a physical problem of any kind, particularly any manner of a sexual one.

She was surprised when Peyton reluctantly agreed to Dr. MacGregory's suggestion that they take a look at sperm donors. But once they got home, he told her in no uncertain terms that he wanted *only* their own biological children. Using a sperm donor was out of the question, as well as adoption. Lily could understand that, even though sometimes she thought it was selfish of her to think that way. She had come to realize that even though many of her feelings about having children were complicated, she did want to see her own blood running through her child's veins.

As she was telling Dr. Atwood this, she could feel tears welling in her eyes.

"I know this whole process has been difficult for you," Dr. Atwood said softly. "It can be so hard on individuals, and on marriages, too. Perhaps you've done everything you can for now."

Lily rubbed her eyes with the back of her hand. "You know how I've always wanted children. I've watched all my friends get pregnant, gone to all their baby showers, seen the bond between them and their newborns. I just can't understand why this is happening to me. Some mothers don't even want their children. It's not fair. I've been having these dreams. . . ."

"Tell me."

It was a recurring nightmare she'd had for the past few months. In her dream, she would wake up to blood gushing down her arm, pouring like her favorite red nail polish on to her white nightgown and white bed sheets. She wasn't in her own bedroom but a sterile room that could be in a hospital, white and blank as a seashell. Lily guessed it might have been inspired by all the times she'd had to sit in the doctor's office, getting her blood drawn.

As she related this, Dr. Atwood nodded thoughtfully, making some notes in the file on her desk. "I'm glad you've continued to come here every week, Lily. Talk is good, and maybe you'll find some answers. Let's try to think positively," she added as she closed

Lily's file. "You're in good health, have a thriving business, and many close friends. Try to focus on that."

* * *

There wasn't much time for Lily Rose to dwell on her sadness. She was scheduled to depart later that day on a flight to Los Angeles, to make a television appearance on a topic that would be difficult for her to swallow. Months ago, her head assistant Amanda suggested that The World of Lily Rose needed to sell a line of luxury maternity wear. Amanda was only twenty-five but ambitious, and Lily saw a lot of herself in the young woman's drive to succeed. However, when Amanda had voiced her idea, Lily had immediately snapped, "Of course not. Why would you even suggest such a thing?"

Looking tearful, Amanda had said, "So many celebrities are doing it. I just thought it might work for our company."

Lily sighed and pressed her index fingers to her temples. Her fluctuating hormone levels due to the fertility drugs often made her feel like she was spinning out of control. Leveling her tone of voice, she said, "Well, Amanda, maybe you could make this your project. Come back with some possible manufacturing ideas for clothing and accessories, and we can try it. We might even pitch a television segment on being healthy when you're pregnant. I won't be the talent, though, you'll have to find someone else for this spokesperson position."

Lily never thought her assistant could do it, but to her amazement Amanda put together some chic Lily Rose–branded maternity items and succeeded in booking segments on several top national television shows. She found a well-known, pregnant television host to talk about how to stay hip and healthy during pregnancy. The only problem was that the pregnant host got sick at the end of the tour and couldn't fly anymore, leaving Lily to take over. As spokesperson for R. R. Peyton's, Lily had done television segments on just about everything fashion and beauty had to offer. But now, given her conversation with Dr. Atwood, the thought of talking about pregnancy made her want to vomit. Still, The World of Lily Rose needed her. She'd fly to L.A. to do one of the daily talk shows, and as soon as the taping was over, she'd be headed back to New York on the red-eye the next morning.

After the five-hour flight, a driver whisked Lily to one of her favorite hotels in Beverly Hills, the Peninsula. Walking through the hotel's lush tropical gardens, she wished that Peyton were here with her. While the past three years of trying to have a baby had been hard on her physically and mentally, she knew that it wasn't easy for Peyton, either. Sometimes she felt he was just indulging her and didn't really care whether they had children or not—or at least not beyond what it meant for the company. Like his father, work seemed to consume his life.

Lily's mantra was "always make the best of it, even if it's work." After entering the elegant hotel lobby, she checked in and headed for her special place. Being a seasoned traveler, she had her favorite things in each city she visited regularly. Here, it was the Salon, which looked inviting as usual with its pristine white sofas and sparkling crystal chandeliers. She slipped into one of the restful white chairs and decided that she might as well enjoy herself. It was high tea time, and soon before her were placed an antique china teapot with tiny tea cups to match, freshly baked scones, ripe red strawberries, and luscious clotted cream. Usually she was watchful of her diet, especially with trying to get pregnant, but this certainly raised her spirits for the moment.

The following morning, Lily sat in the spotlight as the hosts introduced her segment about staying hip and healthy during pregnancy. She was as bright and sunny as ever, explaining all of the ways women could make their baby bump sexy.

"These new stretch pieces will keep you cool, comfortable, and feeling fresh!" she gushed. "And don't forget to apply shades of the newest lipsticks and blush to enhance your natural glow! And be sure to take advantage of your thick, glossy hair during this time by keeping it washed and gently blown dry!"

What bullshit, Lily thought to herself. She was sure that mothers-to-be in their eighth and ninth months who could no longer see their toes were gagging by the time she was finished. But, as the cameramen were giving her the wrap sign for the segment to end, at least she had gotten through this ordeal.

Lily was just about to go back to the hotel when she noticed that Amanda had left her a voice message, breathless with excitement.

"How was the segment?" Amanda asked when Lily called her back.

"It was fine," Lily replied, not wanting to go further into detail. "What's going on?"

"*Good Day Atlanta* wants to do a segment on the Lily Rose maternity line tomorrow morning! Isn't that wonderful?" When Lily didn't respond, she continued, "This would mean you'd have to change your plans and fly to Atlanta. What do you think?"

As much as Lily wanted to say no, the Atlanta store was the latest one to open, and she knew the exposure would help sales. Besides, the World of Lily Rose might be the only thing she had left in the end—she owed it to herself and to her employees to give it the best chance possible to grow. "That sounds fine," she said without enthusiasm.

If Amanda caught on to Lily's reluctance, she pretended not to notice. "Great! I'll make the arrangements and send you the information right away."

That was how Lily found herself back on the plane that night, although this time winging to Atlanta rather than New York as expected. She had her face mask on and was trying to sleep, but she couldn't help recalling all the pregnancy tips she had given out on the show earlier that day. Pregnancy tips that she would never be able to use herself. As the plane began to climb high into the night sky, tears began to fall silently from her eyes.

When she arrived early the next morning, Lily's nerves were shot. She checked into the Ritz-Carlton in Buckhead, which was her favorite place to stay in Atlanta, and soon it was time for her driver to take her to the television station. For the second time in as many days, Lily Rose smiled her way through fifteen excruciating minutes. The moment she got back to her hotel room, she lay down on the bed and slept dreamlessly, only waking when the sun had slipped beneath the horizon.

Thankfully, Amanda had booked a late-morning flight back to New York the next day for her, so she would be able to rest. She had that evening all to herself, but not wanting to stray far from the hotel, she decided to go to the bar downstairs. The spacious room was timeless, with chandeliers glittering from the high ceiling and rich Oriental rugs carpeting the floor. Drinking a single-malt Scotch, with a tiny bit of maple syrup and a sprig of rosemary—a favorite from back in Kentucky—Lily basked in the sight of the cigar smoke rising in the air and the soft murmur of the other guests. The richness of old Southern hospitality fell upon her like a blanket and her soul felt soothed by it. She recalled evenings at Red Rose Farm when Aunt Martha and Uncle Grant would invite their friends, many of them influential people in the Thoroughbred racing world, and they would gather in the sitting room and talk until past her bedtime.

For the first time since she'd stepped out of Dr. Atwood's office, and perhaps even longer than that, Lily felt her present troubles melt away. She'd go home and tell Peyton that she needed to take a break from the fertility treatments. Although they hadn't exhausted every possibility that one had nowadays to procreate—biologically or otherwise—for now, she had had enough. The World of Lily Rose was rapidly expanding; that would be her baby for now. She thought that Peyton would be able to understand at the very least that, the importance of business. With her mind made up, Lily sat back in her comfortable club chair, closed her eyes, and let the sounds of her surroundings wash over her.

After a while, she couldn't help overhearing snippets of a conversation behind her. Although she didn't normally eavesdrop, the subject matter captivated her.

"So she decided to have the baby?"

"Unfortunately, yes. Her poor parents. Here they thought they had a straight-A student bound for Emory, and their daughter turns out to be no better than a high school dropout."

The voices were distinctly female, older, laced with a Southern drawl that Lily normally found comforting, but here it was tinged with an unpleasantness that came from finding amusement in someone else's misfortune.

"What about the father?"

A snort was the reply, without any pretense of hiding scorn. "What about him? She refuses to tell them who he is."

"An immaculate conception, then."

"I suppose you could call it that. Too bad they're not Catholic."

The other woman laughed obligingly, and chills ran down Lily's spine. Without making it too obvious, she turned slightly so that she could see who had been speaking. Two society matrons were sitting a little beyond her, several empty martini glasses covering the small table between them. While they didn't look alike, their appearance suggested a variation on a theme. They were middle-aged but had obviously indulged in measures that gave the illusion of youth, ones that Lily was familiar with from the customers that frequented her boutique: a face lift here, a chin tuck there; a lip injection; blond hair of an unnatural shade. Their makeup was overdone for a weekday evening out, their dresses were very expensive but a bit too short for an upscale hotel cocktail lounge, unless you weren't intending to leave alone.

Sitting opposite each other must be like looking into a funhouse mirror, Lily thought. She wondered what these women's husbands were doing back home, or maybe stuck working late at the office. They must have children, too, she speculated, perhaps the age of the poor girl they had been gossiping about. She thought that the pregnant teenager must be the unlucky daughter of one of their friends, a family they had often hosted at their house for dinner parties, and vice versa, but suddenly persona non grata. And what about the girl? Didn't she deserve some sympathy for making such a difficult decision? Lily almost never thought about her birth parents, but she supposed that it was likely her biological mother was a teenager who had found herself in the same untenable situation.

Inexplicably, Lily felt a warmth toward the unknown girl that these women were gossiping about. Whoever she was, Lily wished she could know that somewhere out there, a stranger was thinking about her and hoping the best for her.

Chapter 13

THE LATE NOVEMBER SUN STREAMED through Anna Jefferson Baker's enormous, mirror-clad bathroom suite as she struggled, hopping from one foot from another, to get into her Spanx. Unfortunately, it seemed to be a size too small and no longer fit. After much pulling and tugging, Jeff gave up with an exasperated sigh of defeat. Noting how her tummy still protruded under the tight elastic garment, a tiny roll of fat distending her waistline, she frowned. Where had her glorious, sought-after figure gone?

Once considered among the most beautiful women in Atlanta, Jeff had graced the cover of *Atlanta Look* magazine, next to the words proclaiming her as "Baker's Beauty." After college she had married William Robert Baker, aka Billy Baker of Baker's Car Dealerships, which could be found all over Georgia. Twelve years her senior, Billy doted on her and treated her like a princess. Since they didn't have any children, Jeff had plenty of time to focus on shopping for designer clothes and chairing society galas, just like she had dreamed of as a teenager. She had always felt superior to other women because of her stunning appearance, imagining herself as one of the forever youthful models she saw in the pages of New York fashion magazines. But now what?

The reflection in Jeff's mirror filled her with dismay. Not only was she starting to get thick around the middle, her once-sharp jawline was beginning to sag and her mouth was beginning to look pinched. Though she had to admit she drank more martinis than she should and needed to quit smoking, she had the definite feeling that her age was catching up to her. She got some solace out of her long blond hair, still thick and shiny, and without a hint of gray, thanks to Antonio, her colorist. Somehow she'd have to find a way to make her face and body match her hair, and soon. She'd just started planning a big fiftieth birthday party for herself on Valentine's Day, which meant that she had only a little over three months to turn back the hands of time. Jeff had the name of one of the top plastic surgeons in the country that her friend used whenever she needed to get a nip and tuck. As much as she'd judged other women in the past for needing a "little help" with their appearance, she had to admit that maybe the time had come for her. She just needed to go to New York and get a consultation.

Having made up her mind, Jeff slid into a soft knit caftan and went downstairs. Although she'd been to New York before after she'd been married, it had always been with Billy, and they'd done things together as a couple. This time, she'd make the consultation trip a holiday for herself. She'd book a suite at the Four Seasons, shop at R. R. Peyton's and Bergdorf Goodman. She decided she wouldn't tell Billy her true purpose for the trip—the makeover would be a present for him, too. Although she knew he saw her as the same person he'd met almost thirty years ago, what man wouldn't want a better-looking, more youthful version of his wife?

As she waited for her husband to come home, Jeff sat down in the living room with an ice-cold martini on the rocks and leafed through a new Peyton's catalog that had arrived a few days earlier, wondering just what she might find for herself there.

* * *

Jeff's college roommate, Haley McKinney, had introduced Billy to Jeff, as her father had worked with him. So small-town Haley was good for something, Jeff had thought. At first she balked at his age and occupation, but Haley wore her down, telling her, "My father says he's a good man. He's just gone through a divorce and he's ever so lonely. Maybe you could help cheer him up."

Why not? Jeff was starting her last year in college with no prospects; if she didn't meet someone soon, she might even have to use her degree. While she went out on occasion, rarely did anyone merit a second date. This didn't mean she spent her Friday nights alone, though. She was a frequent visitor to Buckhead's most expensive watering holes, and some of the sleazier ones, too. Since the Ritz-Carlton wasn't the sort of place where she could just regularly pick up men, she asked her driver, Chad, what bars she and her fake ID could make it into. Although he was older than her, Chad called her "ma'am" and always spoke to her with a straight face. He knew many of the bouncers, as well as a small hotel where she could rent a room without any questions asked. A former marine, and in top physical condition, he stood watch by the door while Jeff went inside with her conquests, to make sure no one tried to take advantage of her.

Jeff couldn't say what drove her to these sexual encounters. Part of it was the thrill, the danger, the knowledge that she could just look at a man across a bar and he'd fall into her lap. She loved the expression on their faces when she suggested they go somewhere else, somewhere quieter, to "get to know each other." It was as if these men were still drunk and weren't sure if she was part of a wet dream. Usually both she and her target were a little tipsy as they staggered out of the bar, arms around each other, and across the street to the town car where Chad waited. They'd make out in the back seat on the way, and Jeff would be half delirious with desire by the time the hotel's sign came into view. Out of the car they'd stumble, into the elevator and to the designated room that had already been paid for, booked every Friday for weeks in advance, and into a haze of stale air and carpet freshener. That was when it became blurry for Jeff. In the dark, their mouths, their limbs, their bodies, became entangled and she lost herself in the feeling she so craved, that of complete release, a complete forgetting of who she was and what had happened to her.

Jeff made sure to use a condom every time. She had a large supply that she kept hidden in a locked box in her dorm room, away from Haley's innocent eyes. She was no longer the naïve teenager that Eric Langvin had seduced at a horse farm, but a young woman who was wise to the ways of the world, and whose heart was hardened because of them. Most of the men she slept with were anywhere from their early twenties to early thirties—she really couldn't tell—but she was sure they had a lot more experience under their belts than the boys at Emory. Still, they were appreciative, even grateful, that someone as beautiful as Jeff, with a body as luscious as hers, would want to spend a night with them. The fact that the sex had no strings attached was even more mind-blowing. A few of the men angled for another meeting, or even a real date, but she refused them all. And if they tried to go any further, Chad was there to send them on their way.

There was one night when a particular man was getting rough with Jeff, insisted on staying longer when she clearly wanted him to leave.

"You owe me," he said, beckoning with his finger as he would a dog.

"I owe you nothing," Jeff snapped, already regretting her choice that night. The sex hadn't even been that great, and he had the nerve to want something more from her.

When she turned away from him, he grabbed her arm, she screamed, and in a flash, the door opened. Chad rushed in, a Glock 9mm leveled at the other man's head.

"Get out now," he growled.

Not knowing that he regularly packed heat, Jeff screamed again, then cowered behind the bed. With the gun still trained between his ears, the man scrambled for his clothes and his life. When he was gone, Chad holstered the Glock and said to Jeff, "It's okay. You can come out."

She crawled from behind the bed, mascara streaming down her face, and clung to him while he stood, impassively, arms at his side. Then he sat her down, pulled her bathrobe closed, and waited until her sobs subsided

"Why are you doing this?" she asked.

He looked at her with a sincerity that she had never seen from another man before—someone who wasn't looking to get into her pants—and replied, "I got your six."

Jeff had never heard the phrase before, but when she found out what it meant, she began to cry all over again. No one, even her father, had ever treated her with such protectiveness.

That was the state of Jeff's love life, so to speak, when she met Billy Baker. Her first thought was that while he was far too old for her, he was not unattractive, with a kind smile and gentle eyes. At least he still had all of his hair. As for Billy, he looked at Jeff as if he had never seen such a wondrous creature before. From that moment on he placed her on a pedestal, and she had never been in danger of falling from it.

With Billy, Jeff finally got a taste of the high society she so yearned for. No matter how he had made his money, it was still money, and there was quite a lot of it. He took her out to the best dining establishments in the city, and she was on his arm for every charity ball and gala of the season. For those events he encouraged her to purchase gowns that previously she could only have dreamed of wearing, and soon they were accentuated with jewels that he gave her for her birthday, their six-month anniversary, and, finally, an engagement ring.

Of course, the first person Jeff told was her mother, who was overjoyed for her, and then her roommate Haley. And then she told Chad, who regarded her solemnly and said, "I guess you won't be needing me anymore, then."

It was true that she didn't need him, since when she married Billy she'd have use of his staff, including his driver, but she was suddenly reluctant to let him go. He'd been a constant in her life for the past four years, the longest of any man she'd known in college. One last time, she asked Chad to take her to the hotel room she'd been in with so many other men, and she convinced him to pull her down on the bed and make love to her, knowing she'd never see him again. That way she could tell Billy, in all honesty, when they slept together for the first time on their wedding night, that there was no one else.

Not long after they were married, Billy started talking about having a family. There were no children from his previous union, and he was anxious to get started. Jeff knew this day would come and had prepared herself for it, including making sure she had a ring on her finger first. With a quiver in her voice, she told Billy that she wasn't able to conceive, that an illness in her childhood prevented her from ever having children.

"I was afraid to tell you about it when we first met," she whispered, eyes lowered. "I thought if I told you the truth, you wouldn't want to marry me."

Billy enfolded her in his arms, his eyes troubled. "Of course I would still marry you." He wiped away the tear she willed to trickle down her cheek. "You've made me the luckiest, happiest man in the world. Not having any children won't change that."

Over the years Jeff stuck to her story, obtaining birth control pills from her doctor that Billy never knew about. To tell the truth, she didn't want children, actually didn't like them, although she never uttered the words to anyone, afraid of what they might think of her. Sometimes she felt guilty, knowing how much Billy would cherish a son or a daughter. He could never know about her past. He thought she was perfect; what if he found out what had taken place the summer before she went to college? So rarely did Jeff recall that horrible July 4th weekend, when she had given birth to a baby girl and given her away the next day, that she was almost able to convince herself it had never happened. Soon, she wouldn't have to worry about getting pregnant ever again. That was one good thing about getting older.

* * *

December 8th was a brisk, cold day in Manhattan as Jeff left the plastic surgeon's office to head to R. R. Peyton's for a celebratory shopping spree. She was elated, having set the date for her upcoming surgery for the beginning of January, which would give her plenty of time to recover before her party. Already she was starting to feel more confident about her looks, walking down the street in her full-length fur coat—a little outdated by New York standards—that Billy had bought her for Christmas. She didn't get much of a chance to wear it in Atlanta. She went into R. R. Peyton's, ready to buy some new clothes to inaugurate her soon-to-be-improved self.

Wandering around the first floor, Jeff looked at the exquisite jewelry, thinking which piece Billy might buy that would make her the envy of all her friends. Toward the back, she stumbled upon a pretty space adorned with red roses in silver chalices and wooden plank floors. It almost made Jeff wish that she had gone into fashion merchandising after college at Emory; maybe she would have ended up working in a boutique like this. She could only imagine the possibilities she might have had; where her great looks might have taken her.

Seeing a store clerk, she went over to him and asked, "What is this place called?"

"The World of Lily Rose, ma'am," the young man replied.

Jeff liked the name—"Lily" instantly conjuring up the elegance of Lillian Langvin, and "Rose" making her think of the South. "I've never seen anything like it," she admitted, then lest the clerk think she was from some backwater, added, "I live in Atlanta."

"Oh, we have a store there, too," he informed her. "It just recently opened."

"I'll have to check it out then." Jeff made a mental note to herself to look it up when she got home. Maybe she'd get a Christmas present for Billy there.

She stayed in the boutique for a while longer, then went through the designer floors and purchased a couple of cocktail dresses she thought would be suitable for splashy dinner parties. The perfect gown for her birthday party eluded her, though. It had to be something elegant and sophisticated, something no other woman in Atlanta would wear. Jeff liked to think she had style and taste far above that of any of her friends, and her party would be the perfect place to prove it.

She was taking in all the sights and sounds of the department store when she happened to look down at the end of the aisle and noticed two young women. The one with long brown hair seemed to be in her late twenties and was listening intently to the other, while taking notes on a tablet. The woman who was giving direction appeared to be slightly older, and she was one of the most striking women Jeff had never seen. She had pale blond hair that was pulled back at the nape of her neck, and was dressed in black from head to toe—a fitted cashmere sweater, slim black trousers, and patent-leather stiletto high heels. Her only jewelry were her wedding rings, an expensive oversize watch, and diamond stud earrings. She was exactly what Jeff used to be and everything Jeff wanted to be now: young, beautiful, and stylish.

Although she wasn't close enough to hear what they were talking about, Jeff assumed from their actions that they worked at the store. Perhaps they were sales associates and could help her find a dress. She had started to head toward them when they suddenly turned and walked away, deep in conversation, without giving her a glance. Jeff looked down at her big, blocky fur coat and felt what she was wearing was all wrong. The giddiness she'd felt earlier walking out of the doctor's office was starting to seep away from her, leaving her dejected. Despite the shopping bags on her arm, the promise of a new body and a new face, she couldn't hide the fact that she was almost fifty, and she was never going to be able to look or feel as attractive as she once had.

Back at her hotel, Jeff decided she would go to the bar that evening. Even though she hadn't been out alone in a long time—always with Billy or friends—she was sure that the men would flock around her as they'd always done. The marble bar was crowded with men and women having after-work cocktails, and Jeff's mood lifted. She ordered her martini and enjoyed the elegant surroundings, imagining herself thirty years younger and a single woman on the prowl. Although she had no intention of cheating on Billy, a little flirtation would do no harm and give her the boost she needed.

After her second martini, feeling all warm and assured, Jeff looked around for a potential target. A couple of empty seats down was a dark-haired man who looked to be in his mid-thirties, head bowed over his drink and seeming in need of some consolation. As if sensing her eyes on him, he lifted his head and looked in her direction, a grin on his face. But before she could make her move, his gaze moved past her to a woman in a business suit, who came up and kissed him on the cheek.

"Sorry, honey, I'm late but I was still working on the case. You know I have that big trial tomorrow."

Immediately, Jeff tuned the couple out. She had naively thought the man might be interested in having a conversation with an older woman like her, while his wife or girlfriend, who was young enough to be Jeff's daughter, must be an attorney. The night was souring fast, and Jeff couldn't wait to leave.

Just as she was ready to sign her tab, she heard a deep voice behind her say, "Leaving so soon? I thought I'd see if I could buy you another martini."

Jeff turned around to see a well-dressed gentleman who looked to be in his early seventies. He had thick gray hair and was well built, except for a slight bulge over his alligator belt and slightly stooped shoulders. He might have been attractive to some, but Jeff felt like she had been slapped in the face. This was the only man who had noticed her all night. Feeling her stomach churn, she quickly raised her hand with its flashy diamond ring and excused herself. "Thank you so much, but I need to leave now. I'm meeting my husband for dinner and can't be late."

Jeff returned to her room and ordered a small salad with shrimp and another martini, resolving to start her diet that night. After a quick shower, she lay in bed thinking about what had happened in the bar. A man in his seventies actually thought that he had a chance with a woman like her? Had she been living in a dream world? She had been married to Billy for so long that she just assumed that every man thought she was as wonderful as he did.

Jeff got out of bed and lit a cigarette. She wandered into the living room, then filled a crystal cocktail glass with ice and poured herself a Grey Goose vodka. She sat watching the flickering fire as it danced in the dimly lit suite. In a bit of a drunken stupor, she began to envision her Valentine's Day birthday celebration. When everyone was gathered in the front hall, she'd walk down the staircase in a tight new dress that showed off just how youthful and gorgeous her new figure was. Murmurs of astonishment and admiration would arise from the assembled guests, among them the wealthiest and most influential people that Atlanta society had to offer. Billy would be waiting for her at the bottom of the stairs, his eyes wide and his mouth slightly open, as if he was seeing her for the first time, until she stepped off onto his arm. The crowd would part as he led her, gliding across the parquet floor, into middle age.

With that final thought, Jeff fell asleep on the sofa, the smell of stale tobacco smoke still thick and heavy in the air.

Chapter 14

IF LILY THOUGHT THAT DECIDING to set aside the whole issue of having a baby would improve her and Peyton's relationship, she could not have been more mistaken. It was as if the discovery made in Dr. MacGregory's office had lit a fuse in Peyton, the truth not setting him free but sending him down his own destructive path of booze and drugs. Lily could do nothing but endure the rising tide of dread she felt waiting for Peyton to come home from work each evening, and watching him drag himself in, his eyes glazed over, his clothes smelling of weed and expensive perfume. He no longer bothered to try and explain away his behavior, and she had long since stopped avoiding confrontations with him about it.

"Peyton, where the hell have you been?" she would say, knowing full well the answer.

He would whip past her, raising his voice to meet hers. "You know I have more responsibility now that I'm president of the company."

Then Lily would chase him into the bedroom, screaming, "What, more responsibility to be drunk?"

Sometimes the argument would stop there; other times they would end up having wild, exhausting sex. *Lily had a virgin nose and had never done drugs of any kind, but even she knew that Peyton's frantically beating heart was cocaine at work. Still, she did everything she could to satisfy him, giving him all of her until her body ached, thinking that maybe this way she could reach him. She wanted him to know how much she loved him, but she knew this was not about love. It was about him "riding high on the white horse," and she could never follow him to the places he went during his coke-fueled binges.*

All of this was taking a toll on her well-being, too. Sometimes Lily would be sitting at her office at work or at home by herself and feel like she couldn't catch her breath. Dr. Atwood, her psychiatrist, told her that she was experiencing panic attacks, which was not uncommon in individuals that had been through traumatic events. After telling Lily she wasn't surprised, considering Lily's past, Dr. Atwood prescribed antianxiety medication, which made Lily feel calmer. Or at least that she could put up with Peyton's depravity for a little longer.

Lily also reached back into the long, pushed-aside religious faith that her family in the mountains had so devotedly followed and started going to church. It seemed to be the only place where her heart stopped frantically beating and the calmness of what she felt and believed was God, and the spirits of her beloved parents, would wash over her. Lily began to make new friends at the church, who embraced her into the fold with open arms. They never acknowledged her social position, whether they were aware of it or not, and she never discussed it. It was a balm in the asphalt jungle of her life.

At home the tension continued to rise and could conceivably have gone on for a while, if not for the fateful night when *Peyton came home to her usual question of where he'd been. He stopped dead in his tracks, his brown eyes looking almost black, cold and dead. "For your information, I've been out for dinner with my father and a few of his colleagues to discuss business that is far above your level."*

As he practically ripped his shirt off and headed toward the bedroom, Lily couldn't control her anger. She ran after him, catching his arm, and said, "Pey, I know you weren't with Daddy Rich because I just talked to him on the phone, and he was at home with your mother."

Peyton grabbed her by the shoulders. "What did you call my father?"

"Daddy Rich," Lily replied defiantly. "I asked him and he said I could call him that. I'll call him what I want."

"He's not your father!" Peyton exploded. "Your father's dead!"

Lily would never forget what came next. Her once warm, loving, charming husband threw her on the floor and started to kick her, like he was trying to punt a field goal but kept missing. She tried to scramble toward the door, but he continued to kick her in the buttocks and legs, then in the ribs and torso, until she finally gave up and lay in a fetal position covering her head, which he hadn't gotten to yet in his blind rage. Then in three or four minutes—she wasn't sure; time seemed to pass in slow motion—it was over. Peyton walked briskly away into the bedroom, as if he'd just finished dealing with a minor annoyance. Feeling dizzy and disconcerted, but most of all afraid for her life, Lily got up as fast as she could and grabbed the keys by the door. Dressed in only a light skirt and skinny tee, she ran barefoot into the night, ten blocks up Park Avenue, until she reached Richard and Lisa Reynolds' apartment.

Within minutes Lily was sitting in the living room of Richard and Lisa's grand triplex. Lisa had grabbed a blanket and wrapped it around Lily's shaking shoulders, then given her some water and a Xanax, which Lily readily accepted. Lily wondered what her in-laws must think had caused the bruises rising red and purple on her fair skin.

"Who did this to you?" Richard demanded. "Did someone break in to your apartment?"

Beside him, Lisa kept her eyes lowered, her hands trembling. As Peyton's mother she had an unthinkable intuition of what might have happened. When Lisa raised her eyes again, Lily looked straight into a mother's greatest fear.

"Your son did this to me," Lily confirmed.

She watched as a mixture of emotions crossed both her in-laws' faces.

Richard's chest seemed to deflate, and almost imperceptible beads of sweat formed at Lisa's hairline, a shade darker than the rest of her hair. Then a screen seemed to come down over Richard's face, and he looked the consummate businessman again.

"Does anyone else know what happened?"

Confused, Lily said, "No, I came here first because I didn't know what else to do."

"Good," Richard said. "If this gets out to the press, it could look very bad for the company. For the World of Lily Rose. I know you don't want that to happen, right?"

After a moment, Lily slowly shook her head.

Lisa tried to give her a smile. "Why don't you stay in the guest suite tonight? I'll have fresh pajamas and a robe laid out, and hot tea sent up. Then you can take a shower and have a full night's rest. We can talk about everything in the morning. What do you think?" She almost sounded like she was pleading, as she looked from Lily to her husband and back again.

In the silence that followed, Lily knew they were waiting for her to make a decision. There were two alternatives: she could either call the police and file charges or pretend that nothing had happened. Neither was terribly appealing. If she did the first, the Reynolds family would be front and center in the tabloids the next day, and if she did the second… As many women in her situation before her, Lily was convinced that this was a onetime occurrence; that her husband would never try to hurt her again. It had been the drugs talking, not his innermost self, the person he truly was. In addition, she couldn't bear to lose everything she'd built with Peyton and her career, not to mention her place in the Reynolds family. And so, she only had one choice, and behind gritted teeth, she made it.

"I guess I'll go home now," Lily said quietly. "I hope Peyton isn't angry with me anymore." She looked from Richard to Lisa, at the relief that spread across their faces. "Thank you for helping me."

Richard spoke quickly. "Of course, Lily. We're so glad that you came to us. Always feel free to come here."

"We're your family now," Lisa echoed.

Every family has its secrets, Lily thought as she allowed Lisa to help her up.

Richard insisted on having his driver take her back to her apartment, ostensibly for her comfort, but in reality, so that no one else would see, and possibly recognize her, in her present condition. As Lily stepped into the elevator and before the door closed, he whispered to her, "Don't worry about Peyton, I'll take care of everything."

There was no time for her to wonder what he meant by that because she was soon being rapidly whisked down to the first floor. When she was safely out of the building, back in their luxurious living room, Richard and Lisa Reynolds held each other and cried.

As silently as she could, Lily let herself into her apartment, finding it quiet and Peyton asleep. She took a long, hot shower, trying to erase the evidence of his violence against her. But after changing into her night-gown, she couldn't bring herself to enter the bedroom, and feared the very thought of getting into bed with him. She sat huddled in an armchair, and her pets came to her—her beautiful Siberian Husky, Sable, and her beloved strawberry blond Himalayan cat, Hollywood—providing comfort that no human could. As Sable lay by her feet, and Hollywood curled up in her lap, she fell into a fitful sleep.

The next morning, she awoke with a start when she heard Peyton's angry voice coming from the bedroom. The events of the previous night came rushing back into her head as, with her heart thumping, she tentatively got to her feet and listened at the bedroom door. Peyton was having an argument on the phone with his father, and from the sounds of it, it was one that he was about to lose.

* * *

That morning, true to his word, Richard Reynolds took care of everything. On the phone call he informed Peyton that someone else would be stepping in as president of the company while he spent six months in rehab in Malibu. Lily didn't know what to say as he packed a small suitcase in a stony, resentful silence. Finally, as he was waiting for the limo to take him to the airport, he turned to her. To her amazement, he was the one who sounded hurt, like a child who had been severely disciplined.

"Why did you tell my father what happened?"

"There was no one else I could have gone to!"

"It was only that one time. You should have told him to give me another chance. But now it's too late."

And with that, he was gone. At least, Lily thought, with Peyton on the other side of the country, she could focus on work and herself. At the department store, Richard occasionally checked in with her about the boutique and, she suspected, to see how she was doing without Peyton. Lily made no pretense that she was greatly relieved by her husband's absence, or that she appreciated the intervention. Richard had bought her a six months' grace period, and she would forever be grateful to him for that. As for the business side, she trusted that he knew what was best for his son and his company. Richard Reynolds and his forefathers were known to be some of the keenest business minds in New York City. They seemed to make the right moves first, always one step ahead of everyone else. That's why R. R. Peyton's had been the top luxury department store for over a century, and it seemed that he was willing to do just about anything to keep it that way, even if it meant taking his own son to task.

With Peyton gone, Lily was able to relax for the first time in months. She didn't realize before how much of a psychological toll Peyton's behavior had been taking on her—not knowing who he was with or what he was doing when he was out at night, steeling herself for their arguments when he returned home. Although the bruises he had inflicted on her body faded, the ones on her mind did not, and she couldn't help replaying the sight of his face—that of a stranger—just before he kicked her to the floor. She heard again the echo of the last words he said to her, that it was "too late," with a finality that took her to the edge of despair. Peyton's rehab did not allow phone calls, or any communication with the outside world, as part of the recovery plan, so she had no way to tell if he was getting better.

Lily continued to go to the beautiful stone church on Fifth Ave. that she had found many years ago when in need of spiritual guidance during her fertility treatments. Sometimes, when she was listening to the voices of the choir soar underneath the arched roof, she felt like she was back in the small white church in Cumberland Falls, watching her father sing while she sat holding her mother's hand. Many times, tears would silently roll down her face when the choir sang her father's favorite hymn, "Amazing Grace." The memory was filled with sadness, but her parents' presence was stronger than ever in those moments.

In late August, Lily planned to pay a long-overdue visit to Red Rose Farm. On impulse, she invited Richard to come with her, as thanks for trusting her with the boutique and dealing with Peyton so swiftly and decisively. Lisa was welcome to join, too, of course, but she made an excuse that she was allergic to horses, and privately Lily was glad that she would not have to spend a weekend in her most favorite place in the world with her mother-in-law. Richard would be the first person in her new family to visit the farm. She told him to bring jeans and casual clothes, and she teased that if he really wanted to look the part, to buy a pair of Frye or Durango western boots on his employee discount at the department store.

As their private jet descended over Blue Grass Airport, over the acres of land crisscrossed by white fences and dotted with grazing

Thoroughbreds, Lily laughed when she saw the expression on Richard's face. "You've never flown in here, have you, Daddy Rich? Doesn't it look like a scene out of a commercial for the best horse farms in the world?"

Shaking his head, Richard said, "And here I am, thinking I've seen just about everything and been just about everywhere. I do remember flying in one day to Louisville for the Kentucky Derby with the governor of New York. We had a few mint juleps, hobnobbed with the rich and famous, watched a few fine horses run, and then headed back home." He gave her a warm smile that few people saw these days. "But my daughter makes for much better company."

They were picked up in a black SUV with the words "Red Rose Farm" colorfully stenciled on the side and driven by Marcus, Ray's son. Marcus had taken over the position of farm manager when his father had gotten too old for the job, although Ray stayed on at a little cottage on the grounds. When Marcus opened the iron gates, before them lay what for Lily had always been—and would be forever—one of the loveliest places on earth. For the worldly Richard, this would be nothing less than a revelation. Lush oak trees stood on either side of the long drive up to the white-brick country mansion. Tangled, old-fashioned red roses climbed the white fences surrounding the house, while pink-and-white hydrangeas bloomed lavishly all around the edges of the property.

When Lily and Richard got out of the SUV, they were greeted by two chocolate Labs and a golden retriever that immediately jumped up to greet Lily. As if she'd forgotten that Richard was with her, Lily sat down on the grass and kissed and hugged the dogs with more affection than she'd shown Peyton the last few months before he'd left for rehab.

After a bit, she looked up and said, "Oh, Daddy Rich, I'm sorry, I didn't introduce you. These are my dogs who have been with us for years. That's Jagger and Scotch," Lily said as she nodded toward the twin Labs, "and this gal," shaking the retriever's head back and forth playfully, "is Charlie," she laughed, as the dog licked at her face, all full of excitement to see her.

"I'm sure we'll get properly acquainted," Richard said with a grin as Lily's four-legged friends led the way into the house.

Lily walked with pride into the living room. She'd spent considerable time over the years decorating the house to reflect her tastes, and this room was no exception, with its peaceful, serene palette of dove white and accents of china blue. White, luxurious sofas and chairs were arranged invitingly in front of a large brick fireplace that had a gleaming white panel. Photographs of horses lined the walls, all Thoroughbreds that had been born and raised on the farm, each distinct and powerful in their own way.

Similar photos were displayed in the guest suite, which Lily had decorated with a masculine touch in mind. In the sitting room, a sparkling chandelier cast a soft light on a classic, tufted black leather sofa. The chairs were covered in a black-and-white herringbone pattern, and the drapes were a deep, royal purple.

"Well," Richard said, turning around the room in appraisal, "I can see where the inspiration for your boutique comes from. This is lovely, my dear."

Lily basked in the compliment. "Thank you. I thought you might want to get settled and have some lunch? Remember to dress casually," she added.

By the time Richard came downstairs, in jeans and a crisp white shirt—over his regular city wingtips—Lily had changed into riding pants and boots. They sat down at the wooden kitchen table for a simple but delicious lunch straight from the garden, starting with bowls of steaming corn chowder. Their main course was a butter lettuce salad with juicy ripe tomatoes, accompanied by freshly brewed iced tea. Richard indicated his enjoyment of the meal by patting his waistline.

"After lunch I've arranged for us to take a ride around the farm on horseback," Lily told him.

"I haven't ridden a horse in a long time, and certainly not some fancy Thoroughbred," Richard protested.

"Don't worry, the horses we're riding today are old and gentle and probably couldn't get up more than a trot. But they love a good walk with kind folks."

Out in the pasture in front of one of the stables, Marcus helped Richard up on a chestnut horse with a white mane, and he and Lily headed off. She showed him the white barns with steeples, the training rings, the old breeding sheds, the elaborate graveyard and the memorials to the famous horses buried there at the farm. It was a world he knew nothing about, but she knew like the back of her hand.

"So where are all the racehorses?" Richard asked.

Lily laughed. "Daddy Rich, this hasn't been a working Thorough-bred farm since my Uncle Jeff passed away. Now we only keep rescue horses, dogs, and cats here, in addition to a staff to take care of them. I sold off a thousand acres of the farm and now we're down to a little under nine hundred acres for ourselves. Just enough for a country home."

"It certainly is something," Richard remarked, looking around at the rolling pastures that shimmered blue underneath the sunshine.

Arriving back at the house a couple of hours later, Lily thought her father-in-law looked a little tired, so she suggested he might want to take a nap before dinner. He agreed and headed up to his suite, while she discussed some business matters with Marcus. When he entered the kitchen at six o'clock, there was a roast chicken surrounded with vegetables just coming out of the oven. Lily poured them each a glass of white wine and they ate at the massive old oak dining table. The three dogs that had greeted them on their arrival lay flopped in favored positions around the large room, Richard laughing when he remarked that their noses were nevertheless still working, presumably to detect any scraps that might fall to the hardwood floor.

After dinner they retired to big, comfortable chairs in the conservatory, which looked out on the grounds, and watched the sun set over the bluegrass. Lily poured them a couple of neat bourbon whiskeys, exactly what one drank in Kentucky after a day on horseback. The golden liquid tasted as smooth as silk.

"This place is wonderful, Lily," Richard said. "Why have you been keeping it such a secret?"

"I haven't, really. Peyton's just never been interested in coming down here or seeing this part of my life, I guess."

"Maybe a little Kentucky might be good for him," Richard suggested.

"I always thought we would bring our kids here," Lily said quietly. "You know how after my parents died, my aunt and uncle took me in here. That's why this farm is so precious to me. It represents all I have left of my past. Just like you have Peyton's Department Store, I have Red Rose Farm. Someday I hope to share this with my children and continue the legacy of my family and this great place."

"I understand," Richard assured her, and together they sat in an easy silence as the last rays of the sun slipped beneath the horizon.

* * *

Peyton was due to come home right before the holidays, always the busiest time for the department store. Lily tried to immerse herself in her work and not think about what might happen once he returned. Yet as the day approached, it became increasingly difficult to put the thought completely out of mind.

The afternoon his flight was coming in, she sat on the sofa in the living room, dressed in a white cashmere sweater and tailored pants, petting Hollywood the cat in her lap and waiting for the sound of his key in the lock. She wondered if she should have gone with the town car to pick him up from the airport, but she didn't want other people around when she saw him again for the first time. She had no idea what her reaction would be—or his, either.

Then there he was. Standing in the doorway, Peyton was thinner than when he'd left, his face almost gaunt and his winter coat hanging off his tall frame, but he was still the most attractive man she had ever met.

"Pey, how are—" she began, rising to greet him, but before she could say any more, he knelt before her, as if he were about to propose again, and pressed his face against her stomach.

"I'm so sorry, Lily. Can you ever forgive me? I don't mean for . . . just for what happened the night before I left. I'm sorry for everything . . . for all of it. Can you give me another chance?"

Looking down, Lily buried her hands in his lustrous brown hair, and somberly rested her chin on the top on his head. "Welcome home, Pey," she whispered.

Chapter 15

WHEN PEYTON REYNOLDS WALKED INTO the apartment he shared with his wife, he felt genuinely happy to be home. Lily had prepared a simple but romantic dinner for them, and as he looked across the candlelit table at his gorgeous wife, he had to admit that he had missed her. She seemed blissfully happy to see him, and he found her new sense of confidence and contentment very appealing. Afterward, they made slow, delicious love in front of the fireplace with some of his favorite jazz playing softly in the background, which Lily had selected. He looked down at her flaxen hair, her pale smooth skin, and into those beautiful aqua eyes, and asked himself what more could he ask for? Except maybe a drink and a snort of coke, but that wasn't happening anytime soon.

The next morning when he got to work, Peyton headed directly to his father's office. Richard Reynolds was sitting behind his massive desk, reading the *Wall Street Journal*.

When he saw his son, he didn't close the paper, much less get up from his chair.

"So you're back. I hope the time away has done you some good."

"Yes, Dad." Peyton said the words he'd carefully rehearsed, "It's given me the opportunity to reflect on how important home and family are, and I'd appreciate your confidence in me. I'm ready to get back to work."

"I'm glad to hear that, but it'll take you a while to catch up on things. I'll set up several meetings for you with the senior staff. I expect you should be ready to take back your role as president again in a few months."

"A few months? I'm ready now!"

"Peyton," Richard said sternly, "you've been in rehab for the past six months. Before that, you were drunk and drugged most of the time—"

Peyton opened his mouth to protest, but stopped when his father held up his right hand flatly, like someone about to take an oath.

"Let me correct that, "Richard continued. "*All* of the time. You only remained president of this company because you were my son. If not, you'd have been sent packing a long time ago. Now we have the chance for a new beginning. For the time being your office will be here on the executive floor where I can keep an eye on you, but you won't regain your title until you're ready."

Peyton was dumbfounded, but when he saw his father turn to his paper again, he knew it was useless for him to say anything. And maybe he should go, just before his seething anger, bubbling just below the surface, exploded beyond his control. If that happened, his father might just make his demotion permanent.

"By the way," Richard added as Peyton was leaving the room, "before you leave today, you should take a look at your wife's boutique."

"The World of Lily Rose?" Peyton couldn't keep the sneer from his voice. "How's that coming along?"

"All of the World of Lily Rose boutiques are best sellers, nation-wide," Richard informed him. "You are one fortunate man, son, marrying that Lily Rose. She's an asset to the store and the family.

Maybe more so than some people who are in the family. Don't you forget that."

Peyton thought he might just punch a wall. He had been down-graded for the second time, and it wasn't even ten in the morning on his first day back at work! Through clenched teeth, he said as pleasantly as possible, "Of course, Dad."

He turned and went straight into the women's restroom, which luckily was unoccupied, broke the soap dispenser off the wall, and hurled it into the mirror, sending shards of glass flying everywhere. Breathing hard, Peyton looked down at the mess he'd made and, as he'd done with so many other things in his life, walked away to let someone else clean it up.

When noon came, he knew he needed an outlet, to do or feel something that made him feel like he was back in control. Lily had called earlier in the morning and suggested they have lunch together, but he made the excuse that he had too much work to catch up on. He told her he'd see her back home, walked out of the store past her boutique without looking twice at it, and took the subway uptown. After he got off, he headed toward the East River to an apartment building he had never been inside before, but in which just a couple of weeks earlier he had secured an apartment.

He rode the elevator to the eleventh floor, stepped out, and turned left. Before he could knock on the door at the end of the hallway, it opened to reveal a young woman wearing a shiny black raincoat, sheer black nylons, and black stiletto heels.

Looking at her quizzically, he asked, "Are you pretending to be a glamorous spy in some James Bond movie?"

Green eyes fixed on him, she pulled him across the threshold and dropped her raincoat. The vision before him made him salivate. The ends of her thick, strawberry-blond hair just brushed the tips of her nipples in a low-cut, lacy bra, and she wore a matching thong and garter belt that made her long legs seem endless.

Before Peyton could make a move, she whispered, "I've been waiting so long for this."

Never taking his eyes off her, Peyton removed her bra, his fingers lingering on her breasts. Then he scooped her into his arms—she barely weighed anything—and whispered into the fragrant curve of her neck, "Me too." Then he carried her into the small living room as all of his troubling dilemmas in Gotham City disappeared from his mind.

* * *

In the beginning, rehab was the most excruciating experience he'd ever had in his young, privileged life. Detoxing put his body through uncontrollable tremors and nausea, leaving him unable to eat, sleep, even think. During that first month, a staff member continually followed him around, monitoring his actions to make sure he didn't slip up. It was like being under house arrest, except he didn't think what he'd done was bad enough to warrant this forced incarceration at all. The person who'd been hurt the most by his actions was himself, wasn't it?

After he'd been through the worst of the detox, and his head began to clear, he began to see the merits of being in a place where he could be somewhat invisible. He'd checked into rehab under a false name, and as "Rick Hammond from New York," he found himself saying and doing things that Peyton Reynolds III would have never considered. Although each day was a struggle, he was determined to stay clean because he knew that it was the only way he would prove to his father that he could remain president of the department store. He had to stay on his father's good side, which also meant trying to make his marriage work. Despite everything that had happened, Peyton still loved his wife, in his own way. Other patients in the clinic were allowed to have contact with their families, even have family conferences, but for reasons he didn't know, this was forbidden to him. He could only conjecture that it might have something to do with how he had treated Lily that terrible, drug-fueled night. He knew that if he'd just had the chance to talk to Lily during this period in his life, he wouldn't have been so vulnerable to the young woman he saw one day in Narcotics Anonymous.

It was in one of those meetings, where everyone is nobody, that Peyton first noticed Gracie Jane Gallagher, and he was sure she was definitely somebody—at least somebody he wanted to know. Most people had similar things to say about how they started abusing drugs—the whys, the pain, the drama, and how hard it was to stop—but Gracie was different. He couldn't keep his eyes off her as she talked, one finger absentmindedly twisted around a strand of her very long, ginger-colored hair. Her face was sprinkled with freckles, and she would occasionally glance up at the group with her beguiling green eyes. She reminded him of the cookies he used to love when he was a little boy, all warm and sparkling with crystals of sugar and powdered with cinnamon dust.

Gracie spoke of how she had grown up in a large family in Boston. Her father, a fireman, had been killed in the line of duty when she was only ten years old. Soon after, her mother moved her and her brothers to Delray Beach, Florida, near their grandmother in the hopes of starting a new life. She had started modeling in Miami at age 15 and was introduced to cocaine; ever since then she'd been on and off drugs, in and out of various programs, with varying success, but always failure in the end.

"I'm not in here this time because of the drugs," she explained, her arms holding her sides as if trying to keep herself from disappearing. "I need to gain weight."

Listening to her, Peyton unconsciously rubbed his finger where his gold wedding band had been. As part of his staying in character, he'd slipped it off and left it in his room. After the meeting, he approached Gracie to introduce himself. She looked to be about 5'10", but it was impossible to tell how much she weighed. As thin as she appeared to be, she wore an old, oversized sweater that hung off her shoulders, over raggedy jeans and once-white sneakers that were now gray. Despite the appearance of her street urchin clothing, Peyton was inexplicably drawn to her. He had never seen someone who was so wonderfully fragile, in immediate need of a man's protection.

As she shoved her hands into her pockets and started to walk away, Peyton caught up with her long stride. "I liked what you said back there."

"You mean how I was introduced to coke when I was barely a teenager?" she said sarcastically.

"Uh, no... I mean, would you like to sit and have dinner together tonight?"

"I can't. They make me eat with my group. Until I gain another five pounds, I'm not allowed to eat with the general population."

Peyton wasn't going to let her walk away that easily. "How about after dinner? They're showing a movie tonight in the rec room."

"No thanks, I'm pretty tired these days. See you around." And with a flick of her light red hair, Gracie walked away.

Peyton stopped in his tracks and stared after her in disbelief. Sure, he wasn't officially Peyton Reynolds here, but no woman had ever turned him down flat like that. He was only thirty-six, and his looks were as striking as they had always been. *What is the matter with her?* he wondered. *Well, she probably isn't much of a model anyway, if she hasn't been in New York* (if she had been, he would have surely met her by now).

For the next week, Peyton followed Gracie around like a little dog. When he found out she went to morning yoga classes, he even forced himself into downward dog for her. Finally she agreed to go for a walk with him on the grounds during the one hour of free time they were permitted after NA. Soon it became their daily ritual. Not wanting to reveal his identity, Peyton talked about his job in New York as a hedge fund trader, never mentioning anything personal, least of all that he was married. So they mostly discussed her modeling career, such as it was. Peyton had been correct in that Gracie had never made it to New York, instead being consigned to local events like car shows and bar openings. Now, at 23, she was afraid that it was too late for her to make it big.

"I just know that if I had the chance, I could go really far," she said, looking at him with her intense green gaze.

Peyton nodded, but he was thinking about something else. It had been about a month since they'd met, and he felt he had to come clean with her in order to get beyond this vague, arms-length friendliness. It might be the only way, since Gracie seemed to look upon him merely as a sounding board for her worries.

"Gracie, I have to tell you something," he said. "My name isn't really Rick Hammond. It's—"

She stopped him by placing her hand on his, the first time they touched, and it thrilled Peyton with a jolt of hope. "I know," she replied, and laughed at the look on his face. "You think I didn't recognize you the moment you came to the clinic? I've known about R. R. Peyton's since I was a kid. When I was thirteen, I read all about your wedding in Palm Beach in some gossip magazine. You're still married to your wife, right? Lily Rose, isn't it? What does she think about all this?"

"One thing," Peyton lowered his voice, "I don't want to hear you ever mention her name, if we're to—"

"If we're to what?" Gracie asked, turning her face innocently to his.

When he grabbed her arm, it felt like with just a little more pressure, he could break it in two. But her lips against his were firm, and she pressed against him with an urgency that went beyond the need to alleviate the boredom both of them were feeling in this constrained place. He didn't know where she summoned such fierceness, such aggressive strength, from within that delicate and seemingly frail body.

It was an affair the likes of which he had never experienced before. The biggest turn-on was that they had to sneak around together. Gracie soon abandoned her uniform of baggy sweater and jeans for little sundresses so that she could fuck him almost anywhere without having to take off her pants. He loved the way she would sit in their NA meetings, so young and innocent, sometimes provocatively nibbling a fingernail, knowing she wasn't wearing any panties. Just minutes after the meeting was over, she'd be helping him get off in a broom closet or a secluded part of the grounds. One night they snuck out of the clinic and went to a nearby ritzy country club, where they slipped through the bushes and onto the grounds, to the undulating warm waters of the swimming pool. Slipping out of their clothes, they fucked in the dark water for hours, while the members were having dinner in the gaily lighted clubhouse on the hill above, but just close enough to make it thrillingly dangerous. It was better than any high.

He and Lily Rose once had had great sex like this, but it had been so long ago. Long before they'd started trying for a baby, when sex had become a chore. He was sick of sex being purely about procreation; it certainly didn't make him feel like much of a man, especially when that doctor had told him he had weak swimmers. As much as he had always loved sex, Gracie brought out an animalistic side to Peyton that he never knew he had. He could do anything he wanted to her, and she eagerly welcomed it, as if it kept her body tethered to this earth. She started to put on a little weight, but he liked the way she felt beneath him, so birdlike and frail. It made him feel all powerful, as if the world was once again his. By the time his six months at rehab were up, he had a new addiction.

Gracie was due to get out two weeks before Peyton, and he knew that he couldn't give her up. Now that he was allowed to make phone calls out of the facility, he decided that he would rent her an apartment in New York and pay for all her expenses, as well as help sign her to a top modeling agency. When he told her this, on her last day at rehab, she clapped her hands like a little kid. She was so excited about going shopping for furniture at Bloomingdale's that she barely resisted when he started to pull up her skirt. One last fuck to carry him through until he would be able to see her again.

* * *

After Peyton had bent Gracie over the arm of her new black leather sofa—his hand wrapped in her long red-gold hair as he pumped her smooth white bottom—they ordered Chinese food from around the corner and ate like two young wolves after the kill. Within the hour, he headed back to work, feeling like the man he knew he was once again.

The afternoon passed without incident, and when he arrived back at his and Lily Rose's apartment that night, he headed straight for the shower to remove all signs of Gracie from his body. The scent of her Opium perfume continued to linger on his skin as he let the water stream down his back. He hoped Lily wouldn't be interested in having sex again that night. It wasn't that he couldn't handle two women in one day, but he knew he wouldn't be able to fake passion with his wife after what he'd tasted that afternoon.

Fortunately, Lily was tired after work. She simply kissed his cheek and said, "I hope you don't mind, but I'm heading off to bed early. Good night, Pey."

He forced himself to smile at her like nothing was the matter. "Good night, Lily."

He was left sulking and feeling overly sorry for himself, yet another time on his first real day home. He thought about going to Gracie's again, but decided that was too risky, and so instead he did what he had been dying to do for the past six months. He started rummaging through the cabinets for some liquor or wine, knowing that Lily had probably removed most of it before he came home. But he was in luck. He found a bottle of expensive French Bordeaux that he suspected Lily didn't have the heart to get rid of, thinking he wouldn't find it. He opened the bottle and got out one of their Baccarat wineglasses, from a set that had been a wedding present.

The wine was exquisite, like having great sex. It slid down his throat and pooled warm in his belly. Peyton downed glass after glass, trying to forget what had happened that day. As he reflected on things, he realized that he didn't know what he might have expected. His father to welcome him back with open arms? His life was to resume exactly the way it was when he'd left it? Perhaps neither of those were in the cards to begin with. At least Lily Rose seemed to have forgiven him. Every word he'd said last night when he'd first seen her was true; he did want another chance at their marriage. Only now, it seemed like their marriage might be what was standing in the way of him getting what he was owed.

The wine was long gone. He took the bottle out into the hall and threw it down the communal trash, then went out on the terrace into the cold December night. With one quick gesture, he smashed the crystal wineglass into a thousand tiny pieces that went flying into the evening sky.

Chapter 16

THREE MONTHS HAD PASSED SINCE Peyton had returned home, and Lily couldn't have been prouder of him. His hard work had led to his father reinstating him as the president of the company earlier than anyone had originally expected. Although she knew how difficult it was for him to resist old temptations, she had not seen a drop of alcohol pass his lips. Given their busy schedules, she didn't see him much throughout the week, but when they did spend time together, he was as attentive and affectionate as when they were first married.

Still, she was surprised and thrilled when one morning he presented her with a bouquet of a dozen, long-stemmed red roses.

"These are lovely, Pey," she said. "What's the occasion?"

"Look inside."

Nestled among the blooms was a small velvet box, similar to the one he had taken out of his pocket a little over ten years ago. Could it be…?

Before her eyes was an eternity ring sparkling with so many diamonds that it eclipsed her engagement and wedding rings.

"I know it isn't our ten-year anniversary for a few months yet, but I wanted to celebrate early," Peyton said, kissing her.

At the office, looking at her new ring, Lily thought about what she and Peyton had endured during their near ten-year-marriage: their infertility issues, his drinking and drug problems, that one horrible night when he had been violent toward her, which she tried to forget had ever happened. But perhaps, in the end, everything was worth it to get to where they were now. Their marriage was as solid as the diamonds that graced her hand. Maybe they could even start trying to have a baby again? Maybe Peyton would be more open to looking at sperm donors now. He had been such a different person since coming back from rehab that she was sure anything was possible.

Lily's assistant knocked on her door; Peyton had arrived to escort her to Richard Reynolds's office. Richard had ordered them to see him that afternoon to discuss an important matter concerning the company.

"Ready to face the old lion?" Peyton asked when he saw her.

"Yes," she replied, and hand in hand they walked down the hall.

When they entered Richard's office, they quickly took seats opposite him.

"Now that you're both here," Richard started, his eyes resting momentarily on Lily's glittering hand, "I can tell you the good news. *New York Tribune* magazine wants to do a story on the legacy of R. R. Peyton's and our family. The photo shoot will be next week, and the three of us will be on the cover."

"What about Mom?" Peyton asked.

A frown crossed Richard's face. "What about her? She's not part of the company."

"I thought the family was the company."

"Peyton," Richard sounded like he were talking to a child, "your mother has many strengths, but a businessperson she is not. As you well know, she was a model when I met her—a successful one at that—but she has never shown any interest in what goes on in the department store other than getting her hands on the designer clothes. Please leave her out of this."

Although Lily was taken aback by the way Richard was speaking so callously about his wife, her heart warmed to the way Peyton had leapt so quickly to the defense of his mother. Then Peyton turned to her.

"If wives aren't welcome, then why would *she* be included on the cover?"

"Don't be ridiculous. Lily has been a vital part of the company since the day she walked in here. Her boutiques are integral to our bottom line and may very well outlast the department store one day."

Uncomfortable that she was being talked about as if she weren't there, Lily leaned forward. "I think the magazine article is a wonderful opportunity to raise the profile of the store, and the boutiques."

"Quite right," Richard said. "So we need to make sure that the cover achieves that purpose. You're the only one here with any design sense, Lily. What do you think?"

Lily thought about how a real photographer, like Eric Langvin, would treat the subject matter. "What if you sit at your desk, with that panoramic view of Central Park behind you, and Peyton and I standing on either side?"

"Or," Peyton spoke up boldly, "it could be me sitting at the desk with you and Lily on either side. After all, I am the heir to R. R. Peyton's."

"At this point, both of you could be considered that," Richard said.

"What do you mean?" Peyton asked.

Richard's eyes flickered once more to the new ring on Lily's finger. "May I remind you that you married Lily without a prenup? That was your decision, not mine."

Again, Lily fought to keep herself in the room. "Maybe we

should just let the photographer decide what's best. I'm sure he or she will have their own ideas."

"Quite right," Richard stated. "Let's focus on what we know, which means you should both get back to work."

In the hallway, Peyton said to Lily, "I hope you didn't mind what I said back there about you being on the cover. Of course you belong there. It just galls me sometimes the way my dad talks about my mom, as if she isn't worthy enough for the Reynolds name."

"I know." Lily placed a soothing hand against the side of his face. "You love your mother, that's all."

"I mean, so what if she was a model? It doesn't mean she isn't . . ." Peyton smiled at her as if he'd just realized he was starting to ramble. "Never mind. I'll see you when I get back home tonight. We have our anniversary to celebrate. Oh, by the way," he added before they parted, "your assistant told me that you're having trouble finding the right models for your fall photo shoot."

"And?" Lily said, arching a brow. "You know anyone?" Once upon a time this would have struck a raw nerve, but now that those days were long gone, she could joke about it.

Peyton grinned. "No, but my mother might. She still keeps in touch with some casting agents."

Lily nodded, thinking Lisa Reynolds probably didn't have any idea who the top booking agents were now, but if it would make Peyton feel better about his mother, she was willing to take anyone into consideration.

* * *

A week later, Peyton arrived at Gracie's door, tired and aggravated. He'd spent all morning in his father's office for the photo shoot, mostly waiting as the hairstylists and wardrobe fussed around Lily. Although he knew she had been in magazines before, even on the cover of *Couture*, he had to admit that she was born for the camera. When she posed, she radiated a self-confidence that would light up any room. His father was his usual, forthright self, and as for Peyton . . . he felt like an imposter. All these months he had toiled to make it back into his father's good graces, and for the most part it had worked. True to his word, his father had turned over the presidency to him, but Peyton sensed that he had done so begrudgingly, even suspiciously, with the unspoken warning that he would be watched very carefully. So what could be wrong? He had everything he'd ever wanted—including a loving wife and a red-hot girlfriend. So why did he feel like it could all be taken away from him in an instant?

Peyton had no idea how the magazine cover would turn out, and right now he didn't care. He just wanted an outlet for his frustration, and he knew Gracie would be obliging. Usually he saw her during his lunch hour, sometimes after work or on the weekend, but he didn't want to do anything that would make Lily suspicious. He felt he covered his tracks well enough, not going out with Gracie where they could be seen together, or allowing her to call him. He liked that they moved within their own special world, enclosed by the four white walls of her apartment. He especially enjoyed the fact that the space was so small she couldn't get a drink, or even get dressed, without him being able to watch her.

Gracie, however, was getting impatient. She was tired of waiting around for him, and the fact was that she had been in New York for three months and hadn't booked a single modeling gig. Where were the jobs he had promised her? How did he expect her to plan her days around when she would see him? She felt like she was back in rehab, except at least in rehab she was able to meet other people! Maybe she should meet someone else, someone who wasn't married and who could take her out properly.

It was enough to make Peyton want to stomp out of the

apartment. He'd taken a mistress so he could get away from all the pressures of home and work, not to replicate them. That was why he'd suggested to Lily that she look at other models for the fall fashion campaign, to get Gracie off his back. He'd handed her booking assistant a number of comp cards, including Gracie's, and it just so happened that Lily was searching for a natural redhead to model a couple of sweaters. The job was pretty much guaranteed at this point, and Peyton imagined just how grateful Gracie would be and what she'd be willing to do to reward him.

But he didn't tell her right away. When she let him into her apartment, he sat down, poured himself a big glass of red wine, and allowed her to go through her usual litany of complaints about how bored she was, how she needed to see him more often, how he should have gotten her a bigger place.

"Do you know how I spent this morning?" he said, abruptly cutting her off.

"I don't know, and I don't care about playing your little guessing games." She glared at him, pushing up the sleeves of her sweatshirt. After the first month or so, she no longer bothered to dress up for him when he came over, reverting to the jeans and sweats she had preferred during her early rehab days. What was the point, she said, when they didn't go out anyway?

Peyton tossed back the rest of his glass. He never drank that much at Gracie's, just enough to remind himself how good it felt. "I was pretending to be someone else."

"Huh?" A puzzled look creased Gracie's face.

"I was at a photo shoot."

"Oh. For what?"

Peyton shook his head. "It doesn't matter. Speaking of photo shoots, what if I told you that I got you a modeling job?"

"Really? Where?" Gracie whipped her head around as if she expected a photo shoot set to materialize before her.

"Where do you think?"

It took her a second to understand. "Your department store? Thank you! Thank you!" she squealed. "That's just the push I need to get myself out there. After that, I know things will just fall into place for me."

She wanted to jump into his arms, but Peyton drew back so he could look at her face, shining with a joy and optimism that had long since been drained from himself. It was the hope of someone who still believed they had a chance at getting what they wanted, what they deserved. Was he what she deserved? She was so young and pure and guileless; he needed that in his life. But did she need him?

A sudden sadness overcame him. Gracie was getting playful, tugging at his belt, wanting to get things moving. Rather than the usual way he treated her, which was to rip off her clothes and fuck her on whatever piece of furniture was closest, before moving to the bed for a second helping, he lifted her in his arms and carried her to the bathroom. He turned on the shower, and before she could protest, set her down gently in the pouring water. She stood there, too shocked to do anything, as he tenderly began to remove her clothes, kissing each part of her body as it was revealed. Her ribs weren't as prominent as before, her hipbones not as sharp, but she still possessed the fragility that he so cherished. As he moved down her body, the look on her face was uncertain; how should she react? Was this a new kink? What did he want from her? She thought she knew how to satisfy his every need, but this came from somewhere deeper.

When she was completely undressed, he wrapped her in a fluffy white towel and carried her to the bed. Surely he would fuck her now, but instead he tucked her underneath the sheets, pressed his lips against her forehead, and without saying another word, left the apartment.

* * *

The end result of the legacy photo shoot was better than anyone could have hoped for, Lily thought as she glanced at the latest cover of the *New York Tribune* magazine. In the photo, Richard sat behind his desk, looking powerful and patrician, framed by a spectacular green view of Central Park. To his left stood Peyton in a well-cut suit, one hand on his father's shoulder. And to her father-in-law's right, sitting on his desk, was Lily in a chic couture dress as a nod to her role in the fashion industry. Across the top, against the rich, dark, wood-paneled walls of Richard's office, marched the words: "The Once and Future Rulers of R. R. Peyton's," and then in smaller print on the side, "A Peek Inside the World of Department Store Royalty." She hoped Peyton would be pleased by it. At the photo shoot she could tell that he was uncomfortable, although she didn't know what was bothering him.

"Lily," an assistant called. "They're ready for you."

At the moment, Lily had another photo shoot to worry about. The fall campaign for R. R. Peyton's involved dozens of models and several different locations in and around the city. Usually Lily did no more than approve decisions from her desk, but on this particular day one of the senior coordinators was absent, so she had taken it upon herself to oversee the photo shoot at a location upstate. She put the magazine away and walked onto the outdoor set, where a model in a Fair Isle sweater was lounging against a stone wall. Lily recalled her as being a last-minute addition; she was inexperienced and a bit older than what Lily had had in mind, but her looks were certainly stunning, her golden-red hair contrasting with her lightly freckled complexion and piercing green eyes.

"You're Mrs. Reynolds, right?" the model asked.

"Yes," Lily responded, disturbed by the brazen way in which the model looked her up and down. "Can I help you with something?"

Indicating the band of diamonds on Lily's right-hand ring finger, she observed, "That's a nice ring."

"It's an eternity ring." When the model looked puzzled, Lily explained, "My husband gave it to me to celebrate being married for ten years."

She snorted. "I guess eternity doesn't mean much to him, then."

"Excuse me?"

"We're talking about the same person, aren't we? Mr. Peyton Reynolds?"

Lily narrowed her eyes. "What do you know about him?"

"I know quite a lot. Like how he used to do coke every night, and how it made him feel. How he has a mole on his lower back. You want to know how I know that?"

Feeling like the world was falling away from her, Lily placed her hand against the stone wall to steady herself. Who was this girl? Sure, she was aware that Peyton knew many models from years ago—had probably cheated on her with some of them, if she was being honest—but this girl was new. And she spoke about Peyton in a way that suggested she was recently involved with him. Perhaps still involved with him.

Remembering herself and who she was, Lily straightened her spine. Pointing at the redhead, she told her assistant, "Fire her," and stormed away from the set, the model's laughter still ringing in her ears.

The fifty-minute ride in the town car back to the city felt twice as long to Lily. Her head was clearer now, and she had moments of calmness, only to be overridden seconds later with a wave of terror. Knowing a panic attack was imminent, she fished in her purse for a pill. After swallowing it and waiting for it to take effect, she stared at the *New York Tribune* magazine cover. She hardly recognized the woman sitting on the desk, businesslike and poised, her head held high. Her gaze moved to Peyton, handsome, self-assured, his hair brushed back. Could he have been with that girl then? That very day? She crumpled the magazine and tossed it onto the floor of the car.

At the department store, she got into the elevator and rode straight up to the executive floor. Striding past Peyton's assistant, she went straight into his office and closed the door.

"Who is she?"

If Peyton had looked confused, or even acted like he didn't know what she was talking about, she might have held onto some hope. But her heart sank when he stared back at her with no pretense in his dark eyes.

"Her name is Gracie. I met her when I was in rehab in California. When I came back to New York, I got her an apartment."

"And a modeling job through me."

"I wanted to make her happy."

Trembling, Lily felt like she was at a crossroads again, like the night she'd gone, battered and bruised, to Richard and Lisa Reynolds' apartment on Park Avenue. She had wondered if she'd made the right decision then, and she didn't know if she would make it now. All she knew was that she desperately wanted to forget that she knew about Peyton's affair, that things would go back to the way they were—to the way they had been over the short but transformative months since Peyton had successfully completed rehab. Or had his rehab been just another sham?

"Peyton," she pleaded. "Tell me you're done with her. Tell me you'll never see her again."

"I've tried. I haven't seen her since the day of the photo shoot, last month. But, I can't give her up. She's the one I want to be with." Tears formed in Peyton's eyes. "Lily, I want a new life with her. I want to start over."

Lily couldn't bear to look at his face. If she did, she would know that he meant what he said, that there was no hope for their marriage any longer. A rage gathered in her unlike any she'd ever felt before. It was as if all of the hurt and confusion and despair she'd felt since learning about her husband's mistress had coalesced into a single arrow that needed to be released.

Her eyes landed on a silver-framed photograph of herself on Peyton's desk. She grabbed it and flung it against the priceless Georgia O'Keeffe painting on the wall behind him, where it made an angry black mark against the abstract red. Peyton shouted for her to stop, but she never heard him. Next, a paperweight shattered the glass top of his desk. Papers scattered all over the floor, chairs overturned. At what point Peyton had snuck out of the room, Lily didn't know. When she was done, his office looked like a hurricane had passed through it.

Catching her breath, she smoothed her hair and straightened her clothes, then walked out past Peyton's terrified assistant. When the elevator doors closed behind her, she knew she would never be back there again.

Chapter 17

LILY FELT NUMB AS SHE walked out of Peyton's office that day. The rage that was draining out of her body was being replaced with deep sorrow that felt like it would submerge her. A dark memory passed over her, of another time she had left Peyton, her body battered and bruised. She had gone to Richard and Lisa Reynolds then, but now that course was impossible. Perhaps there was still a chance that Richard might find a way to fix things, but she suspected in this matter they would take their son's side.

She needed to go somewhere else. As her hands and body started to tremble, she instinctively walked up Madison Avenue to the stone church she'd attended for years. She prayed that Clifton Thomas, her minister, would be home working on next week's sermon.

When she knocked on the parsonage's heavy oak door, Cliff Thomas opened the door. He wore a gray Yale sweatshirt and jeans, looking more like a former quarterback than a doctor of divinity. Lily had eagerly listened to his inspiring sermons over the years, as well as his funny jokes. He and his wife, Helen, had warmly embraced her into the fold of the church and included her in friendly meals, especially when Peyton was in rehab. Her minister was like a beacon of light in those days, when she felt she was left in the darkest depths of stormy waters.

Cliff took one look at the tears that left long, black streaks of mascara on Lily's pale, drawn face and immediately led her into the living room. "Come," he said gently, almost paternally. Helen was playing the piano but stopped and quickly came to her husband's side.

Putting his arm gently around her, Cliff asked, "Lily, what is it?"

Lily started to sob, repeating over and over, "Pey left me, he's gone. They're all gone."

"Who's all gone, Lily?" Helen asked.

"My family." Lily could barely choke the words out. "The Reynolds. My parents. Aunt Martha and Uncle Grant. They're all gone."

Cliff and Helen exchanged a look of concern over Lily's head at her rambling. They made her sit down between them on the sofa and tried to piece together what had happened. Having heard about most of Lily's marital troubles, from issues with infidelity and infertility, to Peyton's physical and emotional abuse that had culminated in his being sent to rehab, they knew that something even more distressing must have happened for her to be completely falling apart this way. After more questioning, they found out that Peyton had a mistress and was leaving Lily for good.

"Help me, help me," Lily entreated, and it wasn't clear whether she meant them, or a higher power.

Both Cliff and Helen put their arms around Lily, embracing her between them as the late afternoon sun streamed through the parsonage's windows. After she had calmed down somewhat, they escorted her back to her apartment, put her to bed, and promised they would return with others who would look out for her.

For the next week, Lily lay in bed. She had no idea of the passing time; the curtains remained drawn over the windows and her surroundings were enshrouded in a perpetual dusk. Since the day she'd left his office in ruins, Peyton hadn't been back to the apartment.

Lily didn't know if she would have had the strength to engage with him if he had. Her only physical comfort were her pets, her dog Sable and her cat Hollywood, who stayed by her side. She'd buried her face in their fur, felt their warm, beating hearts under her hands. If it weren't for them, she was sure that she would be tempted to let go completely.

As she lay in a crumpled mess of sheets and pillows, her mind circled around the many tragedies in her life. The death of her beloved parents when she was only thirteen. The passing away of her uncle and aunt when she was in college and shortly thereafter. So many of her many family members had been taken away from her prematurely. Was the Reynolds family going to abandon her too? While she had never been close to her mother-in-law, Richard had been like a father to her, and she'd even shown him Red Rose Farm, the place that meant more to her than any other in the world. As much as it hurt her to lose Peyton, this wound also cut deep.

And then there was the promise of starting a new family, a hope that had almost nearly been extinguished by her fertility treatments over the past few years. Still, she had hoped to start trying for a baby again when Peyton had come home from rehab. But that woman Gracie had changed everything; her red hair and piercing green eyes haunted Lily in her dreams. Gracie had wanted her life with Peyton and had taken it. Without Peyton, without the family behind him, Lily was not strong enough to fight for her future alone. Perhaps this death of her hopes was the hardest of all to accept, because she knew that the pain from this loss would remain fresh for the rest of her life.

During the week she stayed in her bed, Lily was dimly aware that other people passed in and out of the apartment: her friends, Cliff and Helen, and, in particular, two people from her church who were more acquaintances than close friends. She knew Cliff must have shared her situation with them. They took shifts so that someone was with her day and night, hovering around her like ministering spirits. They took care of her pets and encouraged her to take sustenance, as much as she was able. They talked to her, tried to encourage her to go to the window and enjoy the sight of the summer leaves turning hues of red and yellow. Yet Lily remained in bed, hopelessly held in fear and deep depression.

One of the women from church, Karen, had sung next to Lily in the choir. She had the voice of an angel and was a ringer, which meant she was a paid professional singer who helped the choir to sound more harmonious. Sometimes, when they were singing a hymn at church, Lily would stay silent and just mouth the words, so as not to muddle Karen's clear, pure voice. Other times she would forget to sing and just listened to Karen out of sheer awe.

When Karen sat by her bedside, she would often sing one of Lily's favorite hymns, "Morning has broken like the first morning, the blackbird has spoken like the first bird." Lily would feel a sense of solace, even if just for a few minutes. She would be reminded again of her father, Alexander, singing in the choir as she and her mother looked on in the pew together. In those moments, Lily felt closer to her parents than ever, but this time with an ominous edge. No longer did she wish they were still alive so they could be with her. Instead, she was starting to wish that she could join them on the other side. She dreamt of walking into her childhood church, this time as an adult. Her father beamed down on her when he noticed her, and her mother held out her hand so that Lily could join her. Lily awoke, tears streaming silently down her face when she realized where she was, in the darkness of her bedroom.

The second woman from her church, Christine, was fighting a deadly battle with ovarian cancer. Lily knew she had a husband and young daughter, and she seemed to exude the warmth of family life. When she came and sat with Lily, Christine would talk to her about her everyday doings, a new craft project she had taken up or a delicious recipe she was trying. She spoke of the flowers she grew throughout her apartment, trying to create an oasis in the concrete jungle, and her next family vacation to the Caribbean where her parents had a small place on St. Kitts. Christine confided that she wanted to retire there, where she and her husband could live a simple, slow-paced island life. Not once did she allude to the possibility that she might not live long enough to see that happen.

Together, Karen and Christine were Lily's stranger angels. Once, when she was in a lucid moment, Lily overheard Karen say to Christine, "When do you want to go on the death watch tomorrow?"

Death watch. Did they think Lily was going to hurt herself? Of course, she would never do anything like that. Who would take care of Sable and Hollywood if she wasn't there? Yet the thought hovered: If only she could take Sable and Hollywood with her, death seemed like a peaceful option . . . and Lily drifted off, unaware that she was letting the darkness pull her in deeper. The depression, the despair she felt, was dragging her down unremittingly without her being aware of it. It was truly like being drawn into a black hole.

* * *

At the end of the week, Christine knocked on Lily's bedroom door.

"Someone's here to see you," she said softly.

Lily's eyes strained to identify the person standing in the doorway. A man, standing tall and erect. For a moment her heart beat a little faster, thinking it was Peyton. But then the man spoke, and she realized it was his father.

"Lily, my dear." Richard Reynolds approached her and sat down at the end of the bed.

At this proximity, she could see the shock on his face. For the first time since her confinement, she wondered what she must look like. Karen and Christine had persuaded her to take a shower, but her normally shiny blond hair hung limp on her shoulders, since she could not find the strength to wash it. Her face was sunken, her body thin. He'd never seen her this low before, not even the night she arrived on his doorstep with bruises spreading across her face and arms.

The shock turned to sorrow as he added, "I'm very sorry to see you this way. But I had to come to tell you something."

Lily's heart quickened again as she wondered if Peyton had asked his father to speak with her.

"He wants to come back?" she croaked out. She hadn't spoken in so long that she almost didn't recognize her own voice.

Richard shook his head. "I realize this is hard for you, Lily, but Peyton is living with that other woman now." A look of disgust crossed his face. "Believe me, I don't like it any more than you do. She seems like a—" He caught himself before he could go any further. "Well, who knows how long that's going to last. The point here is that Peyton wants a divorce. I wanted to let you know before the papers are served."

Lily nodded, looking down at the blanket twisted in her hands. So there really wasn't any hope for her and Peyton anymore. Although she had known it for many days from somewhere deep down inside, hearing the words from someone else drove the dagger in further.

"This probably isn't much comfort," Richard continued, "but since my son foolishly insisted on not having a prenup, you could stand to gain quite significantly. As much as half the company."

Lily nodded again, without emotion. While she understood the magnitude of this information, it meant nothing to her in the wake of the grief she felt.

"I want to make you an offer, Lily. I can't pretend that you haven't worked hard and contributed significantly to the company for these past twelve years. That's why I'm willing to give you The World of Lily Rose boutiques—the name, the brand, everything and a significant cash settlement—in exchange for your stock in the company."

Richard sat back as if he'd made a particularly clever business deal, waiting for her reply.

Something stirred within Lily, a spark of self-preservation. "That's not fair. My stock in the company is worth millions. I'm entitled to that as Peyton's wife." Which she still was, she reminded herself.

Richard sighed heavily. "I think it's a very generous settlement. But if you refuse, I only have one other choice. If you're entitled to half of Peyton's assets, he's entitled to yours."

"What do you mean?"

"Peyton's never been to Red Rose Farm and he doesn't care about it, but I know how much *you* care about it, Lily. If you make things difficult, I can take that farm away from you—completely. Do you want that?"

Lily was dumbstruck at the very thought, and lay silent for a long moment. "No," she finally whispered.

"Then I advise that you take into careful consideration the proposal that I've laid out for you."

"I thought," she said quietly, "I thought that we were family."

"I regret losing you as a daughter-in-law," Richard replied, "but I have to think of what's best for my company." He paused and looked around, as if just noticing not only her physical appearance but the state of her bedroom. "I also think you could use some professional help. I know a place you can go to and will contact them immediately."

Barely hearing the last of his words, Lily fought back tears. She hadn't cried when she'd learned about Gracie, she hadn't cried when

Peyton had told her their marriage was over—she hadn't cried all week—but now she was crying over losing someone whom she had trusted like no one else.

"Am I ever going to see you again?" she asked.

"I'm sorry, Lily," Richard said, "but I don't think so."

The last she saw of her father-in-law was him pulling out his phone from his suit pocket and stepping out of her room to make a phone call. She didn't care where he was sending her. All she knew was that the darkness was pulling her under again, to a place from which she might never return.

Chapter 18

WHEN SHE FIRST ARRIVED AT Golden Woods in Connecticut, Lily tried to focus on her present rather than reflect on the past or speculate about the future. Thinking about the past brought up raw memories, most recently of Peyton leaving her. She especially tried not to imagine how he must have met his mistress, in a rehab center that probably wasn't that different from the place where she was now. Her future remained amorphous, hazy at best. She simply couldn't think of where she should go or what she would do after she left this place.

As one month passed into two, however, Lily found that she was able to resume some semblance of living, as much as was possible given that she was basically in the modern version of a psychiatric hospital, hopefully without the dungeons in the basement. After the first week it was determined that she was not a danger to herself, and she was no longer subjected to the hourly check-ins from a nurse at night. She was allowed to take part in group therapy, and recreational activities such as tennis and swimming. In another world, she might have been at a country club—the facility certainly looked like one. The white clapboard buildings with their gray-shingled roofs and wide porches could even have been part of someone's rambling country estate, and she could have been a guest, as country clubs are apt to call their usually well-heeled clientele.

But, she reminded herself, she was a patient here, among other patients, all with their own paths of pain and suffering. Whether it was alcohol and drugs, an eating disorder, or depression, it had led them to the same place. She wasn't interested in hearing these stories during group therapy, of taking on the burden of someone else's past. Her own was enough to endure; she didn't have the energy to absorb any more emotions. Although she sat in the circle during group therapy, and spoke when it was her turn, she closed herself off from getting to know the other patients.

The only thing Lily looked forward to each day was taking long, solitary walks on the facility's generous, wooded grounds. The towering oak and maple trees felt comforting to her, and the flowers—the white hydrangeas that turned light green, then almost purple—were like old friends. She had always been soothed by nature, and this place provided the peace and calm that her soul needed.

The last time she had been to this part of Connecticut, she remembered, was for the photo shoot she had done with Eric Langvin, five years ago. She had thought about how wonderful it would be to have a summer house in the country, where she and Peyton could take their children. There was no hope for those children now. But, looking at the abundant greenery surrounding her, she wondered if it might be possible for her to live in this kind of place someday, where she could escape from the city. She could see how a photographer like Eric might find inspiration in the lushness here, and idly she wondered if he lived nearby.

Since letting her friends know that she arrived safely at the hospital, she hadn't been in touch with anyone from the outside world. No one, least of all any of the Reynolds, had officially checked in on her, although she suspected Richard might be keeping tabs on her condition from afar. While this might have troubled some people, Lily knew her friends were giving her the time to heal. One of them had offered to take Sable and Hollywood to her country home upstate, and although Lily missed her pets terribly, she knew they would be well taken care of there and would be ready for her when she decided to return.

Six weeks into her stay, Lily still had no idea when she would be going back home, or even if she was ready. She had been assigned a psychiatrist, Dr. Hermann, who was the opposite of her old psychiatrist. Where Dr. Atwood was chic and elegant, Dr. Hermann was unkempt and rumpled, but he treated her kindly.

"How are you doing, Lily?" he asked when she entered his office one day.

"I'm feeling better," she replied cautiously. "But I'm still wondering what's wrong with me?"

"From what you've told me, I don't think you have clinical depression," he said. "You're simply suffering from pure grief, from all your losses. Sometimes it can just be too much for one person to bear, and it overflows."

"So what do I do about it? What medicine do I take?"

"Medication isn't always the answer, Lily. While yes, it can help you, I don't think that's what you need here. You just need time to process what's happened."

"How do I do that?"

Dr. Hermann paused. "I think that's for you to decide. You can stay here as long as you need to, but I would advise you, for the sake of your own health, and for the sake of your outlook on life, do not stay here any longer than is necessary. The clinically depressed people are going to want to group around you, and it's not going to be good for you in the long run."

After another moment, Lily asked, "Does that mean I can leave?"

"Whenever you're ready."

* * *

As reassuring as Dr. Hermann's words were, Lily didn't think she was ready to leave Golden Woods just yet. Time here seemed to stand still. She was no one to the other patients, and they were no one to her. For the first time in many years, she was able to focus solely on her own well being—not Peyton, or her work—but herself.

She was also able to recognize that there was nothing to look forward to if she went back to the city. She was sure that Richard was actively looking for her replacement at the department store, and while the boutiques were still hers, their day-to-day running was being done by her assistants, with one of them, acting as a kind of point-person, getting in touch with her, but only as needed. All said and done, she didn't need to actually be in New York at the moment. Thinking about being back in the city made her stomach turn, the possibility of running into Peyton and *that woman*, or anyone that would remind her of them. Her mind reeled at the idea of being confronted daily with the tabloid headlines about the future of R. R. Peyton's now that it had lost its crown jewel.

No, Lily wasn't ready to leave, but at the same time she was starting to feel lonely. There was no one she could talk to inside or outside Golden Woods, not even her friends. As close as she was to them, her friends from the city had not known her in her grief-stricken years after her parents had died. The only person she had felt she could depend on back then—whom she could still depend on—was her first boyfriend, Finn Macarney. They had lost touch over the years, and the lasting memory she had of him was the conversation they'd had on the phone fifteen years earlier, when she told him that she wasn't going to follow him to Houston after graduating from college but would be moving to New York. She wondered if he was still in Houston, whether he'd gotten married and had children. He would be a wonderful husband and father, just as he'd been the ideal first boyfriend.

There was only one way to find out what had happened to him. Lily pulled out her phone and did an Internet search. It wasn't long before his name came up as "Finn Macarney, Director of Aeronautical Engineering at SkyTech," which appeared to be a large aerospace company he'd help start. So he'd risen up in the world and done well in his field, just as she'd thought he would. Calling him would be too intrusive, so she sent him an email, keeping the tone light and impersonal. He replied within a few hours, sounding delighted, and asked if they could find a time to chat that evening.

At 7 p.m. that night, Lily sat in her room as if waiting to be taken out on a date. Although this wasn't a video chat, she had put on makeup for the first time since arriving at the hospital, if just to feel more confident. The hour on the dot, Finn called. The sound of his voice, deep and familiar, thrilled her to her fingertips. After exchanging a few awkward pleasantries about how many years had passed since they'd gotten in touch, he asked, "So how is it in New York right now?"

"I wouldn't know," Lily said. "I'm actually in Connecticut right now. At Golden Woods."

"Is that a spa?"

She gave a bitter laugh. "It's a psychiatric hospital."

There was a short period of silence on the other end of the line, in which she guessed Finn was trying to figure out what to say. But what came next was completely unexpected. "Are you allowed visitors?"

"I haven't had any before, but yes."

"Then I'm going to come see you this weekend."

"Finn, I—"

"I won't take no for an answer, Lily."

After they hung up on each other, Lily sat for a while in her chair, looking out the window at the dark woods beyond. Although the last thing she had dreamed of was seeing Finn again, for the first time in many weeks she felt a spark of anticipation, of life; maybe even hope.

On the day that Finn was set to arrive, Lily went for a long walk on the grounds to settle her nerves. As she entered the main building through the lobby, she saw a man dressed in a handsome tweed jacket, jeans, and cowboy boots, waiting at the desk for the attendant to return.

"Finn?" she asked. "Is that really you?"

He turned and gave her that wide grin that only belonged to him, and embraced her gently. Lily buried her head in his jacket, holding onto him as if he were a life preserver. Then he pulled back and said, "For the crazy girl I've always known you to be, you don't look half bad!"

Lily laughed like she hadn't in a long time. After Finn checked in at the front desk, they went to the visitors' room, which looked more like a den with its couches, armchairs, and television. They sat down next to each other on a couch, not really looking at each other, although Lily couldn't help secretly taking peeks at her former boyfriend. Finn's hair was longer than in the past and he had a well-kept beard, looking more rugged and manly than she remembered. Although he had said she didn't look half bad, she knew she had changed significantly from the girl he'd known in high school and college. She might still have the same blond hair and blue eyes, but what she had experienced since then had hardened her beyond mere physical aging.

Finn reached over and took her hand in his. "So, how did you end up here?"

For the next hour, Lily poured out the past eighteen years to Finn, from moving to New York and the death of her Aunt Martha ("She was a wonderful woman," Finn remarked), to rising in the ranks at R. R. Peyton's and launching her namesake boutique. She spoke about her marriage with Peyton, his struggles with substance abuse and infidelity. If Finn thought anything of how Peyton had treated her, he reserved judgment, merely nodding at times to punctuate her words. Finally, tears welling in her eyes, she told him about her years of yearning to have a baby, only to have to give up on her dream once Peyton had left her.

"I'm sorry you've had to go through all that, Lily," Finn said quietly when she had finished. "It's enough to send anyone to a place like this."

"Well, enough about me," Lily said, attempting a smile. "What's been going on with you?"

"So you know how I started out at NASA? I was there nearly a decade, got the experience of a lifetime there. Then at about year ten, a few colleagues and I decided to start our own company, SkyTech, using all we'd learned from the best in the world. I loved being independent, working for myself. It also gave me the opportunity to spend more time with my wife." Finn looked down at the floor, clasping his hands on his knee. "You see, she only had about a year left to live."

"Tell me about her," Lily said softly.

"Her name was Eve. She was beautiful, like the light. I'll never forget the day we met. A colleague had invited me to a family barbecue, and she was a friend of a friend who'd gotten dragged along. She wore a white dress that had these little green leaves sprinkled all over it, like she'd just laid down in some freshly mowed field and gotten up. When I told her that, she reacted like I'd said something clever rather than used a weird pickup line. That's when I knew she was someone I wanted to get to know. I knew I wanted to marry her, for her to be the mother of my children. We were married only two months later."

"Did you have children?"

Finn just shook his head. He and Eve had planned on starting a family, but a year after they'd gotten married, Eve started to feel extreme fatigue; her hair started to fall out, and she lost more weight than she could afford from her already slender frame. Since she was a nurse, she just thought she was stressed. But it turned out she had a rare blood disease that in most cases was fatal within a year of diagnosis.

"We did everything we could to cram a lifetime of marriage into that last year. We'd dreamed of traveling the world, but now that she wasn't well enough to leave the house, I tried to bring the world to her. Silly things like getting takeout from a different cuisine every night, or I'd dress up in some ridiculous costume, but it would make her smile. Her smile is what I miss the most."

"What did she look like?"

In response, Finn merely took out his phone. The lock screen was the picture of a dark-haired woman whose face was half-turned, as if she had been caught unawares. But the smile on her face, directed to whoever had caught her, was unmistakable, and Lily thought she was indeed beautiful, like the light, just as Finn had said. Under different circumstances, she would felt a little jealous of whoever Finn married, but now she only felt grateful that this woman had given Finn such happiness, if for only a short time.

"How do you move on from losing someone like that?" she wondered aloud. She focused on Finn's sorrowful face. "How *did* you move on?"

"I don't know if I really have. But I just signed a contract to oversee a Sky Tech project in India. I'll be living there for the next two years."

"That's so far away," she murmured.

"Yes, but it'll be a welcome diversion. I need to shake things up in my regular life. Waking up every morning in the same bed that Eve and I shared, walking through the rooms that she walked through . . . I won't pretend it isn't hard. Every moment I'll think I hear her footsteps in the hallway, or her turning on the faucet in the kitchen. It's like living with her ghost."

Lily nodded, remembering her parents. "I know what that's like."

"So I'm putting all the furniture in storage, renting out the place to a nice young couple with a kid, hoping that by the time I get back, the place will feel different. And if not, and if I decide to sell and move somewhere else, start my life over . . . well, thirty-seven isn't that old."

"I wish I could try that," Lily admitted. "I wish I could go thousands of miles away to another country, but I can barely drag myself out of bed in the morning."

"I don't think another country would be the right place for you," Finn said. "You said you don't want to be in New York right now? You should go back to Red Rose Farm. Home may be just where you need to be."

Home. She would have no family left at Red Rose Farm, but it was still where she had felt the most loved, where her most precious memories were kept.

"There's one other thing," Lily began, then paused. Every day since she'd arrived at Golden Woods, she'd taken out that worn slip of paper with her birth mother's name on it. "I've never told anyone about this, not even Peyton, but the day before I left for New York, Aunt Martha gave me the name of my birth mother. My real mother, Carrie Ellen, had written it down for her to pass on to me when she thought the time was right." Lily took a deep breath. "Maybe the time is right for me to start looking for her."

"I think you should," Finn replied. "You'll always wonder if you don't, and who knows, maybe she'll end up being someone you can get to know. It's worth trying. Because if it's one thing I've learned from these past few years, it's holding tight to the people you love that matters most. Who you could love."

Visiting hours were almost over. This time, when Lily hugged

Finn goodbye, she could feel the weight of what he'd just told her, about losing his wife and trying to overcome the grief that came with it. But at the same time, she had every conviction that he'd emerge stronger from it. Maybe she and Finn would see each other again when he came back from India, maybe not, but she'd never forget how he'd had the compassion to visit her at her lowest moment.

After Finn had gone, Lily spent the evening in her room thinking about what he'd suggested. Maybe she should go back to the place that had always been a haven for her, where she felt like she could be her true self—Red Rose Farm. She could just picture the bluegrass and the trees turning color, not in the same way it did up in the northeast but equally magnificent. The horses would be growing their winter coats, and the dogs would be lying in front of the living room fireplace as the weather started to get chilly. That was where she could find her heart again. And then maybe, when she felt up to it, she could pursue the whereabouts of Anna James Jefferson, the only family she had left in this world. What would she look like? Lily imagined an older version of herself but wiser, kinder, someone who could tell Lily what she should do next.

With that image fixed in her mind, she got up and started to pack.

Chapter 19

THERE WAS NOTHING MORE COMFORTING to Lily than waking up at Red Rose Farm in her large, old, four-poster bed surrounded by her dogs. She loved her jewel box of a room, the walls a soft lavender, with Palladian windows stretching from the floor to the ceiling, its cathedral ceiling covered in white bead board. Every window brought nature inside, the morning sun shining through the trees and bringing the promise of a new day.

On the bureau opposite the bed was a signature Red Rose Farm silver chalice filled with luscious pink tea roses. Beside it sat framed pictures of her mother and father, her aunt and uncle, and her beloved dog Rebel, reminding her of how much she missed them. Sometimes she imagined her parents and Aunt Martha and Uncle Grant were just downstairs having coffee. Yet, except for all her sweet animals—including Sable and Hollywood, whom she'd brought with her from New York—Lily nevertheless felt terribly alone. However, after what she just learned from a private investigator in Lexington, she did have one last hope.

Lily had spent the past month recuperating at Red Rose Farm. She sat for hours by the fireplace with her dogs lying at her feet, staring out at the rolling fields beyond the windows. On several nights she had to be transported to the medical center in Lexington with her chest pounding and her feeling faint. For a while panic had been her constant companion. Aside from her farm manager Marcus and his elderly father Ray, she came in little contact with anyone else. Back in New York, the divorce papers had gone through, and Lily had not contested a single line. Perhaps out of pity, Richard Reynolds had given her one of the family's lovely properties in Palm Beach. Lily had fond memories of her wedding in Palm Beach and many joyful and contented vacations there. Someday she would go there, but for the moment she had no desire to be anywhere else.

Just like so many years ago after her parents' death, being at Red Rose Farm reawakened Lily's heart. For the first time in months she felt the stirrings of wanting to return to work, to her real life in New York. But she couldn't go back until she knew who she really was. After thirteen years since her Aunt Martha had placed that worn slip of paper in her hands, she decided it was time for her to find her birth mother. But how to go about actually doing it? Since she'd had luck with finding Finn through the Internet, that was the first place she turned to. But when a cursory search revealed no one by the name of Anna James Jefferson, and she didn't have the energy to pursue it any further, she hired a private investigator to start looking in Lexington, the closest large city to where her parents had told her she'd been adopted. Within two weeks the investigator had handed her a file, which was now sitting downstairs on her kitchen table.

"Let's go, boys," Lily told the dogs that were wiggling and playing on her bed, and it was like racing thunder as they fought for first place barreling down the stairs.

In the kitchen, Lily made herself coffee and started to scan the numbers of how the Lily Rose boutiques across the nation were doing. The CFO had sent his report earlier in the week and needed her final approval to continue. Although she hadn't been in New

York for months, Lily had followed every business move through her trusted associates. With that taken care of, she pushed the report out of the way and opened the private investigator's file in front of her. Of course she'd read it many times since it had been delivered to her, but the facts still filled her with wonder.

Anna James Jefferson had grown up in Paris, Kentucky, a small town outside of Lexington. Her parents had gotten divorced when she was a child, and her mother had later remarried. At eighteen she gave birth to a baby girl and put that baby up for adoption; a father was never named on the birth certificate. Then she started school at Emory University in Atlanta, where she studied psychology. After graduation, she married a businessman named William Baker, and had been known as Anna Baker for the past thirty years. This was likely the reason Lily hadn't been able to find any information about her on the Internet. But there was plenty of local news coverage of Anna Baker the socialite, write-ups of charity galas she had attended—many that she herself had hosted—even a magazine cover where she posed in a ball gown and was dubbed "Baker's Beauty."

Lily scrutinized that image the most. At the time the shot was taken, her birth mother was probably close to the age Lily was now, and she was indeed a beauty. Her long golden hair flowed over her shoulders, her eyes sparkled a bright blue—although a different shade of blue than her own eyes, Lily noted—and her figure was stunning. But it wasn't as if Lily could take one look at her and could immediately see the resemblance. A needle of disappointment pricked her heart, but she moved on. She hoped to find out more from other pictures, but in the most recent photo that had been provided, from a few years ago at the Kentucky Derby, a large hat was covering Anna Baker's face so it wasn't clear what she looked like.

The final piece of information in the file was the most important:

a phone number. But as much as Lily was tempted to call it and tell the woman on the other end that she was her long-lost daughter, she knew that only worked in fairy tales. If she were Anna, she would never believe a stranger calling her out of the blue, claiming to be who she was. No, Lily needed to find a way to see her birth mother in the flesh, to find out what kind of person she was, before she made her earth-shattering revelation. From the photos and articles she had seen about Anna, she seemed to be someone who liked being in the limelight, but probably hadn't been for a while. With that thought, Lily came up with the perfect hook. Confidently, she called the number in the file.

"Hello?" a surprisingly husky voice said on the other end. For a moment Lily's heart skipped a beat—*this was the voice of her birth mother*—before she regained her composure. "Who is this?" the voice sounded again, impatiently.

"Mrs. Baker? I'm an editor with *Luxury* magazine in New York."

"Yes?" The sudden interest so evident in the voice was like a dog pricking up its ears.

"Your name was given to us as someone who might be interested in having their home featured in our winter issue devoted to grand houses in Atlanta."

"Yes. Yes, I would."

From then on, it was easy for Lily to say she was making arrangements for a reporter to come down to Atlanta and conduct an interview the following week. After she set down her phone, she sat still for a moment, her insides swirling with anticipation and anxiety. What was going to happen? Would she tell her birth mother the truth and instantly be welcomed into the fold? Maybe Anna would love her, want her. Lily could imagine it all now, describing the loss of her parents and her aunt and uncle. Anna would say, "Don't worry, Lily Rose, I have always loved and missed you, and it's going to be wonderful when you meet the rest of my family." Although

Lily knew that was a daydream, she couldn't help believing a bit of it. Perhaps Anna wouldn't embrace her immediately, but what mother wouldn't want to get to know her own daughter?

* * *

On the day she was set to meet her birth mother, Lily spent considerable time in the morning pondering her wardrobe and deciding what to wear. She finally settled on her usual fashion armor, which she hadn't worn since she'd been in New York, consisting of a black silk turtleneck, slim-fitting black trousers, and black stiletto heels. The only jewelry she wore was a Cartier watch and her mother's gold wedding ring on her right hand. Her hair she chose to leave down, where it framed her face in pale blond waves. Nervously, she pushed her hair back that afternoon as she stepped out of her car and walked up the long driveway to the house in Buckhead. The Antebellum mansion was every inch a typical home of that area, with a large white edifice and pillars marching around it. Feeling, as the old Southern saying went, like a cat on a hot tin roof, Lily pressed the doorbell.

A housekeeper answered the door and ushered her into the living room. The walls were lemonade yellow, and cathedral floor-to-ceiling windows opened onto a lush green garden. Comfortable sofas and chairs covered in a floral chintz pattern were arranged beneath a sparkling crystal chandelier. On the coffee table sat an enormous vase overflowing with green hydrangeas. It would be perfect, Lily thought, for a magazine spread, if that were the real reason she was there.

"Good afternoon," came the same husky voice that she had heard on the phone. Anna Baker walked into the room and sat down in a chair opposite Lily on the sofa.

At once, Lily could see traces of the woman from the magazine cover. She was still beautiful in her early fifties, with her thick golden hair streaming over her shoulders, a shade too vibrant to be faked. She wore red lipstick and a formfitting Versace dress that was the same color. Lily was not a Versace fan, as she found it flashy and loud, but maybe the apple fell a little farther from the tree when it came to style. The dress did show off Anna's trim figure and her smooth, tanned legs. Her face looked remarkably unlined, although from her work at the department store that brought her into constant contact with women of a certain age and type, Lily knew that this was probably the result of a very good plastic surgeon. Like those women, Anna Baker was most likely trying to hold on to her youth, and from the looks of it, she wasn't doing that bad of a job.

Beyond that shiny surface, Lily searched for any familial resemblance. But as it had been when she'd first seen the magazine cover, she saw less than she had hoped for. Her birth mother was taller, her figure fuller, her voice deeper, although Lily didn't know it was from decades of chain-smoking. None of her mannerisms so far struck a chord, but perhaps more would be revealed after they started talking.

"Thank you for taking the time to speak with me, Mrs. Baker," Lily began.

"Oh, you can call me Jeff."

What an odd, tomboyish nickname, Lily thought, but she nodded. In the silence that followed, a housekeeper brought in a glass of sweet iced tea with mint and placed it before Lily, then set a vodka martini in front of Jeff. After taking a sip, Jeff lit a cigarette and appraised her visitor through a cloud of smoke. Lily resisted the impulse to wave it away.

Jeff leaned in closer, as if intrigued by the chic young woman before her. "Are you originally from New York?"

"No, I'm from…" Lily hesitated, unsure of revealing the truth about her origins. "I'm from Kentucky."

She looked boldly at Jeff to gauge her reaction, but Jeff just said, "That must have been interesting."

Encouraged to speak further, Lily replied, "It was. Have you ever been there?"

"No, never." Jeff abruptly changed the subject. "Where are you staying in Atlanta?"

"The Ritz-Carlton in Buckhead."

"Oh, I adore that place. That's where I met my husband, Billy, when I was in college. Our eyes just met across the bar and I knew he was the one for me." Jeff smiled fondly at the memory. "I had never been involved with anyone before that, not even in high school. Billy is my first and only love."

But what about the man who was her biological father? Lily wondered. The birth certificate had not given the father's name, but that certainly didn't mean his identity was unknown to Jeff. Lily had surmised, given Jeff's age when she'd given birth to her, that her biological parents must have been teenagers caught in a bad situation. But Lily had hoped they'd had some kind of relationship, that at least she had been conceived out of some kind of love, primordial as it might have been.

Before she could think any more about that, Jeff asked, "Are you married?"

"I recently got divorced," Lily admitted.

"I'm sorry to hear that. But I'm sure you can easily find another man." Jeff spoke benevolently to her from the position of an older woman giving advice to a younger one. "Why, a beautiful girl like you? They'll be beating down your door. Of course, if you don't have any children. There are no children involved, are there?"

Lily couldn't conceal the wince in her voice. "Unfortunately no. My ex-husband and I wanted children very much, and we tried very hard, but we couldn't make it happen."

Jeff said graciously, "Well, it was probably for the best. Children just tie you down. Thank goodness I never had any children."

That triggered something in Lily. There was no way she could continue with this charade after knowing so much about this woman that was the opposite of what was being said.

"Mrs. Baker—Jeff—I need to tell you something," she said quietly. "I haven't been totally honest about who I am and why I'm here."

Jeff put down her glass. "What is it?"

"I think you did have a child. You gave birth on July 2nd, thirty-five years ago, to a little girl that you named Lily."

Jeff looked at her questioningly, as if to say, *And?*

"I'm that child. My name is Lily Rose Long."

Jeff threw back her head and gave a long laugh. "You have got to be kidding me." Then she leaned forward and looked more closely at Lily. "I've seen you before. At a department store in New York. You worked there."

"Yes," Lily said simply. "R. R. Peyton's. My ex-husband is Peyton Reynolds. Before I got divorced, I was the fashion coordinator and spokesperson there. I also started a line of boutiques called the World of Lily Rose."

"I know that store. I go to the one in Atlanta all the time." Jeff's eyes strayed to the vase of hydrangeas on the coffee table. "I've even gotten things from there."

"Then you have good taste." Lily hoped to lighten the mood, but Jeff remained dumbfounded. She stared at Lily as if she couldn't reconcile the young woman she was seeing before her as the tiny baby she'd given away.

"You were adopted by a nice family," Jeff insisted. "At least that's what social services told me."

"My parents were wonderful, and I loved them more than anything, but they died when I was thirteen. Then I went to a farm in Lexington to live with my aunt and uncle, who did everything they could to help me while they were alive. I attended school in Lexington before moving to New York about ten years ago. I've known your name all this time, but I never thought about trying to find you until now."

Jeff's eyes narrowed with suspicion. "Why now? What do you want from me?"

Lily could tell what she was thinking. Any stranger walking into a house like this under false pretenses and claiming to be a long-lost relative could only want one thing, especially after a messy divorce: money. Jeff had no way of knowing about Lily's divorce settlement, the success of her business, or her inheritance of Red Rose Farm.

"I don't want anything from you. I just want to get to know you. You're all the family I have left."

"Lily," Jeff said firmly. "I'm sorry, but I'm not the motherly type. I never wanted to have children. You were—you were unintentional, the result of one night with someone I barely knew when I was a teenager. My husband thinks I can't have children, and he certainly doesn't know that I had a child in the past. I don't know what he would do if he found out."

"He doesn't need to know. No one needs to know."

"So you haven't told anyone else? Good. You have to keep it that way."

Lily nodded numbly. "But you and me—can we at least—"

Jeff stood up, her hand trembling as she pointed with a long, red, manicured nail toward the door. "You have to leave now, Lily. Please don't come back, and don't ever try to contact me again."

Tears welled in Lily's eyes. "But I—"

"I'm sorry, Lily, but I'm not the person you're looking for."

Through a haze of tears, on stumbling legs, Lily walked out of the house.

* * *

After Lily had left, Jeff remained seated on the sofa. Her hand shook as she drained her martini glass, and she considered calling for another—how much she wished for another!—but was afraid to move, as if that might bring back the specter from her past.

Not in her wildest dreams or nightmares could she have imagined the baby she had given birth to so long ago would come back and find her. Jeff couldn't even think of the woman who had just left her house as her daughter. How could she, when she had never felt like a mother? When she had hardly ever, in the past thirty-five years, thought about the child she had given away? But now she knew why she'd been inexplicably drawn to the woman dressed in black she'd seen at R. R. Peyton's only two years ago. Although she still thought that Lily took more after her biological father, especially in the color of her eyes, there must have been something beyond her cool elegance, some physical similarity, that Jeff had somehow viscerally responded to. Seeing her again, Jeff could admit that Lily was indeed beautiful, and successful, and all the things that a mother might want for her daughter. But the truth was, *she did not want to know her.* She had never wanted to know her. Nothing had changed from the day Lily had come into the world.

Then, there was the matter of the little lie she had told Billy about not being able to have children. A little lie, she had thought at the time, but one that would have unimaginable consequences if he were to know that not only had she been hiding the existence of this secret child, but that she had refused to give him the one happiness he so wanted. This would change everything between them, she was sure. Billy was kind, and sometimes a pushover, she thought, but he would not tolerate the fact that his marriage and his love for her were based on a falsehood. Where would she go once he kicked her out? Even if she received a generous divorce settlement, she would have to go away to start her life over again. Jeff had already done that once when she was a teenager; she wasn't about to do it again.

As she was mulling over these thoughts, she heard Billy's voice in the hallway. It was later in the afternoon than she'd thought, and he'd returned from work a trifle early. When he came into the living room, she tilted up her face so he could kiss her cheek.

"Everything okay, honey?" Billy asked, glancing briefly at the martini glass and stubbed-out cigarette in the ashtray on the coffee table. He had always disapproved of her drinking and chain-smoking, but these would be small transgressions compared to what she was really capable of.

"Yes, I just have a headache, that's all.

"How was the interview?"

Jeff had excitedly told Billy about the upcoming interview with *Luxury* magazine and how their home would be featured in it. Although he didn't much care, he had pretended to be enthusiastic for her sake. "Oh, it was a flop. The reporter they sent wasn't very good. Unprofessional, as a matter of fact. The things she said. . . ." Jeff shivered at the memory of it. "I don't think they're going to run the piece after all."

Giving her a comforting shoulder rub, Billy said, "Well, that's too bad. I hope you're not too disappointed."

Jeff shook her head. "It's not the kind of magazine I would have in my own home anyway." She looked up at him and said, "You should go upstairs and change, dinner will be ready soon."

Billy kissed her again, and as he walked out of the room, Jeff watched him with anxious eyes. Although he was in his mid-sixties and graying, and he had never been the handsomest man in the room, the sight of him was very dear to her. She just couldn't lose him and the life she had made for herself with him.

Jeff didn't think Lily would come back, but she needed to make sure Lily never bothered her again. The surest way to achieve that was to point her in a different direction, where she could hopefully get what she wanted. Jeff went to the corner of the room to her writing desk and pulled out a pen and notecard. When she was done, she called in her housekeeper and gave her instructions on where the note should be delivered. Then her eyes landed on the vase of green hydrangeas in the center of her coffee table.

"I don't like the way that looks. Please get it out of my sight."

"Do you mean change the flowers?" asked the housekeeper.

"Just throw the whole thing away."

"Yes, ma'am," said the housekeeper, and picked up the vase on her way out of the room with the note.

* * *

Back at her hotel, as evening fell, Lily lay in bed, trying to process the fact that she had just met her birth mother, only to lose her again. Jeff had made it quite clear that she didn't want anything to do with her, and Lily knew that was unlikely to change. And there was nothing she could do about it. She couldn't force a relation-ship where there was none, just as she couldn't have willed Peyton to stay with her. But what would she do now that her last hope for family was gone?

Someone knocked on her door, rousing Lily from her despair.

"A message for you, miss," the bellhop said when she opened the door.

"Thank you," Lily said, taking the envelope from him in exchange for a tip.

Turning on the bedside light, she opened the note and read the words on the small square of cream-colored paper. They were writ-ten in a round hand that looked more appropriate for a teenager than a grown woman.

Dear Lily Rose,

I meant what I said to you this afternoon, but I regret leaving things the way we did. I can't help you, but your father might. The last I knew of him, he lived in Greenwich, Connecticut. His name is Eric Langvin. Good luck with finding him.

Sincerely,

Anna James Baker

PART III: ERIC EDWARD LANGVIN

And then came you...

Chapter 20

AT HIS HOME NEAR BEDFORD, Connecticut, Eric Langvin replayed the message that had been left on his phone a week and a half ago.

"Hi . . . um . . . this is Lily Rose Long. I don't know if you remember me, but you did a photo shoot of me for *Couture* magazine about five years ago, for the opening of my boutique line The World of Lily Rose. The photo shoot was in the countryside in Connecticut."

A pause, then a small laugh that he couldn't decipher the meaning of—amusement over a memory, or sheer nervousness?

"You said that it was near where you lived and that's why you took the job, because it was a short commute. I was . . . um . . . in that area recently and thought of you."

Then the voice turned abruptly serious, guarded, almost businesslike.

"There's something important I need to tell you. Can you please call me back as soon as you can? Thank you."

Eric wondered why Lily Rose had contacted him. Of course he remembered her—he remembered every subject of his photo shoots. It was hard not to, once he had examined each facial expression, each angle of their bodies. Lily Rose, he recalled, was the fashion expert he'd photographed at an old farmhouse nearby. He'd taken pictures of many models and celebrities over the years, but she remained one that stood out to him. He wasn't sure why; she certainly was beautiful, but he'd photographed many beautiful people. It was more of the haunting look in her eyes, an unforgettable, yet indefinable sadness that made you want to do something to alleviate the pain in those pure blue depths.

Eric hoped that her life since then had been happier, although from what he had seen in the media, it didn't sound like it. After he had semiretired from the business, he rarely looked at print publications any more, but he had made it a point to follow Lily Rose. For some reason, he was curious to know what was happening to her. So he'd seen the *New York Tribune* legacy magazine cover (although she had looked striking, he'd have shot it differently), followed by the tabloid headlines about her husband cheating on her with a model. That latter incident was difficult to avoid, as it was blared from the newsstands every time he went into the city. But that had been earlier in the year, and he'd hoped she'd been able to move on from it.

Surely he didn't know why Lily Rose would be contacting him now. Maybe she wanted photographs taken of a party, or her boutique. He was familiar with The World of Lily Rose, as his wife, Gabriella, sometimes shopped at R. R. Peyton's sprawling flagship store in Manhattan. Once she brought home a colorful, glazed earthenware vase, saying that it reminded her of her childhood. It now sat in their kitchen.

Although Gabriella had grown up in a small town in southern Italy, she'd gone to school at La Sapienza in Rome, studying 17th-century religious art history. Eric had met her through a mutual friend the first year he'd moved to Italy. He'd spent a few years in New York before that, after graduating from Harvard with a major in finance, just as his father had demanded. But his degree went largely unused, as he began taking pictures of people on the streets of New York—whoever caught his eye. He could make an ordinary pedestrian look like a fashion model, a nobody look like somebody, and the New York art world took notice. He was beginning to get commissions from big magazines when his father intervened, telling him that he was a disappointment to him and his mother, that he was wasting his life, and so he decided to move across the ocean where his father's voice could no longer reach him.

Eric had always wanted to live in Italy, becoming interested in the language and Italian culture very early in life, perhaps in part because his family chef while he was growing up had come from Rome. He had spent hours at the kitchen table with Claudio and his wife Sophie, going over his homework from language class at school. They had been like second parents to him, warm and helpful where his own parents had been cold and unforgiving. Claudio and Sophie had moved back to Rome by the time Eric had arrived there, opened their own restaurant like they had always dreamed. Eric sat in their big industrial kitchen, taking pictures of Claudio, Sophie, and the other workers as they handled the dinner rush. Then one day Claudio suggested he meet the daughter of an old family friend, whose name was Gabriella Russo.

"She is *bellissima*," Claudio said in the unique blend of English and Italian that made Eric think of snowy afternoons back home at Viking Manor. By this time he had met many beautiful girls, since he was constantly photographing models and actresses, occasionally dated one of them, but none had captured his attention for long. Still, he trusted Claudio's judgment and so agreed to meet this girl.

Gabriella was indeed *bellissima*, with a halo of dark curly hair that tumbled down her back, and her bright laugh was unlike that of any girl he'd known before. When she stood next to him, the top of her head barely reached his shoulder, and he found that she could be easily tucked underneath his arm, like a bird. She also, he discovered, came from a devoutly Catholic family, which he found comforting. He was reminded of the empty days after his sister Mary's death, where some kind of faith—any kind of faith—might have helped ease his mother's devastating guilt. Not long after they met, Gabriella moved into Eric's apartment at the top of a set of rickety wooden stairs in Trastevere, and she finished her studies while Eric continued to make a name for himself in photography.

Then came the telephone call from his father that his mother had passed away. She'd died of an overdose of pills mixed with alcohol—ruled accidental, but Eric knew that she'd been teetering on the brink of tragedy for years. Perhaps he'd even left the country because some part of him knew it was inevitable. Racked with guilt, he went back to Greenwich, joined by his somber father and estranged brother, Christopher, who by then was a doctor in Los Angeles. According to her wishes, Lillian Langvin was cremated. Half of her ashes were buried in the family plot next to her daughter, and the other half was buried at sea, amid the swirling waters just below the bluff where the family house stood, swallowed in the grayness that she had looked at every day from the windows of the Lalique Room.

Upon returning to Rome, Eric felt anew the pressures of fame and time. He was a sought-after photographer now, moving among the fashion capitals of Milan, Paris, New York, and London. Whenever he was in New York, he tried to meet with his father, who looked older and grayer and more morose with each visit. Lars Langvin had retired a few years back and lived by himself at Viking Manor, with a skeleton staff to care for him and the property. Eric was saddened but not surprised when his father died of a stroke, two years after his wife had passed. Going through his father's old things, he discovered a stack of magazines that featured his photos, collected without his knowledge. Gabriella found him doubled over in his father's study, the tears he hadn't shed at the funeral threatening to overflow.

Gabriella had gone back to Greenwich with him this time. Not only did he want to show her where he'd grown up, but he also wanted to see what she thought about living in another country. Although she would miss her family and her culture, she was interested in starting a different adventure somewhere new, with him. Eric and Gabriella were married in a tiny stone church in her hometown, after which they moved to the States. The grand house in Belle Haven was sold, and they bought and renovated an old farmhouse in the countryside near Bedford. Their daughters, Emily and Chloe, were born, four years apart.

As the girls were growing up, Eric realized how much he didn't want to miss their childhood. He was at the point in his career when he could pick and choose assignments, and he started to refuse any that took him too far away or too long from his family. Gradually, he became so selective that he rarely left his property, although he could be seen getting coffee in the town nearby. He was so famous now that the tabloids reported on his every move, as if an Eric Langvin sighting was akin to seeing a mythical creature. He knew people thought he was an eccentric, a recluse, when all he wanted was to be able to live on his own terms.

In almost every respect, he conducted his life in direct opposition to how he'd been raised. The farmhouse he and Gabriella had so lovingly restored was a fraction of the size of the house he'd grown up in, and, although they hired seasonal help for the grounds, there was usually no staff around. The girls were allowed to pursue their own interests, even if those interests changed from week to week: soccer and tennis for Emily; ballet, then tap dancing, then back to ballet for Chloe. Eric drove them to their games and lessons, cleared hallways of barely used equipment and costumes. He didn't care, as long as they were happy.

The constant abiding interest for Emily had always been horses—their house was less than a mile from a riding stable called Green

Meadows. At the age of seven, she took her first riding lesson, and it seemed like she had barely left the saddle since. Over the past ten years she'd become an accomplished equestrienne, winning tournament ribbons that plastered the walls of her bedroom. But Eric and Gabriella had always made sure that she earned the privilege of her passion, that she pulled her weight in taking care of her chestnut dressage horse—whom at age twelve she had named Chessy—and that it never interfered with her schoolwork. Luckily, Emily was a star student and wanted to attend Yale.

Eric thought he knew everything about his oldest daughter's life, until a week ago.

He'd been sitting in his study, looking at some proofs through a jeweler's loupe, when there came a soft knock at the door. Emily slipped in, and as she sat down across from him, Eric was struck by how much she looked like her mother, with her long dark hair and eyes, round face, and full lips. Both of his daughters took after Gabriella in coloring, but he liked to think that in their veins ran the characteristic stubbornness of the Langvins.

"What is it, my dear?" he asked.

Emily looked down, twisting the frayed cuffs of her baggy sweatshirt. Almost in a whisper, she said, "Dad, I'm sorry. I don't know how else to tell you, but . . . I'm pregnant."

Staring at his seventeen-year-old daughter, Eric felt the past rush up to grab him by the throat. He was seventeen himself, sitting opposite a blond girl at a yacht club. A whirlwind of questions threatened to cloud his mind. *Are you sure? Who's the father? How far along....* Automatically, his eyes moved toward Emily's stomach, hidden behind her sweatshirt. She had worn oversize clothes the whole summer, even in the warmest weather, and now he wondered what she had been hiding beneath them.

Emily guessed what he was thinking. "I'm twenty-two weeks along."

Too late for an abortion, even if Gabriella and her faith allowed it at any point after conception.

Eric finally found his voice. "Does your mother—"

At his daughter's nod, Eric thought of course her mother knew. Of course Gabriella was the first person Emily would have told. Gabriella would have wanted to share the news with him, to be with her daughter when she told him, but Emily would have insisted on doing it herself. He knew that Gabriella had taken Chloe out to run errands that afternoon, and it must have been planned deliberately so that Emily could be alone with him. He tried to remind himself that before him was his little girl, needing his comfort as much as she had when she was four and skinned her knee, or ten and taken a fall at a dressage event.

"Tell me everything," he said.

In a halting voice, Emily spoke of how over the spring she'd gotten to know a new worker at the stables, a boy her age from Argentina named Santiago. (Eric felt a sudden, burning desire to crush this Santiago's head.) He had been visiting relatives in the area, and wanted to make some money for school. His family back home raised polo ponies, so he was familiar with horses and loved them just as much as she did. One day Chessy came up lame and Santiago figured out that she had a pebble lodged beneath her shoe. As he expertly removed it, Emily was impressed by his skillful hands and started talking to him about his experience with horses. When he told her about the ponies and their springtime foals that roamed in the fields owned by his family in South America, she felt like she was being transported to another world. Before long, they were hanging out together all the time at the stables.

At this point Eric didn't need to hear any more. He knew what this would lead to—the proverbial roll in the hay. Emily had had a couple of boyfriends before, classmates who had taken her to dances or to the movies, but he'd never had any reason to think that she'd liked any of them very much, or had gotten very deeply involved with them. She wasn't the kind of boy-crazy teenager some of her friends were; she had a level head on her shoulders; she was more interested in studying and horses . . . wasn't she? How could she not know enough to keep from getting pregnant? Eric caught himself. When he was her age, he should have known better, too.

He couldn't blame this Santiago, either. Santiago was out of the picture, had gone back to Argentina at the end of the summer. Emily said they had exchanged a few emails, but he didn't know she was pregnant. She hadn't even known, until two months ago.

"I guess I was trying hard not to believe what was happening," she confessed, staring at her hands in her lap. "Until it was too late."

"Have you been to a doctor at least?" Eric asked softly.

"Mom took me last week."

Last week? He had truly been kept in the dark.

But he didn't have time to reflect on that, as Emily said in a shuddering voice, "I'm so sorry, Dad. I know I've disappointed you. I've ruined my life . . ."

Eric stopped her with a gentle hug. "No, you haven't. And there's nothing you could do that would disappoint me. Now, I want you to go upstairs and rest. We'll figure everything out, I promise."

After kissing her on the forehead, he watched as she left the room, and continued to sit in his studio as the afternoon light waned. Instead of thinking about Emily, however, he couldn't help reflecting on how similar her revelation was with the one that had blindsided him thirty-six years ago. A bitter laugh escaped his lips. What did they say about history repeating itself? Then he felt the sting of remorse—he and his family had abandoned a pregnant seventeen-year-old girl, giving her a check in exchange for putting her baby up for adoption and going away. After Jeff had gone back to Kentucky, he'd wondered at times how she was doing, whether she'd changed her mind and wanted to keep the baby, but then he'd started school at Harvard, and it was easy to forget what had happened in the fall of his senior year in high school. He'd rarely thought about Jeff since. He'd definitely never told Gabriella about her, and, while he didn't think she would never forgive him over a teenage transgression, in light of what was happening to their family, he'd have to tell her sooner rather than later . . . as soon as they figured out what to do about Emily.

Eric heard footsteps in the hallway; Gabriella and Chloe had returned from shopping. He heard Emily's voice float down to greet them, Chloe barreling up the stairs to show her what they'd bought. Chloe idolized her older sister, and at thirteen she had just become a teenager herself, he was reminded. He almost wished he could halt the passage of time, even reverse it to when his girls were still little, and he could protect them and save them from the same sort of mistakes he'd made in his own life.

Opening the door, he caught sight of Gabriella passing by. The look on her face was one of sadness and understanding as she realized that he now knew, and he couldn't be upset with her for keeping Emily's secret. Without speaking, her eyes said to him, *Whatever may come, we will deal with it together.* Grateful to her, for her, Eric stepped outside the room to join his family.

* * *

In the following week, Eric and Gabriella had not been able to come to a decision. Emily should carry the baby to term, that was certain. But whether to give the baby up for adoption, they disagreed.

"She's set on going to school, she wants to be a veterinarian. She has her whole life ahead of her," Gabriella argued.

"This isn't something that can be undone. She might regret it for the rest of her life," Eric retorted. He wasn't ready to tell his wife why he felt this way, why he needed to give his daughter the option that he'd never had, to get to know his own child.

When asked what she wanted to do, Emily simply groaned and said she was too tired to think about it. Eric tried to impress upon her the importance of letting the father of the baby know, and she said she would call Santiago, but Eric suspected she didn't want to add one more person to what was already a complicated situation.

The only thing the three of them were unanimous on was that they should let other people know about Emily's pregnancy. She was so tiny and slim that she was unable to hide her bump anymore; she couldn't hide behind sweatshirts forever. Besides, Chloe was getting suspicious, and once she knew, it would be impossible to keep her mouth shut. In her typical way, upon being told, Chloe gasped in disbelief, then was excited about being the first aunt in her eighth-grade classroom.

With everything going on in his household, Eric was only now reminded that Lily Rose Long had left a message on his phone that he'd never answered.

When he dialed her number, she picked it up on the second ring. "Hello?"

"This is Eric Langvin. I apologize for taking so long to return your call. I . . . had some family business to attend to."

He could just hear the constriction of breath on the other end. "Thank you for calling back, Eric. Would you be able to meet me in the city one afternoon this week? I need to talk to you, but it has to be in person."

Ordinarily Eric would have required more explanation, but something about the quivering note in Lily's voice, as if she were afraid to let go of something massive behind it, made him agree. "Of course. Where do you want to meet?"

"How about the grand salon at the St. Regis Hotel? Do you know where that is?"

"Yes." He'd done photo shoots there many years ago when he was just starting out in his career. "What time?"

"Three o'clock on Wednesday?"

"That's fine."

"Thank you so much, Eric. I promise I'll be able to tell you more when I see you."

After hanging up, Eric thought this might be a welcome diversion from his current family drama. In any case, whatever Lily Rose Long had to say, it couldn't be more earth-shattering than what his daughter had so recently told him.

Chapter 21

LILY ROSE SAT NERVOUSLY AT a table in the grand salon at the St. Regis Hotel, facing the entrance. Although the room was glittering with glass and crystal, she only had eyes for the guests that came in, her heart jumping a little if she saw a man of a certain height and age and coloring arrive. She knew she would recognize him, but despite their brief time together, she didn't know if he would recognize her. In her all-black outfit and subdued jewelry, she blended in with the well-heeled tourists and businesspeople waiting for clients. No one would think that she was waiting for the one person who could change her life.

Ever since she had learned that Eric Langvin was her biological father, Lily hadn't been able to stop thinking about him. In her mind she kept replaying their one and only meeting at the *Couture* magazine photo shoot. She had been in a dark place at the time, despairing over ever having a baby with Peyton. Somehow, Eric had convinced her to forget about her worries for most of the afternoon, focusing on herself and her love for her dog, Sable, who had accompanied her on the shoot. He had taken a photo of her and Sable and sent it to her, and she'd had it framed, where it sat on her desk along with other pictures of her dear family members.

When Lily had left Red Rose Farm and gone back to New York, the first thing she'd done was go find that picture in her apartment. In it, her hair was loose around her shoulders, her arms were thrown around Sable, and she was laughing. "Remember this moment," Eric had told her. Sometimes, when she'd looked at the photo, she'd remembered its photographer, too, and wondered about him. How strange that because of this photograph, he had been with her for so many years, even without her being aware of it.

She didn't need a private investigator this time; she had only to go through the many media articles about Eric's career, look at the hundreds of photographs he'd taken. Now that she was back in New York, she was able to pull a few strings with people she knew at *Couture* magazine to get his phone number, pretending that she was looking to hire him for her boutique's spring campaign.

"You'll never be able to get him," she was told. "He works only with a very select few people."

"Oh, I think he'll be interested," Lily replied, although deep down she was afraid that Eric's reaction to being told she was his daughter would be to reject her, just as Jeff had done.

For the time being, she busied herself with work. Being back felt better than she had anticipated; as close contact as she had kept with her assistants while she had been at the farm, seeing the World of Lily Rose in person made her realize how important her boutique was to her. Although it was hard to bring herself to step inside R. R. Peyton's again, it was worth it to see how well the fall line was doing. She was able to walk down the street again without fear of running into Peyton or his father, her head held high.

After working up the courage to call Eric and leave him a message, Lily spent an agonizing ten days wondering whether he was going to call her back. If someone had left her a cryptic message like that, she would have assumed blackmail or worse. When he returned her call, though, he didn't sound like he suspected anything. Lily had lain awake the night before they arranged to meet, too agitated to sleep.

Finally, she caught sight of him. He stood in the entrance of the grand salon for a moment, scanning the room. His thick blond hair was slightly graying at the temples, but his jawline was as strong as ever, and age had only made him more ruggedly handsome. Casually dressed in blue jeans and a tan barn jacket, he still commanded attention wherever he went. Some of the hotel's guests turned their heads to stare at him, wondering if he was a movie star, not aware that he was indeed someone, just not the person they'd imagined.

As when she'd last seen him, Lily immediately noticed the color of his eyes, which were like the sea on a calm day. This time, though, it came with a jolt of realization—the odd shade of blue was the exact same as her own. This genetic similarity heartened her; at last, she had some visual evidence that she was related by blood to someone.

Seeing her, Eric smiled and maneuvered around the other tables until he reached her. Lily suppressed the natural instinct to jump up and hug him, and held out her hand instead.

"It's nice to see you again, Lily," he said as he took it and sat down across the table from her.

"It's nice to see you, too," she echoed shyly. "How was your trip?"

They spoke briefly about his train ride into the city and the weather as they waited for the tea they'd ordered to arrive. When it did, Lily stared at the scones and bowl of clotted cream, too anxious to take a bite; if she did, she was sure it would stick in her throat. She didn't want to carry on the pretense too long, as she had done with Jeff.

Taking a deep breath, she said, "Eric, I want to tell you about a trip I just took to Atlanta. I was looking for my birth mother. I'm not sure if I told you that I was adopted?"

Eric shook his head.

"I'd known her name for years, but I never felt the need to look for her until what happened to me last year. . . ."

At this, Lily glanced downward, aware that Eric would know from the tabloids exactly what she was referring to. When she raised them again, she looked back into a gaze that was as penetratingly blue as her own, and was encouraged to continue.

"I hired a private investigator, who found her in Atlanta."

She paused, and Eric asked politely, "What did you find out?"

"After she'd given birth to me and put me up for adoption, she went to college there. Emory University, actually. She went on to do quite well for herself."

"She remarried?"

Lily gave him a curious look. "She married a wealthy businessman, but it was her first marriage. My birth parents were just teenagers when they met, they never married."

Eric nodded. "Of course not."

"I traveled to Atlanta to see her." Lily went on to describe the woman she'd encountered—a brassy blond, statuesque—who asked to be called by her nickname. "It was strange, a boy's name, not something I would expect at all."

She paused, and Eric simply said, "Jeff."

His face did not betray a single emotion. Whether it was because they were in a public place, or he'd subconsciously thought about this for years, his expression remained unchanged, as if he were sitting still for a photograph.

Then he asked, "So how is your mother?"

"She's not my mother. She's my biological incubator. She doesn't want anything to do with me. She said," Lily caught her breath, "that she never wanted any children."

Eric gave a low, wry laugh. "That sounds like Jeff." Leaning forward, he took Lily's hand in his own. "My dear, I know that must have been hard for you to hear. But I have to explain what happened. We came from different worlds, Jeff and I. In my senior year, my high school organized a poverty awareness tour of Appalachia. At our last town, some students at a local school held a party for us. That's where I met Jeff.

"We were . . . instantly attracted to each other, but that's all it was. We . . . made a mistake, and she got pregnant. We were both so young, intending to go to college, that we didn't think it made sense for us to stay together. Both of us thought it was best if she gave the baby up for adoption and we didn't see each other again."

"And you didn't keep in touch?"

"Lily, you have to understand that Jeff and I hardly knew each other. We'd met up maybe all of three times before I had to go back home."

"But that was enough for her to get pregnant." Lily couldn't keep a note of bitterness from entering her voice. "And now you have your own family."

"I do, but if I hadn't met Gabriella, I think I would be quite alone in this world. I had a sister who died young, my parents are now gone, and my brother hasn't spoken to me in years. My wife and my children are everything to me now."

"At least you have that." Lily turned her sad, luminous eyes on him. "You see, Eric, I don't have anyone. My adoptive parents passed away when I was barely a teenager, as did my relatives who took me in afterward. I'm sure you've heard about what happened with my husband. We didn't," here her voice choked up, "we didn't have any children. When we got divorced, not only did I lose him but also my father-in-law, who until then treated me like one of his own. Or at least I thought he did, until he made it quite clear his company was more important. Then I found out about Jeff, and you know how that turned out."

"But she led you to me." Eric's grip on her hand was warm and firm. "You have me now."

"Do I?"

"Lily," Eric said slowly, "this is a lot for anyone to take in. In the back of my mind, I guess I always knew this was a possibility, that my child with Jeff—that *you*—were out there and would find me. But I've never told my wife or children what happened when I was only a teenager. I owe it to them to let them know when the time is right. And right now . . . things are a bit difficult. I need to ask for your patience."

"You wouldn't be ashamed to tell them about me?" Lily whispered.

"About you? Lily," Eric held her gaze with his own, "I'm not like Jeff. I won't say that we can be a proper family now, but you won't be alone. Not anymore."

"Thank you, Eric. Thank you." Lily lowered her eyes, not wanting him to see the tears in them. When she lifted them, she saw reflected in his own the same feeling, blue against blue, like the ocean.

Eric had a train to catch. When they stood up, not knowing what to do, Lily extended her hand again. This time, Eric pulled her into his arms, and she buried her head against his shoulder, holding onto the warmth and strength of him for a moment before releasing him with some reluctance. Of course she and Jeff had never touched when they'd met; before that, she'd fantasized about being held by her biological mother, by someone who shared the blood that ran in her veins. She'd never imagined that it would be her biological father with whom she'd have that moment.

"I'll be in touch," Eric told her, and then he walked away.

As when he'd arrived, the other hotel guests turned to watch his departure. Not being close enough to have heard the real story, they could only look at Lily's tear-streaked face and assume that she'd been jilted.

Lily sat down again, the tea cold and the food unappetizing, but her entire being was awash in emotion. For the first time since she'd returned to New York, she felt a sense of real hope.

* * *

On the train ride back to Bedford, Eric's head swirled with thoughts running as fast as the scenery that passed by his window. He'd kept a calm face for Lily's sake, and part of him was still in disbelief over what she had told him, but now that he'd had a couple of hours to digest the news, it was beginning to hit him in a completely different way.

That Lily was his daughter, he had no doubt. He didn't need a DNA test to prove it. He knew there must have been some reason he had been so drawn to her during their photo shoot, why he'd wanted to follow her in the media. Her eyes, he realized upon seeing them again, were the same color as his, the same as his mother's. Even her name . . . Jeff must have had Lillian Langvin in mind when she'd signed the birth certificate. While Lily didn't look much like Jeff, or even himself, Eric could see the physical similarities between her and his mother, in her fine facial features and the elegance of her figure. More so, she uncannily resembled Mary, his sister who had died in a skiing accident at the age of twelve. If Mary had lived, he thought, she would have grown up to look just like Lily.

Lily Rose was his daughter . . . but how could he be a father to her? He could hardly be a father to his own daughters, he thought; look at what had happened to Emily. Certainly, Lily was grown and did not need the kind of guidance that a teenager did, but she needed him for something. He recalled their parting embrace, the way she'd clung to him so fiercely. She had admitted to him that she had no one left she could turn to. She needed him for family. It was a cry for help that he simply could not reject.

And then, there was the matter of his own family. No matter what kind of relationship he and Lily Rose would have, his wife would need to know first.

Before Eric could think more about this, he was already at the Bedford train station. He had asked Gabriella to pick him up, and he could see their car idling at the curb. Squaring his shoulders, he walked over to it and got into the passenger seat.

"Can you pull into the parking lot?" he asked Gabriella, after giving her a quick kiss.

"Sure." After she had cut the engine, she asked, "What's going on?"

Eric looked at her for a moment, as beautiful as she had been when he'd first met her at Claudio's restaurant in Rome. He knew how big her heart was, taking on an awkward foreigner who expected to make a living from taking pictures, even following him to another country. So he told her everything, from meeting Jeff, to her coming to Connecticut to tell him she was pregnant, and his father paying her to give up her baby for adoption. This was the part that he had not been able to tell Lily, that a financial transaction was why she had been put up for adoption. But now he did not hide the fact that he had taken no responsibility, had been relieved that his family's money had been able to make the problem disappear. While the conditions of Jeff's contract had been that she never contact the Langvins again, there had been no clause about him contacting her. The truth was that he hadn't wanted to see Jeff again, to find out what had happened to her and their child. He had just wanted everything to go away, and it had . . . for thirty-six years.

"But I can't ignore it anymore," Eric said. "Not after what's happened to our daughter, and now that Lily Rose has come to me."

During the entire time he had been talking, Gabriella had been silent, staring ahead through the windshield at the reflection of the streetlights that had started to go on in the parking lot. Now she turned to him, her dark eyes full of sorrow and compassion.

"There's only one thing you can do," she said.

"What's that?"

"You have to invite her to dinner."

Chapter 22

LILY ROSE STOOD AT THE end of a driveway nestled in the deep woods of eastern Connecticut. At its end was Eric Langvin's house, but for some reason she was reluctant to get any closer. She needed to take a moment to gather her thoughts about what meeting his family meant to her. So much had happened in the past several weeks that she couldn't believe she was standing here, about to enter a world that she had long thought was denied her.

After leaving the St. Regis Hotel, she had tried to rein in her anticipation for what might happen next. While Eric's response to the news that she was his daughter had gone as well as could be expected, she didn't know how long it would be before he contacted her again. He had said he needed time to talk to his wife and daughters, and she respected that. Above all, she trusted Eric—she knew that he was a man of his word, that he was a kind man, that he was a good husband and father. She knew his family came first, and she would never want to do anything to jeopardize his relationship with them.

It was difficult, however, for her to not think about them, especially his daughters. For so long she had focused solely on the idea of meeting her birth mother, and then, when she'd learned of his identity, her birth father. Only then did she consider the fact that she had other, living relatives. With Jeff it was a dead end, in more ways than one. But Eric's two daughters were her *half sisters*. Growing up as an only child, Lily had longed for a brother or sister; it was, in part, why her parents had allowed her to have so many pets. Many times she'd listened to friends talk about their siblings and envied their closeness, especially the bond between sisters. While she knew Eric's daughters were young, more age-appropriate to be her nieces, she couldn't wait to meet them.

So she was surprised and overjoyed when Eric contacted her a few days after their meeting to say that he'd told his family about her and that his wife had invited her to dinner the following week. Standing at the end of the Langvins' driveway now, Lily tightened her grip on the bouquet of flowers she'd brought, squared her shoulders, and walked forward.

A converted farmhouse sat at the end of the driveway, framed by the last rays of the setting sun filtering in through the surrounding birch and maple trees. A lot of care had obviously gone into the restoration of its softly weathered red plank walls, gray-shingled roof, and front door with glass panels. It looked warm and inviting, the perfect place to raise a family. Lily could see why someone like Eric might want to leave the bustle of the city for a quiet residence like this—the pull of nature and solitude that she herself had always felt.

At her knock, Eric opened the door and asked her to come in. As she hesitated at the threshold, she saw a small, dark-haired woman with a pretty smile come down the hallway. She knew at once that it was Gabriella, Eric's wife, but before she could say anything, she found herself pulled into an embrace with an intensity she would not have expected from someone so slight.

Gabriella drew back to look at her. "Welcome, Lily," she said in a lilting, faintly accented voice. "I am so happy to finally meet you."

"It's nice to meet you, too." As she spoke, Lily couldn't help looking over Gabriella's shoulder.

Knowing what she was looking for, Eric said, "Emily is picking up Chloe from her dance lesson. You'll meet them soon enough. In the meantime, let me show you around."

Lily followed him through the high-ceilinged living room with its exposed wooden beams and into his study.

"I thought you might like to see this," Eric said, gesturing toward a framed photo on the wall.

She knew without being told that this was a photo of his family when he was young: Eric's image beamed from roughly the center of the print, while around him stood a tall man, an icily beautiful woman, a boy that looked like a slightly older version of himself, and a girl with braids. Everyone was gleamingly blond and appeared, at least at this point in time, to be happy. Without being asked, Eric started to talk about them, how strict his father was, how sporty and loving his mother. His brother, Christopher, was highly competitive, and then there was his sister, Mary, whose death had forever driven the luster from his mother's eyes and shaken the family apart.

"My mother never recovered from that," Eric said. "I don't think my father did, either. None of us did."

Lily nodded, understanding how the loss of a family member had repercussions that never went away. She had endured the sudden passing of her beloved parents; she could only imagine what the death of a child must be like. "I wish I could have known your sister . . . I wish I could have known all of them."

"Well," Eric said, "you'll have the chance to meet your half sisters shortly." He paused. "There's something you should know about Emily. She's five months pregnant. Ironic, I know," he added with a dry smile.

"What is she going to do?"

"Adoption is our best choice at the moment. At least Gabriella thinks so, and Emily is starting to agree with her."

"And you?"

"I don't know anymore. Of course I want the best future possible for Emily, and she was set to go to college before this happened. But to give up your own child. . . ." He trailed off, unable to meet her eyes, and Lily understood the immense guilt he must have felt for so long, even if it was subconscious, for abandoning her.

"I always wanted to have children," Lily said quietly. "That's what I wished for the most in life. I felt my biggest failure was not being able to become a mother." She raised her eyes to his. "I don't believe that there is ever an unwanted child."

Before Eric could respond, they could hear a car pull into the driveway, doors opening and closing, the hardwood sounds of pounding footsteps and young, bright laughter.

"They're here," he said. "Let's go into the living room."

Gabriella must have intercepted the girls upon their arrival, and both of them were sitting properly on the sofa when Eric and Lily entered the room. Lily could see immediately how they took after their mother, miniatures of her dark beauty and grace. Chloe's limbs seemed barely able to contain her energy, while Emily was more sedate. Then she stood up to greet Lily, and Lily could see the curve of her bump beneath her T-shirt, contrasting wincingly with her sweet, childlike face.

Gabriella said that dinner was ready, so they all went into the dining room, where Lily's bouquet reigned over the center of the table in a glazed earthenware vase. Lily was also touched that the main course was a rich Tuscan white bean soup (that Chloe immediately told her was called ribollita), as she'd told Eric when he'd invited her to dinner that she was a vegetarian. The ribollita was accompanied by thick slices of fragrantly warm homemade Italian bread.

Talk during the meal was pleasant but inconsequential: Lily asked Eric and Gabriella about their renovations to their house, while Gabriella remarked how much she enjoyed visiting the World of

Lily Rose boutique. Once, when Lily brought up Red Rose Farm, Emily asked with wide eyes, "Do you really own a horse farm?"

Remembering how Eric had told her that Emily loved horses, Lily said, "Please feel free to visit whenever you want. I think you would really like it."

"It's going to be a while before you can ride again, young lady," Gabriella interjected, looking pointedly at Emily's stomach, and Emily subsided, face red.

That was the only reference anyone made to Emily's pregnancy, except when dessert was served and Emily and Chloe squabbled over who got the last slice of Gabriella's delicious pistachio cake.

"I should get it because I'm eating for two, silly," Emily said, surprisingly unabashed.

"That's not fair!" Chloe protested. "She always gets everything! She's even getting a baby!"

"Hush," Gabriella said, but Lily could only think how young Emily seemed. It was hard for her to believe that her own birth mother was this age when she was pregnant with her. How could anyone expect a teenager, even with all the support in the world, to raise a newborn baby?

After dinner, the girls went to their rooms to do their homework, and Eric and Gabriella and Lily lingered at the table with digestifs. At one point, Lily stood up to use the bathroom and was directed upstairs. On her way back, she couldn't help but notice that a door at the end of the hall was partly open, with light streaming from it.

When she peered inside, she saw Emily lying on her bed, headphones on as she wrote in a notebook. Emily lifted her head at Lily's knock and removed her headphones. "Can I come in?" Lily asked, and Emily nodded, clearing some space on her bed for Lily to sit down.

Her room looked very much like what Lily would imagine for a horsey girl—walls covered with ribbons, shelves with trophies,

and a framed picture of her on a chestnut horse. The pink horse-
shoe-printed coverlet on the bed looked like something that had
been picked out many years earlier, and kept out of habit.

"Is that your horse?" Lily asked, indicating the photo.

Emily told her about falling in love with Chessy when she was
twelve, and begging her parents for months to be able to have her
own horse. Chessy was a Dutch warmblood, specially bred for dressage. "Do you have horses like that on your farm?" Emily wanted
to know.

"It's mostly retired Thoroughbred racehorses now," Lily told her,
"along with a bunch of rescue dogs and cats."

"It sounds amazing. I wish I could go there. I want to get out of
here so badly, now that everyone at school knows about *this*." She
rubbed her stomach with the gesture Lily had seen done by many
pregnant women, and envied. Although Lily didn't feel envy this
time, just a surge of protectiveness over Emily and her unborn child.

"I guess your father told you all about me, how he met my birth
mother," Lily started cautiously.

"Yeah," Emily replied. "He was seventeen like me, and it was at
some party. They weren't in love or anything."

"Were you in love?"

If she were startled by the directness of this question, Emily
didn't let on. "No. I thought I was, at the time. I had never met
anyone like Santi before, you know?"

Recalling how she had felt with Finn, her first boyfriend, Lily
nodded. "I do."

"He was the first person outside of my family that I felt like I
could really be myself with."

"I'm guessing he's kind of cute, too."

Emily laughed, the reaction Lily was hoping for. "Yeah, he's not
too bad. Especially compared to the guys at school."

"Does he know about the baby?"

Emily shook her head. "I haven't told him yet. Dad says he has the right to know, and I guess I believe that, too. But I don't want him to, like, come up here or anything. He's going to school and has his own life. Whatever happens to the baby is *my* decision," she said with a sudden fierceness that Lily also understood. "Not his, and not my parents', either,"

"What do you want to do?"

"I guess I just want to graduate and spend the summer at the stable, and go to college in the fall. But at the same time I don't want this baby to be adopted by just anyone and disappear from my life." Emily looked at Lily sideways, twirling a long, curly strand of hair around her finger. "How did she do it?"

"Who?"

"Your mother. How did she decide who to give you to?"

"She . . . well, my birth mother didn't care who I ended up with. I don't think she gave half as much thought to it as you and your parents are doing right now. It just so happened that I ended up with two wonderful parents, the best parents I could hope for. I always wanted to pass on what I learned from them to my own children, but . . . that wasn't to be."

"Why not?"

"My ex husband was . . . well, he was physically unable, and he refused to consider a sperm donor. He was against adoption, too. The strange thing is, I understood how he felt about it, because even though I was adopted, I also wanted to have a child that was biologically mine."

"And now?"

They locked eyes, and at that moment, Lily heard Gabriella call her name up the stairs. Lily didn't want to look away from Emily, but the moment had been broken.

"You'd better get back or Mom's going to think you've fallen into the toilet," Emily said, giggling and rolling her eyes.

"It was nice talking to you," Lily said.

"Same here. There are some things I just can't talk about with my parents."

Lily hesitated, hoping she wasn't coming across as too intrusive. "I know you don't really know me yet, Emily, but if you ever want to talk, I'm here for you."

"Okay, I'll do that." Emily put her headphones on and turned back to her notebook.

Lily placed a gentle hand for a moment on her half-sister's shoulder, then went back downstairs to where her father was waiting for her.

Chapter 23

OVER THE NEXT MONTH, AS the weather grew colder and leaves fell from the trees, shrouding his house in a cocoon of red and gold, Eric watched his family grow closer to his new-found daughter. Lily had a standing invitation to dinner every week, and on some weekends, the entire family would go into the city to see her. While Eric and Gabriella went out to lunch, Lily would take Emily and Chloe shopping, or they'd hang out in her apartment. Although they referred to it as "babysitting" as a joke—the girls were old enough to look after themselves—in reality it allowed them to get to know each other better. Emily and Chloe were enchanted by their older, glamorous half sister, and Lily spoiled them with gifts.

During the week, Eric would call up Lily to see if she was free for the afternoon. If so, he'd take the train down and they'd have coffee or go see an art exhibit. Sometimes they would walk through a gallery, and Lily would listen raptly as Eric talked about the different angles that composed a photograph or painting. She seemed eager to learn from him, and he appreciated her perspectives on design as well. Other times they would take a walk in Central Park in near silence, letting the sounds of the city wash over them, simply enjoying being in each other's company. Although Eric felt the pressure of compensating for more than thirty years of absence from his daughter's life, he was trying to make the best of the time they had now.

One day, when Eric came home from an afternoon in the city with Lily, Gabriella met him at the door. She had taken Emily for her gynecologist's checkup, and Emily was now resting upstairs in her room. Emily was in her third trimester by now, experiencing more fatigue and discomfort, and talking about the day when she'd finally start feeling and looking more like herself.

"How did the appointment go?" Eric asked Gabriella.

"She is fine. The baby is fine, kicking up a storm. How was your afternoon with Lily?"

"It went well. I've really been enjoying my time with her. I know it doesn't make up for—"

Gabriella placed her hand against his cheek. "I know. The important thing is that you are spending time with her now. You never know what is going to happen in the future, and you can't change the past, so you might as well do what you can in the present. Right?"

"Right." Eric smiled at the wisdom of his lovely wife. "It means a lot to me that you've accepted her, and that the girls get along with her so well."

"They do, especially Emily." Gabriella paused. "You know, I have been thinking about something. When I was growing up, I knew this girl. She was my best friend in primary school. The woman I thought was her mother was actually her aunt. Her real mother had been very young when she had gotten pregnant, and wanted to finish school, so her mother's sister agreed to raise her. I don't think it was a formal adoption, but the entire town knew the truth, and no one blinked an eye."

Eric shook his head slowly. "Gabriella, this isn't a small town in Italy, forty-some years ago. If you're suggesting what I think you are . . ."

"Think about it," Gabriella entreated. "It makes so much sense. The baby would stay in the family, it would be a Langvin. Emily could go on to school and have the future she has always dreamed of. And Lily . . . you told me that her biggest regret in life was not having children. Now she has the chance."

"Gabriella, I just don't know."

"Of course we have to talk to Emily about it first, but can you at least make the suggestion to Lily?"

With a sigh, Eric finally said, "If Emily agrees, then I'll approach Lily."

Gabriella gave him a kiss. "Things will work out, Eric. I just know they will."

Wishing he had her optimism, Eric sat deep in thought in his study. He looked at the framed photograph of his family that was the sole picture on the wall. At first he had considered Gabriella's idea to be preposterous, something out of a fairy tale, but the more he meditated on it, the more it seemed to tie together the various threads that made up the tapestry of his life. The loss of his sister Mary, the loss and recovery of Lily, Emily's dilemma . . . could it all be answered by one simple act? As Gabriella had said, Lily's adoption of Emily's baby would keep the child in the family. Looking into the eyes of his father and mother, sister and brother in the photograph, Eric knew that he owed it to them to try to keep what was left of their family together.

* * *

Eric asked Lily if she wanted to visit the place where he'd grown up. She responded with enthusiasm, so he agreed to meet her in Greenwich, and from there proceed to Belle Haven. As they drove down the quiet streets lined with magnificent houses, caught between the changing seasons of fall and winter, Eric occasionally glanced at Lily's face, looking for her reaction. She seemed to calmly take in all the grandeur; of course, she must be used to East Coast luxury from her ex-husband's family. He himself had rarely come back to Belle Haven after his father's death, even to show his wife and daughters. Although he'd grown up here, this place didn't represent who he was then or who he'd become.

Finally, they arrived at the guardhouse that was the last barrier before Viking Manor, but it was empty; it hadn't been manned for years. The black iron gates were uncharacteristically wide open. The current owner, Eric knew, was a foreign investor who rarely set foot in this country, so the mansion was unoccupied and essentially abandoned. Indeed, there was a spooky air about it, surrounded by the almost bare branches of trees, as he and Lily approached on foot. They walked across the grounds, where his mother had once cultivated a flower garden before Mary's death, now covered in brambles and underbrush. Then their path ended in a cliff that descended sharply into the sea, and they could go no farther.

"That was my mother's favorite room," Eric told Lily, pointing up at one of the dark windows. "She spent more time there than with my father and myself." For a moment he imagined he could see a glimmer of light, a reflection from the glass figurines within, but he knew that was impossible. When the house was sold, so was everything inside it, including Lillian Langvin's prized collection of Lalique crystal.

"You told me she never recovered after your sister passed away," Lily said. "What ended up happening to her?"

"She grieved herself to death." Eric's face was hard. "Pills and alcohol had a hand in it, but she just stopped caring. Her body was there, but her mind was caught back in time when my sister was still alive and she didn't feel such guilt. She forsake the people in her present to live in the past. That's what I swore I would never do." He took Lily's hand in his. "That's why I want you to be part of my family. And that's why I have something important to ask you."

"What is it?" Lily asked, her face reflecting his seriousness.

"You've told me about how much you wanted children, to become a mother. Emily told me why you'd never considered adoption, because you wanted to be biologically related to your child. Well, Gabriella, Emily, and I have talked about it, and we're all in agreement." Eric paused, giving the moment the weight it required. "We were wondering if you would be interested in adopting Emily's baby."

When Lily remained silent, he continued, "All of us, especially Emily, would want to know the child and play a part in its life. But you would be the legal parent. I know this is more involvement in our family than you expected, but I hope you'll think about it."

Covering his hand with her own, Lily turned to him, her eyes bright with tears. "I don't have to think about it. The answer is yes."

She leaned on his shoulder, and he laid his head against her soft blond hair, as together they looked out onto the churning waves of the gray ocean.

Chapter 24

On a sweltering morning in mid-August, Lily Rose was in her New York City apartment, packing for a trip. Although she wouldn't be away for long, she carefully considered the clothes she had laid out on her bed, trying to decide what would make a good first impression.

She turned her head and asked, "What do you think, Baby Rose?"

Nearby in her playpen, six-month-old Ruby Rose Langvin looked up at the sound of her mother's voice and gave her a beaming, toothless smile. She was a beautiful baby, with her birth mother's dark curly hair and her birth father's brown, long-lashed eyes. But she was unmistakably a Langvin, with the same delicate facial features, and determined expression that was most often seen whenever a toy was just out of reach. Although Ruby had been named for Lily's grandmother—Carrie Ellen's mother—Lily had felt strongly that her last name should be Langvin, as her own might have been.

Since the day Ruby was born, Lily had been in heaven. At the hospital, she'd held Ruby's tiny, warm body in her arms and felt a connection unlike any other. It was an all-consuming, boundless love she had never experienced before—a love that grew every day she was with her daughter, feeding her, bathing her, rocking her to sleep. At night she would look at Ruby in her crib, at the soft flutter of her eyelashes against her cheeks and the gentle rise and fall of her stomach, and she couldn't believe the miracle that had entered her life.

Of course it wasn't all sunny days, and Ruby could get fussy like any other newborn who was learning about the world around her. But just being close to Lily would be enough to soothe her, and Lily made sure that they were never parted for long. While Ruby had a nanny, she would often visit Lily's office, and she would watch everything Lily did with alert, darting, curious eyes. Lily would quite seriously explain business decisions to her, laughing afterward, "You're going to be a fashion expert when you grow up, just like Mommy," and Ruby would coo and clap her hands.

Today, however, Lily was going on a trip without Ruby. She was planning to spend a week in Palm Beach, opening up the house that she had received from the Reynolds in her divorce settlement. Richard and Lisa Reynolds had given it to them as their tenth wedding anniversary present, but of course they had gotten divorced before that would ever happen. Lily had fallen in love with the old 1926 Mediterranean, framed by two giant banyan trees and royal palms. The stone house, with its rich mahogany floors and trim and its floor-to-ceiling Palladian windows, brought a jungle of foxtail palms, bougainvillea trees, and sunlight inside every room with the shining deep blue sea in the background. She could imagine she and Ruby and all the Langvins bringing the house back to life this winter. So, redecoration Lily Rose style was ready to begin! The fashion business basically shut down in New York in August, so it was the ideal time to head to the island.

As with all new parents, Lily was nervous about the first time she was going to spend so much time away from her baby. But, she reminded herself, it wasn't like she was leaving Ruby with a stranger. Eric and Gabriella were coming down from Bedford to pick up

Ruby so that she could spend the week with them. They'd offered to take Lily's dog Sable and her cat Hollywood as well, and Lily gladly accepted, as Ruby loved these animals; she had never gone a day in her life without them. Since Emily had already started at Yale, and Chloe was still at summer camp, this would be an opportunity for Ruby to spend some quality time with her grandparents.

For the past six months the Langvins had been very involved in Ruby's life, either spending weekends with her in the city or having her and Lily come out to see them. Lily had wondered whether Emily would find it difficult to be around the baby, but she seemed to treat Ruby more like a little sister or niece. Emily had gotten in touch with Santiago, Ruby's birth father, in Argentina and sent him videos of her. They'd even talked about him possibly visiting over winter break so that he could meet her. All of this, Lily welcomed with enthusiasm and relief, reasoning that the more people Ruby had around her who loved her, the better off she would be.

Just as Lily finished packing her suitcase, the doorbell rang; Eric and Gabriella had arrived.

"Is she ready?" Eric asked, as Gabriella scooped her granddaughter into her arms and gave her a kiss.

"Everything is right here." Lily pointed to a suitcase at least twice the size of her own. "There's extra formula, diapers, clothes if it gets hot, clothes if it gets cold, her favorite stuffed animals, her favorite books, the mobile she likes to look at before she goes to sleep..."

"Don't worry," Eric said. "Gabriella and I have done this before. It's only for a week, and you deserve some time to yourself. I've never seen anyone who works as hard as you, and as a single mother, too. You should enjoy yourself. Especially if you hit it off with Christian." He raised his eyebrows, and Lily had to laugh.

When he had found out that she was going to Palm Beach, Eric had suggested that Lily meet up with a sailing buddy of his who had retired early and now lived in Palm Beach most of the year. His name was Christian Walsh, and he was older than her and divorced, Eric said, somewhat apologetically. Lily reminded him that she was divorced, too, and she didn't mind older men. She got in touch with Christian and he sounded pleasant enough, so they arranged to have dinner the first night she was in Palm Beach. While she didn't have any expectations—and this wasn't quite a date, she kept reminding herself—she couldn't help feeling a mixture of nervousness and anticipation at the thought of meeting him.

"I'm looking forward to it," she said to Eric now. "From what you've told me, he sounds very nice."

"He's really someone special. But even if nothing comes of it, you can still enjoy the beach and the water."

Then the moment she had dreaded all week had come. Taking Ruby in her arms, she whispered into her shell-like ear, "It's time for you to go now. Have fun with Grandpa and Grandma, and Mommy will see you when you get back." She pressed her lips against the silky top of Ruby's head and let Gabriella take her again.

After seeing everyone off, Lily went back inside her apartment, feeling as if her heart had been wrenched away from her. Was this what it was going to be like every time Ruby left her, for however long or short the duration? She thought about Ruby starting school, having her first sleepover, going off to college, as Gabriella must have experienced with Emily just last week. And what if, for whatever reason, she and Ruby were separated permanently? That would be devastating. And while that may have seemed an odd thought, Lily had experienced so many permanent separations herself, in one guise or another. For some reason, Lily thought of how her biological mother must have had to give her up right after she'd been born, likely to never see her again. She was sure Jeff hadn't had a problem with it.

Lily hadn't thought about Jeff in months, but the thought of her left a bad taste in her mouth as she called a car and headed off to the airport. During the three-hour flight, though, she settled down and by the time the plane touched down, she was ready to take Eric's advice and enjoy herself.

* * *

When Lily arrived in Palm Beach, she found it as lush and tropical as when she'd been there last with the Reynolds. Except they'd usually come in the winter, and in the middle of August, the island seemed almost deserted, save for a few locals and the odd tourist here and there. The weather was sunny and hot, with a cool breeze blowing off the ocean.

In her rental car, she drove down streets where only glimpses of grand houses could be seen behind manicured hedges. As she pulled into the circular driveway of Villa Banyan she realized just how beautiful it really was and now she ready to make it a second home for her, Ruby and her new family, but for now, she just wanted to relax. Since it was late afternoon, she went for a walk on the beach, she sat for a long time on the sand, just letting the sound of the waves wash over her as the wind battered back her hair.

By the time evening came, she was starting to look forward to some company. She and Christian had arranged to meet for dinner at The Waves, which happened to be where she and Peyton had gotten married. Lily arrived early and sat at a table on the terrace that overlooked the waterfront, taking in the sunset. Although she hadn't planned it, the last rays of sunlight turned her hair into pure gold and highlighted her figure, clad in a simple silk white sheath. To anyone seeing her for the first time, she looked like the epitome of elegance, and more importantly, a woman comfortable in her own skin.

As Lily sipped at her drink, she noticed what seemed to be a bridal party taking up a few tables at the other end of the patio.

They were loud and boisterous, probably due to the freely flowing alcohol. However, she also noticed what she presumed to be the bride and groom—a couple that appeared to be in their mid-to-late twenties, sitting in the midst of their friends, lost in each other's eyes, as if they were in an oasis of their own making. She and Peyton had once been like that.

Lily thought about that day at The Waves, surrounded by pink and white flowers, where it seemed like she and Peyton were each the most important person in the other's world. Ten years later, it had all fallen apart, disastrously so, and she had been left with nothing. Well, not nothing. She had the house, and she'd do everything she could to make it her own—hers and Ruby's. Already she had fantasies of taking Ruby here for many years to come, watching her play on the beach, learning to swim in the ocean. They'd create their own memories to take the place of the past, turning pain into beauty.

"Lily Rose?"

Lily looked up to see a man who appeared to be in his mid-fifties. He was tall, broad shouldered and quite attractive, with thick wavy, hair that was so dark it was almost black, shot through with silver. His eyes were a sparkling, emerald green, and the corners of them crinkled as he smiled at her. It was clear from the way he looked at her that he thought she was stunning.

Conversation came easily with Christian. They talked about New York—he had worked there for many years—and his sailing trips with Eric on the Long Island Sound.

"Have you spent a lot of time in Palm Beach?" Christian asked her.

"Quite a bit, " Lily admitted. "I was married here, and I came down sometimes with my ex-husband's family. And I'm hoping to spend more time here in the winter."

"Once you do, you'll find that it's more down-to-earth than many people think. I also started coming here because of my ex-wife. It was something she expected, as part of our lifestyle. I never thought I would like it here, but now I can't imagine living anywhere else in the winter, especially after retiring early."

"Why did you retire?" Lily asked.

"I'd spent my whole life working, and so had my parents; they were immigrants from Ireland. My childhood was about rising to the top of wherever I was—school, church, sports, you name it. Naturally, it continued once I entered the business world. But that way of thinking can wear you down. In fact it can break you. A few years ago I realized there was more to life than that. My wife and I had been unhappy for a long time, so we decided to part ways. She, of course, was not in favor of early retirement. But once I made the decision to retire, and live for myself, I felt free."

"I understand," Lily murmured. "I fell apart when my husband left me, but now I know it was the best thing that could have happened to our marriage. If we hadn't gotten divorced, I might never have had the opportunity to adopt my daughter. She's the most important thing in the world to me. I don't know if Eric told you—"

"He explained it all to me," Christian said softly. "You haven't had it easy, Lily. But look where you are now and how far you've come. You've made it. You don't have to be afraid anymore."

As they gazed at each other across the table, Lily was grateful for the candlelight that hid the tears in her eyes. Christian knew everything about her, and he still accepted her for who she was and what she had been through. Eric was right; he was someone special indeed.

A gust of wind threatened to extinguish the candles on the tables, accompanied by some shrieks from the bridal party. Lily and Christian enjoyed a quiet dinner that lasted much later than most first dates and Lily realized just how comfortable and safe she felt around Christian Walsh. It was a feeling she hadn't felt since her first love Finn McCarney.

Christian and Lily talked about meeting up in New York the following week when he was there, and he walked Lily to her car. There weren't any seconds of awkward silence, or moments of what would happen next. Christian just simply kissed her softly and gently hugged her, and Lily folded herself in his arms.

On her way home, Lily felt unexpectedly buoyant. Eric would be so happy to hear that her date with Christian had gone well—yes, she could call it a date now. And come next week, she'd see Christian again. She didn't know why the thought of that filled her with such hope, like she was a little girl. Except this time, she would use her wisdom and experience to keep her heart safe. Still the thought of it made her feel blissful, a bit giddy even, as she turned onto her street.

Once inside, as she got ready for bed, Lily thought about what Christian had said. Had she really come that far? She thought about how last year around this time, she'd been getting ready to leave Golden Woods for Red Rose Farm, broken but on the path to recuperation, clinging to a single thread of hope that was a name on a slip of paper. What a difference a year made. Now she was surrounded by love and laughter—by family—and nothing could take that away from her.

For the next few days, she'd throw all her efforts into her redecorating plans. And at the end of the week, she'd be home with Ruby. Lily longed to hold her daughter's small, chubby body in her arms. While she had been out to dinner, Eric had texted her a photo of Ruby asleep in her crib, to show she was doing fine with her grandparents. Looking at it now, Lily pressed her lips against it, turned off her phone, and went to sleep.

Chapter 25

LILY STOOD AT THE LIBRARY window at Red Rose Farm, looking out at the bluegrass sparkling with snow, while the tree branches glistened with tiny crystal droplets, all set against a clear blue sky. Memories from her childhood flooded her, of the many Christmases she had spent here with her parents and Aunt Martha and Uncle Grant. If she closed her eyes, she could hear her mother and Aunt Martha in the kitchen making fudge and other treats for the sweets table that was a tradition in their household at Christmastime. It was set in foyer for friends that would stop by to visit, while her father and Uncle Grant discussed horse business before the roaring fireplace. In an ethereal moment, the farm manager Ray would come into the room to tell her that her German Shepard, Rebel had snuck outside the regular fencing again, and should he be allowed to play with the horses grazing in the fields?

Lily sighed, turning away from the window. So many family traditions had come to a halt with her parents' and aunt and uncle's deaths. For the past ten years she had spent the holidays with the Reynolds, her new family—or so she'd thought. The Reynolds had always decamped to their home in Palm Beach for Christmas, which was festive in its own way, combining the sun and the sand with twinkling lights and palm trees. They would open up their house at the end of the summer, and when the holidays rolled around, Lily and Peyton would join Richard and Lisa for the season's charity galas and societal events. Lily could not deny the place its charm, and was now going to spend a lot of time in the winter there giving she and Ruby had lots of happy options. But at Christmastime her heart belonged to the Bluegrass and Red Rose Farm, the dogs lying before the fire, the knowledge that the horses were warm and snug in their stalls. She had never been able to convince Peyton to come to the farm with her at any time of year, let alone Christmas, and after she had parted ways with the Reynolds, the thought of being at the farm alone during the holidays had not appealed to her.

Now, however, it was time to start a new tradition. This year Lily had invited the Langvin family to spend Christmas with her at Red Rose Farm, and they'd happily accepted. As she had anticipated, Eric and Gabriella had marveled over the house's rich but under-stated equine architecture, while the girls had been so excited by the horses and other animals. She had made a coordinated effort with Ray and his son Marcus to make sure the house was fully decorated, with wreaths of blue spruce and red holly on every door, even those to the horses' stalls, as it had been when her aunt and uncle were alive. All the silver chalices and crystal bowls that rep-resented former trophy-winning horses were on display and filled with red roses. There were even a couple of Kentucky Derby win-ners trophy chalices on display in the front hall to celebrate the holidays. All the fireplaces were lit and the grand old farmhouse was alive with laughter again.

Lily wanted to make this an especially joyous occasion, as there was plenty to celebrate besides the holidays. Ruby Rose was all dressed in a red velvet dress and crawling everywhere with Sable, Lily's Siberian Husky following not far behind, and Hollywood was curled up purring by the fire. In addition, Emily had just found out she'd been accepted early admission to Yale, her dream school.

She'd be able to spend time with the baby on holidays and in the summer. More than anything Lily wanted Emily to know her biological daughter, although she was also glad that Emily would be able to lead her own, independent life. Lily anticipated that this would be just the first of many holidays spent with the Langvins. For the first time in her life since her adopted parents had passed away Lily finally felt whole again. It seemed almost to good to be true…but this time it was.

A gentle knock and the sound of the door opening interrupted her thoughts.

"There you are," Eric said. "Chloe wants to know if you can go sledding with her and Emily, Gabriella is reading by the fire and refuses to be moved from her comfort zone."

"How about you?" Lily asked with a smile.

"I could be persuaded to join." Eric perused the gold-embossed spines of the books lining the walls. "That's quite a collection you have here."

"It belonged to my aunt and uncle." Lily paused, her face pensive.

"What are you thinking about?"

"Just how much they would have liked seeing the house full of people again. They entertained quite a bit with the other farm owners and friends in the community. While I was growing up, I used to spend my summers and holidays here, and it was always a fun, busy time. All of that changed after my parents died and I came to live with them for good, and their health began to fail." Lily shook her head as if to clear it of unhappy memories. "It means so much to me that you and your family are here during this time of year. How are you finding the place?"

"It's absolutely beautiful. As you know, I've only been to this part of the country once before"—*when I met Jeff,* he didn't add but Lily understood—"and during that time I visited quite a few farms like this one. I was just so impressed by their size and history. Each of them seemed grander than the next, and I kept imagining what it would be like to live in one of them."

"I'm happy to hear it," Lily said. "Because there's something I'd like to discuss with you in private, without Gabriella or the girls."

"Yes?" Struck by her serious tone, Eric moved toward her, a concerned look on his face.

"While I was going over the adoption papers with my lawyers, I asked them to change my will. Of course, I want Ruby Rose to eventually inherit Red Rose Farm. But I've also named you as trustee until she comes of age, in case something happens to me before then."

When Eric started to say something, Lily held up her hand. "I know you have your own house in Bedford, but I want you to think of this place as your home, too. It deserves to have a family—to have children—live here again. I hope you'll come whenever you want, as much as you want, with or without me."

"Thank you, my dear," Eric said. "I never thought I would want to live in another family house, not after Viking Manor. But," and he made a wide gesture, taking in the lit fireplace, the book-lined walls, the snowy vista in the window beyond, "I think I could get used to it. Now, should we go join Chloe?"

"You go ahead, I'll find you in a moment."

After the door closed behind Eric, Lily took a final look at the room she'd spent so many hours in as a child, reading by the fire, her dog Rebel lying at her feet. She'd dreamed of so many things back then, of leaving Kentucky and moving to New York, although she'd had no idea of what she'd do there. And she had done exactly that, and while there had been tragedy and heartbreak, she was still standing here, in the place she loved, with people she loved.

When Lily looked out the window one last time, she saw Eric and Chloe in the yard. Chloe was pulling behind her an antique wooden sled almost as tall as she was, which Marcus must have dug up from somewhere on the grounds. The farm dogs raced around them, creating a whirlwind of snow flurries. Laughing, Eric and Chloe paused to pet the dogs, and gladly, Lily went out to join them.

Acknowledgments

This book was inspired by a true story—my story—but then it became fiction.

I have had many angels throughout my life who have rescued me during dark times and are still here to laugh with me in the good ones.

Thanks to the late Beulah and Cassell Caudill and Susan Caudill, to the Late Bernard and Minnie Banks, Virginia and Meryl Banks for their love and devotion to my parents. Thanks to Earlene John Williams and all my dear friends from Eastern Kentucky who gave me the seeds for my soul.

Thanks to Roy R. Crawford III for Chanel Number 5.

Thanks to Jean Haskins Dalmath, Diane Lloyd Roth, Dr. Patricia Yarberry Allen, Dr. Glenora McCoy and Dr. Frank McCoy, Armand and Sara Harris. Margaret Luce, Suzy Goldsmith, Isabelle (Belicia) Beckett Smith Molly Kellly Wiegel, Jennifer Howk Roe, Todd Howk, Greg Betkinsky, William Howe, Troy Revord, Pierre Matta, Ellie Malmin, and Dr. Charles Alexander for being there when it wasn't always easy and doing a lot of listening.

Thanks to the late F. Ross Johnson for being my dear friend and mentor.

Thanks to the late Annette Allison, John Reynolds Allison, and J. Richard Allison for letting me be an extended part of their family.

Finally, thanks to the three angels who saved me so I could tell this story, John and Sharon Crouch and Dr. Thomas Clifton.

I love you always, Edward J. Robinson.